Selvage

by

Nell DuVall

Nell DuVall

**Published by
Melange Books, LLC
White Bear Lake, MN 55110
www.melange-books.com**

Selvage ~ Copyright © 2012 by Nell DuVall

ISBN: 978-1-61235-461-3 Print

Cover Art by Caroline Andrus

Selvage
Nell DuVall

A bank scam, a series of accidents that end as murders, and police too ready to accept simple explanations for deaths push freelance writer Brooke Beldon and systems programmer Paul Counts ever deeper into a tangled conspiracy. She struggles to clear her brother's name. Paul, a sucker for a blue-eyed blonde, initially wants to help her, but also ends the chief suspect in murder. He must clear his name and unravel the bank theft to identify the culprits.
The only clue they have is the name of a sleazy strip club. Paul gets stonewalled at the club, so Brooke enlists the help of a sympathetic hostess. Going undercover, she tries to learn all she can about her kid brother Stan and the woman who left with him the night he died.

Nell DuVall

Chapter One

The prickling of Brooke Beldon's scalp raised the fine hairs on her neck. That sensation always had signaled bad things happening to her brother Stan—the last time had been when he'd wrecked his car. He hadn't called her in over a week. Lackadaisical about many things, he phoned every week.

She speed keyed his number, drumming her fingers on the table as she waited for him to answer. Ten rings and even his voice mail didn't cut in. Her worry moved to the edge of panic. Frustrated, she disconnected and switched to her PC. Maybe an email would reach him.

Stan, you didn't answer your phone. Your answering machine is either overfull or off. Please call me. If you're gaming online or whatever, take a break. I have a friend who wants to meet you. She's cute, nice, and into computers and computer games, too. CALL ME! If you don't, I'll break down your door tomorrow. ☺)
Love, Brooke

Stan always read his email, so she expected him to respond. She'd taken responsibility for him after their parents died in that horrible car crash. With few friends, he spent so much time online he often forgot to eat or feasted on junk food. His addiction to gaming had caused him to skip work a few times. She wanted more in his life than computers and work.

Ding! Ding!

The alarm signal from her computer startled her. *Reminder* flashed on the toolbar. She had set it earlier to alert her to leave on time for tonight's concert—the Beethoven Choral Symphony. One of her favorites, it would kick off the Columbus Symphony concert tonight. She smoothed the skirt of her black dress, grabbed her purse, and headed for the car.

5

Friday evening traffic downtown could be murder for those who didn't arrive early. As for parking near the Ohio Theater, forget it. Stewing over Stan wouldn't add to her enjoyment, so she struggled to push her concerns aside. Surely, by the time she returned, he'd reply. If only he didn't get so engrossed in those stupid games. Other people had hobbies. Look at those OSU football fanatics, but they got out on Saturdays for the games. Stan didn't; he remained in front of his computer. No wonder he'd put on a bit weight. She sighed and focused on the traffic.

* * * *

"Well, boys, what do we have here?" Detective Milton Meyers squatted down to get a better look at the corpse. From the stench, he'd guess the man died of an overdose. A hint of crack underlay the stink of body fluids. Experience had hardened Meyers to such scenes, but he remained glad he'd eaten breakfast more than an hour ago. The early morning call had caught him on his way to headquarters and directed him to this east side address.

The paramedic, kneeling beside the awkwardly sprawled body on a tan couch stained with vomit and discharge, looked up at Meyers. "We got a 9-1-1 call at oh-five-hundred. When we arrived, we found the victim lying here, dead."

"The cause?"

"Not certain without tests, but from the gear on the table and the state of the body, I'd say a drug overdose." The medic shook his head and pointed toward the plastic envelopes and the glass crack-pipe on the low coffee table in front of the couch. "We get a lot of those, but not in this neighborhood."

Pulling on a pair of gloves, Meyers, careful not to smear fingerprints, sniffed the pipe. "Smells like crack to me, too. Get the lab on this one. Any witnesses?"

The paramedic shook his head. "No, but the dispatcher said a woman called. Probably partying with him, he OD'd, she panicked, dialed 9-1-1, and then split."

"Sounds likely; I'll talk to the dispatcher later. Any I.D. on the body?"

"A wallet." The gloved paramedic opened it. "Says his name is Beldon, Stan Beldon." He passed the wallet to Meyers.

"Thanks." Meyers took the billfold and shuffled through it. He found about fifty dollars in cash, the usual assortment of credit cards with some receipts, an American Express card—green, not gold—an insurance card, several professional society memberships, a driver's license, and a wallet I.D. card. The back of the last carried the name of a person listed as sister and an address on the other side of town.

"Well, at least we have the next-of-kin. I'll contact her later to tell her about Beldon. Perhaps I can ask her a few questions. Anything else on the body?"

"Nope." The paramedic shook his head. "Just a man's handkerchief. Guess you won't need us any more, so we'll get back to the station. Gus said the medical examiner will be along shortly. The corpse isn't going anywhere." The paramedic unhooked and packed up the monitors, closed his bag, and scrambled to his feet.

"Yeah, if we need you, we'll call or stop by the station. Oh, tell Watkins to get his butt in here and quit loafing. We've got work to do."

Meyers continued his perusal of the wallet's contents. The credit receipts bore the imprint of some local restaurants, including a couple for the Club Lido. Most were for less than twenty dollars, but a couple of the Lido slips showed a hundred. Either a heavy drinker or maybe the guy liked one of the dancers Meyers concluded.

Satisfied with his initial survey of the billfold's contents, he surveyed the one-bedroom apartment. It contained functional, inexpensive furnishings and a few books and pictures. The couch, a modern three-cushion variety, once had tan nubby upholstery. Beldon either didn't much care about style, or didn't have taste.

The victim, a somewhat fleshy man, probably in his early thirties, with lank brown hair and reddish skin with a touch of acne, wasn't particularly attractive, and even less so in death. Some people never learned. Play with fire and eventually they either got burned, or the smoke inhalation did them in. With crack, the smoke did it. Get a little too high and that ended it. The inhaled smoke reacted quickly, kindling a brain reaction and changes in brain activity that sent erratic pulses to the muscles, caused the heart to race, and profuse sweating. Hyperventilation followed with involuntary shaking and ultimately convulsions that killed. Not pretty. Meyers only wished the kids could see it happen. The reality might scare some of them straight.

Maybe the woman caller had left some trace of her presence, but Meyers found nothing that gave any clues to who had been with Beldon when he died. The apartment appeared clean, yet not particularly neat. Discarded clothing lay on the bedroom floor and the bed remained unmade. Still, he saw no surface dust and no fuzz balls in the corners. Unwashed dishes filled the sink and appeared to have come from breakfast judging by the remains of dried egg and bread crusts on the plates.

He checked the wastebasket in the compact kitchen and the bath, but found no tissues with lipstick, or anything likely to have been used or left by a woman. Maybe the Crime Scene Unit would turn up something.

A noise at the bathroom door drew his attention. Blaine Watkins, his partner, stood in the doorway. With his receding hairline, emerging paunch, and stained raincoat he looked like a down-at-the heels P.I. or a young Colombo, but not a city homicide detective.

"Where the hell have you been?" Meyers greeted Blaine.

"Finishing my coffee, I don't like drinking around stiffs; you know that. Besides, what's to look for anyway? The paramedic told me the stiff OD'd. It's not a homicide, so why waste our time?"

Meyers sighed. Blaine always looked for an easy out. "Because, we won't know it's an overdose for sure until the coroner completes all the lab tests. What if it turns out the guy didn't OD? The Chief hates sloppy work. You want to end up back on the beat writing parking tickets? I'd rather investigate this scene than face that mountain of paper on my desk."

Blaine flashed him a lopsided grin. "Yeah, you've got something there."

* * * *

As Meyers remembered, the neighborhood where the sister lived contained a mix of university people, business types, and professionals. Her house occupied a corner lot. A gingerbread Swiss chalet, it looked a little out of place among its more sedate Victorian neighbors. He parked his car on the street and strolled slowly up the front walk, noting the neat flower beds and trim lawn. He rang the bell and waited.

After several rings, the door opened partway to reveal a casually dressed young woman.

"Brooke Beldon?"

"Yes?" she answered warily and opened the door a bit wider.

"I'm Detective Meyers." He pulled out his badge for her inspection

"Stan. He's okay, right?"

The worry in her eyes made him wonder whether anything specific made her ask about the victim. "May I come in?"

"Yes, of course." She stepped back, opening the door fully so he could enter. After closing the door behind him, she led him into the living room. "Won't you sit down"? She frowned and stared at him.

Meyer sat on one of the two dark gray leather armchairs flanking the sofa. By habit, he took his time to survey his surroundings to learn what he could before delivering his news and to put that off as long as possible. He never knew how a woman would react. Some raged at him, hysteria vying with wild frenzy. Floods of tears came from some, and he'd even met with raucous laughter from a few.

In his view, her home reflected better style than the brother's place and it probably cost a bundle, too. From his quick review, it appeared she had a good income and taste. The striking abstract picture with deep swirls of blue over the fireplace drew his eye at once and must have determined the large room's color scheme. The pale gray carpet blended well with the soft gray walls while the blue and beige flecked drapes at the large double front windows echoed some of the blue tones of the painting. A glass coffee table sat before the sofa. The colors and the style suited a woman of style and sophistication.

"Stan," the sister asked again.

Reluctant to begin, he focused on her. She perched on the black leather sofa facing him. Rather pretty too, deep blue eyes and blonde hair, but in a somewhat severe style pulled tightly back and wound in a knot behind. She wore a sweater with a sort of abstract design, expensive looking, but the jeans showed wear. She sat tense and stiff, rubbing one hand over the other.

"I have some bad news for you." He hated this part of his job. "Your brother Stan Beldon died this morning."

A gasp escaped her. Her rosy cheeks faded to bone white. For one long moment, she stared at him. If he read her fleeting emotions right, logic and denial warred.

"Not Stan. How?" Her blue eyes took on a blank, dazed look.

At least hysteria hadn't taken hold yet. From the signs, she'd gone into shock. "We're not sure yet, but we suspect a drug overdose. A 9-1-1 call came in at five this morning. The paramedics found him dead when they arrived. According to the dispatcher, a woman called."

Frowning, she stared at him in shocked silence.

"You need to arrange with the coroner's office to I.D. his body. The coroner needs permission for an autopsy. It's automatic in cases like this. I also have a few questions to ask about your brother's friends, but that can wait until later, if you'd rather."

"What?" She tried to brush a phantom strand of hair from her eyes and shook her head maybe trying to clear away an internal fog. "Wait a minute. My brother never did drugs."

"So far we haven't officially determined the cause of death." Meyers took out a small notebook and pen and entered the time, date, names—Stan and Brooke Beldon. "When did you last see your brother?"

She wrinkled her forehead as she considered. "About two weeks ago. We had dinner at the Spaghetti Factory. He always phones me weekly, but I hadn't heard from him yet this week." She shivered and rubbed her arms.

"You didn't see him last night?"

"No, I went to a concert and a reception afterwards. I got home about one and went straight to bed."

Meyers paused a moment to add her comments to his notes. "Did your brother have any girlfriends?"

"None I knew about." She laughed, not quite hysterical, at least not yet. "Stan's always been a loner."

He nodded. "Have you any idea who might have been with him, or who would have called 9-1-1?"

She gave an emphatic shake of her head. "None whatsoever."

He closed his notepad and slipped it along with his pen into his inside pocket. "If you remember anyone, or think of anything else that might help, please call me." He handed her a business card. "At present, we see nothing unusual in the death, but when drugs are involved, we try to trace the source back to the supplier in hopes of preventing someone else from dying."

Taking his card without looking at it, she set it on the coffee table in front of her. "I'm sorry, I can't help you there." Shaking her head again, she frowned. "Stan never used drugs. Someone killed him." She searched his face a moment. "I'll call you, if I learn anything or hear of anyone."

He rose and she stood, as if drawn to her feet automatically and unconsciously by his action.

"Thank you, I'm sorry for your loss." They walked toward the entry door where he stopped. "Can I call a friend for you? A death like this comes as a shock. If we can do anything, let us know." He paused, uncertain, and, as always, somewhat awkward. It never got any easier. "Good-bye, Miss Beldon."

He hadn't learned anything to further his case. Too bad she knew so little about the victim; still they were brother and sister. Sometimes, the family was the last to know about drug use. Pity that, when it ended like this. Remembering the pudgy body in the nondescript apartment, he concluded she had all the looks in the family.

Brooke watched Detective Meyers stride toward his unmarked car. As a writer, she automatically pegged him as a pleasant looking man in a conservative dark blue suit. Short golden brown hair framed an open face—someone to trust and who could find Stan's murderer, if he looked hard enough.

An air of unreality enveloped her. After closing the door, she wandered back to the living room and sank on to the sofa. Numb, she hugged herself, trying to absorb what Meyers had told her. She couldn't dismiss the policeman's presence and his questions, but Stan dead? No way. Shivering, she struggled to find her balance.

Except for their occasional dinners now and then, she had seen so little of Stan. She had relied on his weekly phone calls to reassure her. Drugs made no sense. Such things happened to other people, not to her and Stan.

Images whirled through her mind. Stan at the lake with a toy boat at age five. Him holding an award plaque from the local chapter of the computer society. His grin when she unwrapped the red china cat he'd given her for Christmas. The two of them at the Christmas party last year given by the bank where he worked. For a few moments, the memories overwhelmed her. None of them would bring back Stan or tell her what had really happened and why he died.

Guilt assailed her. She shouldn't have ignored that nagging sensation last night. It wouldn't have hurt her to skip the concert. If she had, could she have saved Stan? He wouldn't take aspirin, so why something so lethal?

And a woman? Always too engrossed in his computers and puzzles, he didn't have many friends, let alone a girlfriend. The only name that came to mind was Paul Counts, a programmer at the bank data center where Stan worked. Stan had introduced them at that last Christmas party and had spoken highly of him. She couldn't remember anyone else. Tomorrow she would call the data center and ask Mr. Counts about Stan.

Frozen, she wondered when this paralysis would lift. Tears refused to come.

* * * *

For systems programmer Paul Counts, Mondays always came as a day to recall where he had left off on Friday—a day to rev up the old brain cells and strive to make some tangible progress before the week's interruptions grew too steady.

He placed his coffee cup beside the workstation screen and sighed at the paltry desk space. The formulas used by the data center planners didn't meet his needs. They allocated office areas and furnishings based on the employee's status or work function, but never recognized how they might differ. Programmers, especially systems programmers, needed room to spread manuals and listings, but policy mandated any extra space went to supervisors and managers so they could hold time-wasting meetings in their offices. That left the worker bees with barely room to turn around.

With limited space, Paul declared war on useless CYA memos and kept only essential reports and memos. Most mail hit the circular file as soon as he picked it up. His wastebasket often overflowed by day's end. He disliked the people who generated unnecessary paper. Ditto their emails. Luckily, today's mail hadn't arrived yet.

Leaning back, Paul stared at the one thing that gave his space something more than company issue sterility. The bank's policy limited personal decorations. His favorite Delacroix lithograph, a rendering of Faust's duel from Goethe's *Faust*, symbolized his favorite sport and. always fascinated him. It provided an alternative to a blank computer screen or the bland panel behind it as a focus when he worked to sort out a troublesome program bug. The three figures in the drawing featured the Devil, Valentine, and Faust. The Devil forced Valentine to parry one last thrust as Faust, a horrible, triumphant grin on his face, skewered Valentine. Paul always wished Valentine would respond with an impossible acrobatic move and skewer the two villains. Two against one didn't sit well with him.

This morning the office buzz rose in volume beyond the normal low level hum. The raised voices carried over the freestanding screens separating the workspaces and over the white noise. Curious, Paul picked up his empty cup and walked to the coffee station. Joining the group there, he reached for the coffee pot, and filled his cup.

"Too bad about Stan," Sharon Belling, a systems programmer, said.

"What about Stan?" Paul stared at her, puzzled.

"Didn't you hear? He died Saturday night."

"You're kidding, right?" Paul considered Stan a first-class programmer and hard worker. His death would leave a gaping hole among the programmers, and Paul would miss him.

"No, I saw it in the paper, but they didn't give any details."

Paul shook his head. "He couldn't have been more than thirty."

"The worst is we have to pick up the pieces. Sure hope Cramer has someone to take over Stan's work."

"Yeah." Paul understood Sharon's concern. Downsizing left too few people to do too much.

He took his coffee back to his cubicle. Death didn't figure much among the lives of most people he knew except for their elderly relatives. He'd always liked Stan. Having someone he knew die so suddenly left an empty place in work schedules, but also in his life. Morbid thoughts wouldn't solve his current problems. With work waiting, he pushed those thoughts away.

Gradually the buzz of talk died as people returned to work. Paul dug into the weekend problem reports on his screen until the shrill ring of the telephone interrupted him. Annoyed, he picked up the phone.

"Paul Counts here," he snapped.

"Mr. Counts, this is Brooke Beldon, Stan's sister. We met last year at the bank's Christmas party. Could you meet me for lunch today? I'd like to ask you a few questions…about Stan."

Empathy filled Paul as he remembered the morning conversation at the coffee station. "I'm really sorry about Stan. A friend said this morning he died Saturday. As for lunch, of course, what time?" She had a nice voice, and he vaguely remembered a blonde with Stan at the Christmas party.

"Eleven thirty at the Court Door? It's not far from the data center."

"I'm not sure there's anything I can tell you, but I'll see you there."

When he replaced the phone, the image of her in a dark green dress at the bank's Christmas party rose in memory. Cool and elegant in his view, but they hadn't exchanged more than greetings before his pager went off. System bugs didn't operate according to a holiday calendar, or rather they did, at the worst times.

Discussing Stan's death with her wouldn't make for a fun lunch. Besides, he and Stan moved in different circles, so he couldn't imagine what she hoped to learn from him. With plenty of work still facing him, he turned his attention back to the problem reports.

Promptly at eleven fifteen, Paul grinned at the Delacroix Devil, filed away the manual he had been reading, and left to meet Brooke Beldon. A cool sunny March day with high, scattered clouds met him as he left the data center. The restaurant Brooke had chosen occupied a site only a few blocks away, so he walked.

The crisp air invigorated and refreshed him after a stuffy morning. Setting off at a brisk pace, he regretted he didn't have a longer distance to go. As he savored the fresh air, he thought he really should get out more at lunchtime. Then, he remembered the reason for this lunch and slowed his pace. He had no idea what he could say to Stan's sister. 'I'm sorry' sounded so trite.

Nearing the Court Door, Paul remembered this restaurant as small with booths set in scallops around a central serving area to minimize the distance the servers had to walk, but requiring a long arm to serve. He grimaced because the last meal he'd eaten had tasted adequate, but not particularly special. Reminiscent of some mediocre frozen entries or even those old coffee shops, not the current pseudo-retro-diner style, best described it. He preferred honest food, not overcooked, over-seasoned, or over-sauced. Trendy food annoyed him.

An attractive woman waited at the front entrance; probably Stan's sister. Blonde and blue-eyed, she looked more mature and self-assured than he had remembered. Maybe the tailored suit and the creamy blouse, or the lack of jewelry, did it. She wore her blond hair wound neatly into a crown atop her head.

"Mr. Counts?" She extended her hand and appeared to take in everything about him in one steady glance. "I'm Brooke Beldon, Stan's sister."

"I'm sorry for your loss. The news this morning shocked me," he said, shaking her hand briefly. "Call me Paul."

Her firm grip surprised and pleased him, but her appraising look amused him. No doubt she expected the traditional accountant or bank manager type in a dark suit and white shirt, surely not a regular guy in Western shirt and jeans. He could almost see her thinking, 'not the attire for a bank.' At least fencing practice kept him in excellent physical condition. With Stan for a brother, she must know about programmers. Most had a maverick streak and the systems programmers went beyond that.

After her initial survey, she smiled. "I reserved a booth in the corner, if that's all right with you?" She gestured toward an empty table at the rear of the restaurant.

He followed as she led the way, struggling with what to say. Helplessness rushed over him. Programs he understood, but people often confused him, especially when dealing with attractive women. He hoped she wouldn't cry.

As they seated themselves, the server came to take their drink orders. Brooke, ordered hot tea and he asked for the same. After the server left, she waited a moment as if weighing what to say.

"I appreciate your coming. I know none of Stan's friends. You're the only one I've met."

'Yes, at the Christmas party, wasn't it?'

She nodded. "He spoke highly of you."

Paul blinked in surprise. "He did? Nice of him. Your brother was one of the best programmers at the data center. He'll be missed."

"Thank you. I'm not sure what he did; he never discussed his work with me."

"I don't know about his current assignment. The last I heard someone said he was working on changes to accounting routines. Our paths crossed only when we had system problems. My job's to keep the systems operating without glitches."

She took a deep breath and brushed at her eyes. "The police say Stan had been smoking crack with a woman and OD'd. For them, it's a simple overdose, so they have no reason to investigate his death. I talked to Detective Meyers again this morning, and, as far as the police are concerned, the case is closed unless something unusual turns up. They don't even plan on looking for the woman who called 9-1-1." Discouragement and anger colored her voice.

The drug use surprised Paul. "And you disagree?"

Staring down a moment at her hands, she rubbed one across the other, and then gazed up at him. "Paul, I know my brother. He never stepped out of the box and never messed with drugs even in college. He didn't even have a girlfriend." She shook her head. "No, something's wrong." She looked at him, expecting an answer.

"Well..." He paused, undecided what to say to her. "I don't know if he had any women friends. Some programmers smoke a joint now and then, but Stan and I didn't cross paths often. The news shook me, but you don't always know as much about people as you think you do."

He wanted to help her and hated his ignorance. He'd never heard about Stan and drugs or women. In fact, he couldn't say he knew much of anything about Stan's personal life at all. They had never discussed anything but work.

The server returned with their drinks and took their luncheon orders. Brooke waited until he left before saying more.

"The police found nothing at Stan's apartment, but he might've had left something in his office that would help. When I called about cleaning out his office, the Human Resources person told me some secretary would do it, and I could pick up his personal things when she finished. I doubt she would even know what might be important. I realize it's an imposition but perhaps you could go to his office, pack it up, sort of nose around, and see if he left anything unusual. As his friend, that would be normal. Please, I need your help."

Paul wanted to refuse, but found the pleading in her dark blue eyes hard to resist. Anyway, she had a point. He didn't owe Stan anything, but helping his sister wouldn't involve much. In any event, doing her this small favor couldn't hurt. Besides, blondes with blue, blue eyes always intrigued him, especially intelligent ones.

"Umm, I'll see what I can do, but don't expect too much."

The server returned with their food. To Paul's surprise, he actually enjoyed his lunch and looking at Brooke added an indefinable something. The juicy hamburger tasted like good beef seared on an open grill and the crisp French fries melted in the mouth more than the usual pre-cut, frozen spuds served most places. He drank the last of his tea and reached for the check.

"No," Brooke insisted, picking it up. "I asked you to lunch."

"Okay, but only if I pay for the next one." He smiled.

Her answering smile lighted her face. She opened her purse for the money to pay the check. Pulling out several dollars for a tip, she then slid out of the booth. Paul followed her to the front of the restaurant and waited while she paid the cashier. He held the door for her as they left the building.

Outside, he paused, wanting to prolong her presence by even a few minutes. "I'll call you, if I find anything, but don't get your hopes up. The bank discourages keeping personal stuff in the offices, so I doubt I'll find much."

"I understand, but I'd feel better if I knew we'd considered everything. I really appreciate your help. Thank you, Mr. Counts." She shook his hand.

"Paul," he corrected. "Glad to help."

Wanting to offer some comfort, he held her hand just a moment too long and released it with reluctance. "Well, I'll be in touch."

"Good-bye." She turned and walked away at a brisk pace. He watched her head toward the parking lot a block away where she must have left her car and noticed several men give her appreciative glances as she passed. He agreed with them.

Strolling deep in thought back to the bank, he mused on the two Beldons. Not anything like Stan, his sister Brooke epitomized style, class, and sophistication. He'd always considered Stan something of a slob, but intelligent and good at writing clean, efficient code. He shook his head, finding it hard to believe they had the same parents. At least he could do this for her. It wouldn't take much time, and it offered the chance to help her in a small way.

Chapter Two

Driven by innate curiosity and an urge to help out a gorgeous blonde, Paul followed up on his promise to Brooke when he reached his office after lunch. He called Cramer Seymour, Stan's boss.

"Cramer, Paul Counts here. I just spoke with Brooke Beldon, Stan's sister, and she asked me to pack up his personal stuff and send it to her. Any objection?"

"None," Cramer responded in a tired voice. "In fact, it'll save Marilyn some time if you would. She's overloaded just now. You can leave the program listings for Kent Carpenter. He's taking over Stan's assignments on the branch accounts project."

"Thanks, I'll stop by there soon."

Paul replaced the phone and strolled the short distance down the corridor to Seymour's section and Stan's office. The empty secretary's workstation indicated Marilyn had most likely gone on an errand. He picked up an empty box next to the desk with Stan's name on it. He'd use it and check with Marilyn later. Box in hand he entered the cubicle labeled *Stan Beldon*.

For a moment he paused, almost expecting to see Stan's pudgy form hunched over the computer display. Paul shook his head. What a waste of good talent. He set the box on the floor next to the paper covered work surface.

This office reflected the same basic layout as his, but the similarity ended there. Stan had the same space as Paul's, but somehow his had degenerated into heaps of papers overflowing every available surface and almost hiding the computer screen. Programmers had an unbreakable addiction to paper. At least the boxes of floppies, punched cards, and tapes had long gone.

Most of the paper represented program listings. Fortunately, the dates on the printouts provided a way to identify the latest versions. The programs fell into four major areas: some general utilities, a few data base subroutines, the branch account code, and other general customer account modules. Paul shoved the piles to one side to clear space. As he reviewed the listings, he stacked them into separate piles.

Next, he focused on the desk drawers. The shallow middle drawer contained pens, pencils, scissors, a letter opener, a book of matches, and a couple of bank memos. The top left hand drawer held miscellaneous paper supplies. A dirty coffee mug, some packets of dried soup, and a few candy bars; the usual programmer's emergency supplies for late hours or skipped lunches filled the second drawer. The deep file drawer below contained more program listings and some coding sheets.

Computer security rules forbade leaving logon codes or passwords lying about, but few programmers took the prohibition seriously and most kept a copy of the latest set somewhere nearby. Sure enough in the file labeled *Procedures,* Paul found a sheet with Stan's logon code and password. Turning to the keyboard at his right, he entered the codes. Now, if only Stan hadn't gotten around to changing his password recently.

The system waited as Paul typed, checked its files, signaled its acceptance, and then waited for his next command. Sys Admin hadn't deleted Stan's authorizations yet. Most likely, they would soon transfer his programs and data files to Kent. At that thought, he debated what to do. If he copied Stan's files into his own, he could check them later and see if any showed something interesting. At least he wouldn't have to worry about Kent changing passwords or updating them.

Finished with the drawers, he looked at the shelves over the work surface. A set of company-issued programming and systems manuals, a couple of books on software design, and one on financial accounting formulas occupied the lower shelf. A couple of paperback action novels, including a graphic novel of the X-men sat to one side. He shook his head surprised Stan read such juvenile stuff although he'd been told the graphic novels had improved.

A framed snapshot of Brooke and Stan taken during the summer reposed next to the novels. He picked up the picture and studied the differences between the two. They made an odd couple, and Paul failed to see any family resemblance. Stan had grinned at the camera while the wind ruffled his receding hair. Brooke stared straight ahead—no smile, her hair neat and fastened close to her head. Stan wore a rumpled shirt,

Brooke a neat and crisp blouse. His arm rested on her shoulder.

Paul leafed through the technical books. The one on financial accounting covered basic accounting principles and techniques. Nothing odd there. He'd review Stan's program code to cover all the options, but expected to find the usual stuff. It shouldn't take much time.

Thus far, he had turned up little of a personal nature. He checked the paperback books which all had Stan's name in them, so he put them in the box for Brooke along with the snapshot, the coffee mug, and the miscellaneous soup packets and candy bars. He left the manuals. The librarians would come for those later. Tomorrow, if he had time, he could tackle the program listings.

Picking up a black matchbook with lurid red lettering, Paul stared at it, surprised. Club Lido? The nudie bar? Had Stan gone there? He'd never impressed Paul as the type to go to such a dump. Maybe someone had given them to him. Paul opened the matchbook and noted the name written in blue ink inside, *Topaz Laval*. Showy name—a dancer? If she worked at the Lido, maybe she called 9-1-1. Paul put the matchbook in his pocket and packed the rest of the personal things in the box. Finished, he picked up the sorry lot and left the office.

Marilyn Johnson, Cramer's graying, efficient, and inquisitive secretary, glanced at him over the top of her granny glasses as he stopped at her desk. She eyed the box.

"Cramer said it was okay to pick up Stan's personal things. You can check them over, if you like."

"Real sad." Marilyn shook her head. "I saw that bit in the paper about him. Someone said he overdosed. It surprised me. He didn't even smoke so far as I know or go out with the other programmers for drinks after work. He never talked much to the rest of us, just work things really. I guess you never know about the quiet ones." She sighed, a solemn look on her round face.

"Yeah, I heard the same. Tell Cramer I'll finish here tomorrow. Stan didn't keep much in his office. You may want to call the library and ask them to pick up the programming manuals and library books. I checked all of these paperbacks and they're Stan's, so I'll take them to his sister."

"I'm glad you volunteered to sort things out." Marilyn smiled, looking like a mischievous Whooppi Goldberg. "It not like I don't have enough to do with all the downsizing around here, and, besides, you know a lot more about the programs and files than I do. I'd have pushed most of it off on Kent."

"I won't do much with the programs except sort them out. Kent will have to decide what he wants to do anyway. I didn't find much personal stuff."

Never good at chitchat and uncomfortable with the entire situation, Paul had too much work waiting to chat with Marilyn. An excellent secretary, she knew everyone and everything happening or about to happen. That made him cautious about what he said to her. The fact she didn't know about Stan and drugs added more weight to Brooke's doubts.

"Anyway, I'll stop back tomorrow and finish up. See you then."

Paul picked up the box of Stan's belongings and headed toward his own cubicle. Once there, he put the carton on his one visitor's chair. He'd take it home tonight and drop it off at Brooke's when it suited them both.

He dialed her number, pleased when she answered almost immediately.

"Brooke Beldon." Her confident voice matched the image he had of her.

"Paul Counts here. I checked Stan's office, but didn't find much—a few personal belongings—some books, a picture of the two of you, his coffee mug, the usual. I can drop them by whenever it's convenient. I'll go through his program files tomorrow, but I doubt there's anything unusual there."

"Oh." A long pause followed. "Thank you for taking the time. Let me know where and when to get Stan's stuff from you. I hate to impose on you."

"No, it's no bother. I'm more than happy to drop it off at your place. Just say when."

"You could stop by Saturday morning, if that's okay."

"Fine. Hopefully, I'll know a little more by then." He paused a moment, wanting to help her, but uncertain what more he could do. Then he remembered the matchbook. "Oh, by the way, would you have a snapshot of Stan? I have the one of the two of you, but one of him alone might be better to use for identification purposes. I found a matchbook from a nightclub and a good picture might help jog memories there."

"I have one somewhere. You can pick it up when you drop off the box on Saturday."

"Right, see you then." He'd completed that little chore. He had his own work, including that system fix Kincaid had asked about. All afternoon, whenever Paul paused, he kept seeing a pair of blue eyes. Yeah, Brooke had his attention all right.

* * * *

Saturday didn't exactly dawn—it more or less crawled up, crotchety, damp and depressing, as if loath to leave a nice warm bed. Paul could sympathize. Even Shadow, his dark gray cat, closed her eyes, snuggled down on the bed, and refused to budge.

The gray sky and rain only added to his gloom. Feeding Shadow, eating his own breakfast, and then picking up the weekly clutter occupied him until mid-morning.

He pulled on his windbreaker and picked up the box for Brooke. "Okay, Shadow, guard duty until I get back."

Shadow stared up at him as if to say 'Don't I always?' Reaching down, he scratched her ears, and she twined between his legs. Her loud purr lightened his spirits.

Fortunately, the drizzle stopped as he parked in front of Brooke's house. He picked up the box from the passenger seat and walked toward the door. Stan's paltry belongings looked pitiful—not much to show for thirty odd years of life. Then Paul remembered most of Stan's things would have been in his apartment and so much of his life revolved around computers and the virtual world he occupied.

Paul stopped for a moment struck by how his few belonging would look to someone else. He had streamlined his life and eliminated non-essentials. What would they make of Shadow, his fencing gear, books, and the Delacroix? He considered himself more than the sum of his belongings. He shouldn't judge Stan by this box.

He rang the bell and Brooke, dressed in gray slacks and a bright turquoise blouse, answered at once. "Paul, thank you for coming. Please, come in."

She closed the door behind him and led him to the living room. He set the box down on the coffee table and stood uncertain whether to sit or remain standing.

"Have a seat." She motioned toward the black leather couch as she perched on one of the gray armchairs.

"I didn't find much, and none of it answers your questions." He pulled the Lido matchbook from his shirt pocket. "This is the only interesting thing; it says 'Club Lido.' I thought I'd visit." He handed the matches to Brooke.

Frowning, she examined them front and back. "The police inventory of Stan's belongings listed some credit card slips from this place, so he must have spent time there."

Her frown deepened as if she puzzled over why her brother would frequent such a place before returning the matches to Paul. "It seems so…so out of character. Stan mostly focused on his computer games. Detective Meyers suggested I look through Stan's apartment, which I did, but I didn't find anything."

Sighing, she picked up a picture from the table. "I found this snapshot among some old albums, and I thought it might do." She handed Paul a shot of Stan with a good view of his face. Smiling, with a park barbecue behind him, Paul assumed it had probably been taken during the summer. While not particularly flattering, it looked like Stan.

Paul nodded. "Yes, the picture's great. I'm not sure we'll learn much at the Lido though, but I'll give it my best try. I'll call and let you know what I find out." He stood, feeling a bit awkward. "Well, I have some errands to run, so I guess I'd better get going."

Brooke rose. "Oh, right. Thanks so much for your help. Listen…" She paused a moment. "It's nice of you to volunteer, but you don't have to go the Lido. I could do that."

Her clear blue eyes swamped him and triggered his protective instincts. No way could he see someone like her in a place like the Lido. "Considering its business, I'd have a better chance of learning something, that is, if there's anything to find out."

She searched his face perhaps seeking some hint as to how he felt, and then looked down. "It's an imposition. Please, don't bother."

"Nonsense," he said. He'd do a lot more if she would let him.

Brooke raised her eyes to gaze at him. He could easily immerse himself in those eyes. Lakes or seas, he wasn't sure which, but suspected more likely the restless nature of the ocean.

"Not at all, I'm curious myself. Besides, it'll give me a good excuse to see the insides of that place. I've always wondered what it was like." He laughed, a little embarrassed by his admission.

"Oh, in that case…" She gave him an impish grin, making her eyes sparkle in amusement.

"Yeah, well, thanks for the snapshot." He shoved it into his windbreaker pocket. "It may help jog a few memories. I'll let you know what happens. Bye, Brooke."

Maybe he wouldn't find out anything, but at least he would have tried, and she appreciated what he was doing. Elated, he strolled to his car. Somehow, the Lido just didn't seem like Stan's kind of place. Curiosity spurred Paul to learn what Stan had been doing there.

Marilyn's view of Stan agreed with Brooke's, and she was a good judge of people. Maybe Brooke was right, but if so, why would anyone want Stan dead? He hadn't made enough waves at the bank to have any enemies. No one Paul knew had a reason to kill Stan.

* * * *

Most people would call Club Lido a seedy dive. Dark—intimate its owners claimed—it reeked of beer, sweat, and cheap perfume. A constant base thrum from the hip-hop music kneaded the air. The loudness and the heavy bass made it impossible to even guess the song title. The little light came mostly from the multicolored ones around a small stage in an adjoining room and a few strobe lamps above the bar. Through a large, partially closed doorway in the middle of the facing wall, a dancer with little on besides sequins thrust her pelvis forward in a lascivious invitation to her small audience. Several women, in various states of display lounged against the bar and chatted with the hard-faced bartender with the obligatory peroxided mane. So far as Paul observed, she served drinks and washed the empties.

He slid onto a stool and ordered a beer from her. As he sipped it, he wondered where to start. The more he considered it, the more it appeared like trying to carry water in a sieve or looking for the proverbial needle in a haystack.

"Buy me a drink," a throaty voice echoed in his ear. "Call me Suzy."

He looked at the straw haired woman clad in a blue, clinging dress. Her skirt, slit to the hip, revealed a well-rounded thigh, and the neckline, dipping to her waist, exposed a generous expanse of flesh. Her full breasts brushed his arm as she settled herself.

Paul gave her a long, thorough appraisal. "I might...for a little info."

"Like what?" She leaned closer, an invitation in her green eyes.

"I'm trying to find a friend of mine, Stan Beldon. I'm told he used to come here."

She looked thoughtful. "Umm, can't say I recognize the name, but that don't mean much. Lots of the guys don't tell us their names, at least not their real names. I've only been here a couple of weeks myself, and, if business doesn't pick up, might move on." She motioned to the

24

bartender. "Vodka Collins."

Paul paid for her drink and continued to sip his beer. "So who has? Been here a while?"

"Topaz, the bartender, she runs this place, and Misty, that dark-haired girl in the blue sequins." She nodded toward a group of tables near the doorway and facing the dancer. "But you won't get nowhere with her. She leaves 'em at the door. Now me, it depends on the guy." She ran her fingers up his arm. "You, I could make an exception for. I get off at two, how about it?" She gave him a toothy smile.

Some invitation, but she wasn't his type; good body, but too hard and way too easy. "Thanks, I may look you up later, but I really need to find this guy. He owes me some dough, and...I kind of need it."

Suzy shrugged, the motion almost spilling her breasts out of her low-cut dress. "Suit yourself, I'll be around, if you change your mind." She slid off the stool, displaying even more thigh, picked up her drink, and walked to the doorway to survey the tables with their occupants focused on the small stage.

Paul looked toward the blonde bartender. Topaz Suzy had said. Topaz Laval?

"Another beer?" the bartender asked, holding up a glass.

He nodded. "Suzy says you know most of the guys who come here."

"The regulars, yeah, but we get a lot just passing through, come in one night and never come back." She placed another beer in front of him.

"Know a fellow named Stan Beldon?" He sipped the watery brew.

"Can't say I do. What's he look like?" She wiped the bar next to Paul.

"Flabby, five ten, about thirty or so, brown hair."

She laughed, harsh and hard-edged. "That describes most of our clientele."

"I have a picture." He set his beer down and pulled out the small snapshot Brooke had given him.

Topaz took the photo and peered at it. "Can't see it in this light." She walked over to the bar light and looked again. "No, don't think I've seen him here. Why're you looking for him?" She returned it to Paul.

"He owes me some money, and well...I need it." He replaced the picture in his wallet.

"You a loan shark?" Her voice hardened.

"No way." Paul shook his head. "Just a friend. Anyone else here

25

who might know?"

"Not really. The girls come and go; most don't stay long. It's hard to keep them, even though the money's not bad. Some are just passing through; others don't like the hours." She wiped the bar once more and looked up briefly. "Sorry, I can't help you." She went back to washing the dirty glasses and tidying the bar.

Can't or won't, Paul mused. He watched her for a moment, then picked up his glass of beer, and wandered over to the small tables edging the stage. The dancer finished, and the spotlight dimmed somewhat. The woman Misty sat by herself.

"You a dancer?" Paul stopped next to her.

"Me?" She laughed. "No, too much work." Her shiny black hair reflected the blue spotlight and the glittering sequins of her dress. The dress, like Suzy's, short and cut low, teased the eye, promising soft, yielding flesh beneath. Never good at guessing women's ages, Paul had no idea how old she was. He saw no telltale wrinkles about the eyes or the mouth. She looked more like someone he might like to know, less hard edged than either Suzy or Topaz.

"Okay if I join you?" Paul pulled out the chair next to her and placed his beer on the table.

She looked up at him, studying him as if assessing how good a mark he might be. Apparently satisfied, she nodded, giving him a wide smile. "Sure, but you have to buy a drink, or Topaz'll think I'm not working."

"Topaz?" Paul thought ignorance might get him more, so he said nothing else.

She nodded. "Yeah, Topaz Laval, the bartender; she runs this place."

He guessed right on that one, but then Topaz wasn't a common name. "What'll you have?"

"A Scotch on the rocks."

Paul nodded and walked to the bar. He returned carrying a fresh beer and a glass of Scotch. Placing the glass in front of her, he grabbed the chair next to her, and slid onto it. He rested his arm lightly on the back of her chair.

"Suzy says you've been here quite a while."

"About three months, since Topaz took over. She and I go back a ways." Misty sipped her Scotch.

Paul drank some of his beer and then set it down. "I asked the bartender—Topaz?—about my friend, guy named Stan Beldon." He watched to see her reaction to Stan's name.

"Stan? Let me think." She looked toward the dancer and frowned.

"We've kind of lost touch. I know he used to come here." Paul paused, considering what might convince Misty to say more. "How's the Scotch? Would you like another?"

"Sure, why not?" She took a last swallow and handed him the glass. "Thanks, it's nice to meet a gentleman. We see too few of those." She grinned at him.

Paul retrieved another Scotch and hurried back to Misty. "Look, I only need to know if he was sweet on one of the women here."

Sipping her Scotch, Misty studied his face. "A guy by that name came in now and then. For a while he was kind o' sweet on Topaz, but she doesn't have time for anybody, except Harley. He owns the place and her."

"Do you remember the last time Stan came here?"

"Probably about a week ago, why?" She looked at him, slightly puzzled.

"He died just after that from a drug overdose."

"Jesus!" She set her glass down with a slight thud. "Sorry to hear that. I never saw him do drugs—a beer now and then, but nothing else." She stared down at the table. 'I hate druggies."

"His sister asked me to find anyone he knew. She says he didn't do drugs." He watched her over the top his glass.

Misty frowned a moment, as if uncertain what to say. "Look, I don't know anything. You should talk to Topaz. She'd know more about him than I would." She sipped her drink.

"She told me she didn't know Stan; said she'd never seen him." Paul cradled his beer and continued to monitor her reactions.

Misty glanced over at Topaz busy behind the bar. "Probably didn't want to get mixed up with the cops, particularly if the guy is dead. She hates cops."

"I understand that. I'm not over fond of them either, but I'm not a cop, and wouldn't she rather talk to me than them?"

"Depends on what you want to know. She's got a thing about nosy people." She raised her glass and studied him a moment. "Why should she trust you?" Underneath, he heard 'Why should I trust you?'

"I'm a gentleman, remember?" Paul grinned at her and then leaned back, his face serious. "I just want to know what really happened to my buddy and who called 9-1-1." He sighed, wishing yet again the police had acted; he didn't even know the right questions to ask. "If it weren't for his sister's blue eyes, I wouldn't be here. It's not really my scene."

"Yeah." Misty grinned. "That's obvious."

Paul grinned back. "Well, thanks for talking to me anyway." He put his empty glass down and glanced at his watch. "Hadn't realized it's so late. I have to get to work early, so I'll try Topaz again, but not tonight."

Nodding to Misty, he rose and strolled toward the door, waving to Suzy as he passed the bar. At the door he gazed back at Misty a moment before opening the door and leaving.

Carrying her glass, Misty strolled over to the bar and slid onto a stool.

"Something bothering you?" Topaz looked up as she dumped some empties into the pan of soapy water in the sink.

"That guy that just left asked about Stan Beldon." Misty sipped the remains of melted ice and weak Scotch. "He said you told him you never heard of Stan. How come?"

Topaz snorted. "Look, the guy's dead. It was in the papers; he OD'd. I don't need to get mixed up with that. You know how Harley is."

Running a finger around the rim of her glass, Misty nodded. "Yeah, but I got the impression he was a friend of Harley's."

Topaz glared at her. "Listen, Misty, this is Harley's bag. We stay out of it. That guy comes nosing around again, don't talk to him. We got enough problems." She began collecting empty glasses, clinking them together angrily. "Besides, maybe he's a cop."

"Nah." Misty shook her head. "He's not the type, and asking questions up front, the undercover fuzz doesn't do that. They're too smart."

"Maybe, but we don't need trouble, so let it be. We got customers to take care of." Topaz wiped the bar in front of Misty and picked up another couple of empties. She walked over to the sink.

Frowning, Misty shook her head, and looked around for any prospects. Spotting a lone man sitting near the dance floor, she left her empty glass and sashayed over.

* * * *

As Paul drove home, he decided he hadn't totally wasted his time. Stan had been to the Lido on a number of occasions. If he had some way to get Topaz to talk about what she knew, maybe she would provide the answers Brooke wanted. Anyway, he still had Stan's program files to review. Something about the code nagged at Paul, but he couldn't quite place his finger on what. Stan hadn't limited himself to activity on new accounts.

Paul considered calling Brooke to update her on what he'd learned, but decided to wait. He'd rather talk with her in person than over the telephone. She was the kind of girl to take home to Mom, but only if Mom had fought in the women's wars. His had, so he felt they would get on just right. She had brains, beauty, and confidence. Still, it did his ego good to be needed, even if he hadn't learned much.

Chapter Three

At work Monday, Paul again tackled Stan's program files. They intrigued him. While most of them performed ordinary utility functions, one subroutine appeared to do something more. Invoked as part of the interest calculation, it truncated the amounts instead of rounding and stored the results into a separate file. That implied Stan shorted some customers of a penny on their interest. Those unaware of what such a change could mean would consider it trivial. However, if it happened often enough on enough accounts, it added to a tidy sum, but enough to cause someone to kill Stan?

Nothing indicated whether Stan had installed the routine or what he had done with the stored file. He might have created it just to see the results. A vague unease and lack of information made Paul reluctant to act yet. Making false accusations wouldn't do his reputation as the best the bank had any good, nor would it make Brooke happy if he accused her brother of theft.

Maybe Cramer, Stan's boss and section manager, knew about the routines, but then he would insist on knowing exactly what they did and Paul had no idea. At best, he had only fuzzy suspicions. He wanted to discuss them with someone, but if his hunch of a scam proved right, it meant serious consequences for the bank—way beyond his experience and responsibility. The question loomed to whom should he pass the information—ideally, someone with the brains and position to act if necessary. No way did he want this mess to rebound on him. Frowning, he leaned back and stared at the Delacroix, straining to consider possible names. He wanted someone he knew and trusted.

Maybe Morgan could handle it. As a corporate officer, the Vice President for Information and Data Systems, Morgan had the authority to deal with any high-level consequences. He'd assess the options and protect the bank's reputation. Paul punched Morgan's number and spoke with Sally Morris, his assistant. Luckily, Morgan had an open slot right now.

Hands in his pockets, Paul strolled down the hall. He wanted to raise possibilities without overstressing problems. Stan might have never installed the questionable subroutine or had dumped the results file. Paul hit the up elevator button, waited a moment, then changed his mind, and took the adjacent stairs instead. The executives had offices one flight up on the third floor, and Morgan's office had convenient access to the elevators.

When Paul approached Morgan's office, Sally, a vivacious brunette, greeted him with a warm smile warm. She motioned him toward the open door.

He smiled back and then sauntered into Morgan's walled office; only senior executives had the luxury of those. He closed the door.

Morgan didn't look up as Paul entered, but focused on a computer screen sitting on a small table to his left. Striking in appearance, Morgan had risen rapidly at the bank, and at thirtysomething, was the youngest vice president in an old conservative company. Noted as a stylish dresser, his navy suit, suitably bankerish, contrasted nicely with his pale green shirt and a gray striped tie. He wore his dark wavy hair suitably short. Everything about him reeked of success. His aura of confident authority reassured both his superiors and his own staff.

The stacks of papers on the credenza behind Morgan almost made Paul laugh. Even executives accumulated too much paper. He eased into one of the side chairs in front of the oval table Morgan used as a desk.

Others spoke of Morgan as a good organizer with a broad understanding of technology, but Paul didn't consider him a programmer, despite his position. Senior executives didn't need to be techies; they only had to know how to use technology to increase profitability and market share. Paul had no idea how Morgan might react to vague suspicions. Still pondering how to approach the matter, he gazed out the window at the tall skyscraper next door and waited until Morgan finished.

"Just catching up on my e-mail," he said. "Some people spend all their time sending messages and copying me on all of them. Maybe you should rig the system so only every sixth message is allowed." He grinned, surveying Paul, and then sobered.

"Sally said you wanted to see me about Stan Beldon." His tone implied both a question and a sense of 'what's the bottom line?'

Leave it to Morgan to cut to the core of things. "Yeah, I've a hunch something doesn't fit about Stan's death. I've gone through his papers and files, and it appears he was doing something odd. Do you know anything about his current project assignments?"

Morgan frowned and studied Paul. "Only what's in the monthly report and in the project schedules. As I remember, Cramer had him working on integrating the customer account information from the branches into our new consolidated customer file." He placed the tips of his fingers together, flexing them up and down, and leaned back in his chair as he considered Paul.

"Did he have anything to do with the account balances?"

"Not so far as I know." Morgan narrowed his eyes. "Why? Something questionable about his work?"

"I'm not sure yet." Cautious, Paul didn't mention the special subroutine. No way did he want to accuse Stan of anything right now. If he did, Brooke would most likely blame him for destroying her brother's reputation as an honest man. Without solid evidence, he preferred to say nothing.

"Look," Morgan leaned forward. "If anything affects the bank, or the accuracy of our reports, tell me now. Our customers rely on us to honor our fiduciary responsibilities to ensure the accuracy of their transactions. We don't want any adverse publicity." He grimaced. "It's bad enough having a bank employee die of a drug overdose."

"I know; I'll keep you updated. I've no idea about the installation status of Stan's recent work. There's probably nothing to worry about. If you hear anything that applies, let me know. I'll tell you if I find anything. Thanks for talking with me." He pushed his chair back and got to his feet.

Morgan gave him a searching look and nodded. "I'm relying on you. We have to protect the bank." He stared at Paul a moment as if thinking. "Have you talked to Cramer?"

Paul shook his head. "I thought I'd get the facts first. Should I?"

For a moment, Morgan sat flexing his fingers and then shook his head. "No, not until you know whether we have a problem. Keep this confidential."

"Of course, I'll give you a full report when I've finished, or sooner if I uncover a problem. Thanks."

"Thank you, I'm glad you have the right priorities." Morgan's dark eyes narrowed and remained on Paul as he opened the door and left.

Uncertain he'd done the right thing, Paul headed for his cubicle with a slow step. Alerting Morgan to his suspicions seemed the wisest course, but he couldn't bring himself to tell him much. Morgan might think he chased ghosts or had too much imagination. At least if he learned anything adverse to the bank, Morgan could deal with what came next.

Now, he'd better spend some time looking at the subroutine. Since Documentation scheduled all program installations, he'd check with them whether Stan's routine had been installed and get a record of which programs used it. He also needed to tell Brooke about his visit to the Lido. Maybe he could talk her into lunch.

He keyed Brooke's number and waited for her to answer, hoping he'd caught her at home. The phone rang twice before she answered.

"Hello, Brooke? Paul Counts here. How about lunch?"

"Hello. Have you learned anything more about Stan?" She sounded anxious, yet hopeful.

"Not much, but we can discuss what I've found." He glanced at the clock sitting on his desk. "Would 12:15 at the Hunan Lion work?"

"Sure. If you get there first, try for a table with a little privacy, okay?"

"Fine. See you then." He disconnected and wished he had more to tell her. At least he had verified the link with the Lido. Topaz might be the woman Stan had liked. As for telling Brooke about the programs, he wanted to know more first. She wouldn't welcome any hint of Stan doing something illegal.

Next Paul called Carol Coates in Documentation. "Carol, Paul Counts here. Can you tell me the status of some work Stan Beldon had underway? If I give you some subroutine names, I need to know which programs invoke them and what the current version numbers are."

"How many are we talking about?"

"Maybe six or so."

"Sure, but things are a little hectic down here right now. Send me an email with the names and when I have time, I'll look them up and email you back."

He paused a moment, wishing he had the data now and could reassure Brooke that Stan had done nothing wrong. However, things never went as fast as he wanted. Carol would respond as soon as she could.

"That's fine, thanks." Paul disconnected and entered an e-mail message to Carol with the subroutine names. Hopefully, she would get back to him later today. That finished, he went on sorting his mail. He managed to clean up various odds and ends before noon and left, anticipating a pleasant lunch with Brooke.

The drive to the restaurant invigorated him, particularly now the trees carried a pale green fringe and some of the fruit trees had decided not to wait for the late spring. White and pink blossoms against the dark trunks brightened the drive. Sunshine added to his happy mood.

Like Stan, he'd let work take over his life. Office romances presented too many complications, and he hated the bar scene. He kept his private life private. The few women he met at his Saturday fencing class didn't interest him—teenagers and a few naïve university students. These days, life moved at a furious pace, but he'd ignored it, and now it ignored him.

Brooke's intelligence and warmth, paired with the fact she didn't work for the bank, attracted him. But something else about her made his heart twist with nervous excitement every time he saw her and teased him with visions of a different future than the one into which he had stumbled.

Reaching the Hunan Lion parking lot, Paul left his car near the restaurant. Inside the upscale eatery, the upholstered armchairs and tables covered with snowy cloths offered an atmosphere of comfort. The staff all wore black suits, white shirts, and black bow ties. The walls, in soft greens and peaches, reflected from large mirrors. Definitely not fast food or even typically Chinese, he hoped his choice convinced Brooke he had more sophisticated taste than the usual nerdy programmer.

He glimpsed her waiting for him at a table near the entrance to the kitchen. He admired her sense of style and elegance. Her dark brown suit set off her blonde hair and fair coloring. Her pale green blouse framed her face and neck and added to her sophisticated aura. He sat on the opposite side of the table, content just to gaze at her.

After greeting him, she looked at him, expectation written on her face. "Well?" Her throaty voice carried a sense of urgency.

"So far, I haven't found much. I've identified what programs Stan worked on and have begun to sort through those. I talked with one of the VPs about Stan's work, but he didn't know much about it. My visit to the

Lido confirmed Stan spent some time there. The woman who knew him best, Topaz Laval, won't talk about him."

"I can't help with Stan's work, but maybe I could do something about this Lido place. What do we do next?" Frowning, she looked to him, as if expecting a suggestion.

"I'm not sure." He ran a hand over his hair smoothing it toward the back. "We could talk to the police again, but we really haven't anything more to tell them, other than your certainty Stan didn't do drugs. One of the Lido hostesses said the same."

Brooke gave him a wide grin. "I told you."

The server arrived to take their drink orders. They both ordered Chinese tea and then studied the menus.

Paul noted with pleasure a number of Hunan and Szechwan dishes. "Do you like Hunan?"

Brooke nodded. "In small amounts, but not for an entire meal."

"I'll select a spicy entree and you pick something else." He grinned at her over the large leather covered menu.

"Okay, maybe the Hunan combination."

"With the Hunan chicken, we have, one neutral dish, one spicy."

The server returned with their tea and Paul ordered for them.

"Would you like steamed or fried rice?" the server asked, pad at ready.

"Steamed," they both answered almost in unison.

Brooke laughed. "At least that's one thing we have in common."

She said nothing more until the server left and then focused on Paul. "So, what about this club?"

"The Lido features hostesses in tight, low-cut dresses hustling men for drinks and dancers wearing…" He stopped, embarrassed. "Uh, not much. Brooke, the place is a dive. It depresses me to see people wasting their lives that way. It's hard to believe Stan went there."

"What about the women who knew him?"

"Only a hostess named Misty and the bartender, Topaz Laval. Stan or someone had written her name in his book of matches. Misty remembered your brother, but said he talked more to Topaz. However, Topaz claimed she didn't remember him, but she's skittish about anything to do with the police, so she wouldn't talk to me. Didn't trust me, I guess." Paul grinned.

"Why not?" Brooke studied him with curiosity.

"Uh, according to Misty I didn't fit. Besides, the turnover is high and none of them talk about much except to say 'Buy me a drink.'"

The server returned and placed heaping dishes before them, with a small bowl of steamed rice for each of them. For a few moments, busy with the food, they didn't speak. Brooke placed only a small serving of the Hunan chicken on her plate, while Paul filled his with both dishes.

"Good choice," Brooke said after sampling the chicken. "It's not as hot as I expected."

After a few minutes, she set her chopsticks down. "Do you think I might have a better chance of getting Topaz to talk about Stan?"

Paul shook his head. "I doubt it. She doesn't know you, so why would she?"

"Because I'm a woman and...Stan's sister." She grinned at him, an impish twinkle in her eyes.

"I doubt it. Those people don't trust outsiders. You'd have to be a pole dancer or a hostess."

"That's not a bad idea. So you think I could pass for one?" She gave him a crooked grin.

Paul's stomach lurched and his eyebrows shot upward. For a moment, he smelled stale air, sweat, and spilled beer and saw all the drunken men and sleazy hustlers. Brooke didn't belong there.

"No way, you're not the type. Not that place. The men want sex without subtlety—as unadorned as possible. It's no place for you. This isn't like the movies."

"Why not?"

"Have you watched any reality TV or those cop shows? This is worse."

"You don't know me very well, Paul. I'd do almost anything if it helped find out what happened to my brother."

"I understand that, but undercover work takes guts and knowledge. Even the language can trip you up. You just want to play Mata Hari or Lara Croft."

"Sure, why not?" Brooke grinned, but then sobered. "I owe it to my bother to try. Anyway, the clothing can't be worse than what's worn on the beach these days, and I've managed amorous men before. " She picked up the chopsticks absently.

The vision of Brooke in a skimpy bikini or even less made him pause. He'd like to see that, but to share her with the drunks at the

Lido—no frigging way. A woman like her had no idea about the Lido and its gritty ugliness. Movies and television always glamorized such places. How the hell could he convince her?

"No," he snapped. "You'd need someone to vouch for you. They don't admit unaccompanied women—too much competition to the hired help."

"I meant as an employee. You said the turnover was fairly steady."

Groaning, Paul stared at her, eyes wide. "It's a lousy idea. Forget it."

"What about this Misty? She knew Stan. Maybe she'd help us."

"Brooke, I know how much this means to you, but it won't work."

She set the chopsticks down and aligned them perpendicular to the table edge before looking up at him. "Either you help me, or I'll do this myself. Which is it?" Her narrowed eyes had a determined glint, and she sat as stiff and straight as a dancer's pole.

He sighed, resenting his lack of options. No way did he want to antagonize her. Of course, Misty would laugh outright at the notion and that would end it.

"All right, I'll talk to Misty and see what she says. We'll find another way."

"Okay, but just ask her to talk to me. Don't squash the whole thing. Promise?" She took his right hand in hers and forced him to look in her eyes.

Gazing into to those dark blue depths, Paul read icy determination. Her insistence on such a dangerous and risky scheme worried him. Feeling pressured and having nothing else to suggest, he stared at her. At last, unable to think of an alternative, he yielded with reluctance.

"All right, I promise, but I don't like it. Maybe she'll tell you a bit more."

Brooke squeezed his hand and released it apparently satisfied he would keep his promise. Then, she picked up the chopsticks and resumed eating.

"Yowouch!" She grabbed for the tea.

"Are you okay?"

"Yeah," she gasped, eyes watering. "I just bit into one of those peppers. Much worse than Mexican chili peppers." She drank the tea, a glass of water, and another cup of tea. "Remind me to be more careful next time."

"I will." He grinned, glad she thought they had a future together.

This time he insisted on paying for their lunch. Outside the restaurant, he lingered not wanting to say goodbye.

"I'll call you after I talk to Misty."

"If you convince her to talk with me, I'll owe you dinner."

"Now that's an offer I can't refuse. Leave it to me and I'll let you know what she says."

"Thanks, Paul, I appreciate it." The warmth of her smile held him as he watched her leave.

On the way back to the bank, he mulled over how to raise Brooke's idea with Misty. His gut reaction told him she'd laugh in his face. Maybe he should let Brooke ask her. In any event, it meant another trip to the Lido to talk with Misty.

* * * *

After eight that same evening, Paul returned to the Lido. The place appeared even seedier than before. No way could he picture Brooke working here. Tonight, the clientele looked drunker and scruffier than the last time. Disgust foremost, he sauntered toward the bar.

"Back again so soon?" Topaz looked up as he approached. "Did you find your buddy?"

Paul shook his head. "No luck. Guess I'm out a couple of C's. How about a beer?"

"Coming up." She took a glass from under the counter and proceeded to fill it with no wasted motions.

Leaning against the bar, he glanced around the place and sipped the cold beer. As before, a few men sat at tables in the far room and watched the dancer. Another two occupied stools at the bar. He wondered how the Club stayed in business with so few customers. The hostesses hung onto their particular marks, each nursing a drink. Misty sat with one yuppie-type, chatting quietly.

"Hey, nice to see you again," purred a husky voice to his right. As he turned, Suzy slid onto the stool next to his. "Come back to see me?" Tonight her ruby red dress clung in all the interesting places, framing her generous breasts with a deep vee, but this time, instead of a thigh-high slit, the short skirt barely covered the essentials.

"You, and a couple of others, including Topaz here."

"Aw, the boss-lady has to keep track of the liquor supply. I've got time to play." She reached for his hand, "Let me tell your future." She peered at his open palm in the dim light. "Yeah, says here you're gonna have a good time, a real good time. This is your lucky night."

"Well..." He squeezed her hand before releasing it. "Since you're here, it must be. Let's see, Vodka Collins, wasn't it?" He motioned to Topaz who slid a drink toward Suzy.

"Right on, that's what I like, a guy who remembers the little things." She took a long swallow from the tall glass. "Sitting makes me antsy. How about a dance?"

"I'm a little rusty, but why not?" Paul left his unfinished beer and followed her to the pocket-sized dance floor near the stage.

Suzy knew how to move, no doubt about that. Supple and hypnotic, she looked lost in the music, but her movements focused on one thing, tantalizing him. She moved with smooth ease, but each dip threatened to spill her jiggling breasts beyond the deep vee.

"You're not bad," she said as Paul did his best to follow her lead.

"With a strong drum beat, I'm okay, but don't get fancy. I'd never make it on 'Dancing with the Stars.' Acrobatics aren't my strong suit."

She moved closer, and Paul backed a bit, but with a small floor and two other couples, she left him nowhere to go. As she thrust her hips forward, he breathed in barely avoiding contact. She didn't appeal to him and forced intimacy didn't solve his problem. He had to talk to Misty, not Suzy anyway. The rhythm changed to a Latin beat, and he pulled back.

"Whoa, enough." He stopped moving. "This music isn't for me. I'll buy you another drink and then I have to split. I work tomorrow and that means getting up early." He steered her to edge of the dance floor and grabbed a cocktail napkin from a table to mop his face.

"Scared?" Her disappointed pout teased and challenged him.

"No, just not into this music," Paul responded.

Suzy's pout turned to a smile. "It was fun anyway." She followed as he strolled back toward the bar.

"Another round for us," He said to Topaz and dropped the wadded napkin on the bar. "Dancing sure works up a sweat."

"That depends on how you do it, Hon." Suzy picked up her tall glass, took a quick swallow, and faced him with a flirtatious smile. "Sure you don't want to stay?"

"Can't. I work tomorrow, but don't let me keep you. Topaz wants you to hustle a few, so maybe I'll see you tomorrow or next week."

"I sure hope you change your mind, but you're right. She likes to hear that cash register ring. Guess I'd better move, or she'll be on my case. See ya next time." Taking two more swallows from the tall glass, she slid off the stool and swayed over to another man farther down the bar.

Paul looked around for Misty and saw the man she had been sitting with head for the john. He grabbed his glass of beer and approached her table. She looked up as he neared her.

Smiling down, he pulled out one of the chairs and sat, stretching out his legs. "Hello. We talked the other night about my buddy Stan, remember?"

"Yeah, but it didn't make Topaz happy. She said he OD'd, and she doesn't want the cops in here." Misty watched him from half-closed eyes.

"Can't say I blame her about that. I'm not so fond of them myself. I came to ask if maybe you'd talk to Stan's sister. His death has upset her, and if you talked to her about Stan, it might ease her mind. She doesn't believe he did drugs, and the police see no reason to pursue the case."

"Yeah, when it comes to drugs, they only care about the dealers. I can't tell her much." She lifted her glass and finished off her drink.

"Maybe not, but talking to you would make her feel better." Paul looked around at the dispirited men and the jaded women. "Somehow this isn't the kind of place for her. Could we meet you somewhere else?"

"I sleep late."

"How about lunch?" Noting her hesitation, he sighed. "I'll make it worth your while."

She looked at him for a moment and then nodded. "Breakfast for me. All right, meet me at the Clock. It has booths and some privacy."

"Sounds fine to me. Tomorrow at eleven-thirty?"

"Make it noon. Otherwise I'll be late."

Paul nodded and set down his empty glass. "Thanks, see you there."

He left his unfinished beer and walked to the exit, glad to leave the Lido behind. He couldn't see Misty telling Brooke much or treating her proposal with anything except a hearty laugh, but he'd kept his promise.

Chapter Four

Paul eyed Brooke with appreciation as she entered the Clock restaurant. They had agreed to meet a few minutes early to ensure they got there before Misty arrived. Brooke, always well dressed, had gone causal in jeans and a satiny shirt with a Western jacket.

"Nice jacket," he said in greeting.

"Glad you like it. I don't want to intimidate Misty."

"I hope she makes it, she said she sleeps late." Paul looked to the door. "Let's sit in back. It's quieter there."

Brooke led the way and Paul admired the smooth movement of her hips as she walked. They passed along the diner counter on one side and high backed booths on the other. They sat in the last booth on the right.

He left Brooke facing toward the front and returned to the entrance to watch for Misty. When a dark haired girl with a pert ponytail approached him, he did a double take for a moment, surprised to see how young Misty looked in daylight with only minimum make-up.

"Thank you for coming." He slipped her two twenties. "We're in the last booth; more private that way." He led her toward Brooke at the back of the restaurant.

"Misty, this is Brooke Beldon, Stan's sister," Paul said as Misty took the seat opposite Brooke.

"Thank you for coming." Brooke's look of surprise as she appraised Misty's neat navy skirt, sweater, and red blouse amused Paul. "I guess..."—she groped for words—"I mean...I expected someone older."

Misty sniffed. "Hey, I work at the Lido 'cause the money's good, lots of tips, and I leave 'em at the door. I'm not a prostitute, despite what some people think. Yeah, some of the girls use drugs, but they don't last long, and I've got a little girl. The Lido pays more than fast food or data entry. Besides, I never learned to type. So what do you want from me?"

"Paul, Mr. Counts," Brooke began, nodding at him, "said you remembered my brother Stan. I want to find out what happened to him and why. The police say it's a case of too much crack, but Stan never used drugs. His credit card receipts show he visited the Lido the night he died. Some woman called 9-1-1 asking for help." She paused a moment and then, with a grim face, skewered Misty with a firm look. "I have to know what happened to my brother. The Lido and that woman are the only leads we have."

"Hello, folks, care to order?" A stocky, middle-aged woman stood beside the booth, pad at ready.

Misty ordered breakfast, and Brooke and Paul asked for cheeseburgers. They waited until the server left.

"I'm sorry about your brother," Misty said. "Like I told Paul here, I can't tell you much. Your brother came in a few times, and linked up with a woman, but not one of us. I had customers to worry about. The two of them drank a bit. He talked some to Topaz. He spent no time with me. This other woman kept him occupied. Topaz keeps an eye on the customers, so she'd know more than me."

Brow furrowed, Brooke remained silent for a moment as if pondering what to say. "Would Topaz talk to me?"

"No way. She chewed me out for chatting with Paul here. Unless she sees something in it for her, she won't talk to anyone. Besides, she says this is 'Harley business.'"

"Harley business?" Brooke looked at Paul and then at Misty. "What's that?"

"He owns the Lido and Topaz. I couldn't prove it, but I'd say Harley deals small time drugs on the side. That makes Topaz touchy. She pays me well, so it's not my business."

The server returned with their orders and a bottle of catsup. "Anything else for you folks?"

"No, we're fine, thanks," Paul replied.

For a few minutes, they all concentrated on the hot food.

When Brooke finished, she took a deep breath. "Misty, what if I…uh…hired on as a hostess at the Lido? Could I learn anything?"

"You'd learn a lot, but not the things you'd want to know." Grinning, Misty sipped her coffee.

Brooke nodded. "I'd need an 'in.'" She looked at her tea and frowned. Paul worried what she might suggest, certain he wouldn't like it.

"What if you said I was a friend from out of town who needed a job?"

"Look, this is too much." Misty opened her purse and took out a pack of gum. Unwrapping a stick, she shoved in her mouth and chewed it for a moment. "One look at you and Topaz would spot you for a phony."

"Ya think so, huh? Like, I kin, sort of, ya know, fake it a bit. Like, 'buy me a drink han'som', is like m' best line."

Stunned, Paul stared at Brooke's sudden transformation as she lounged against the booth back. Her face looked different—sexier with an open invitation written there.

Misty grinned and deposited her gum on her plate. "You're laying it on thick, but maybe for a little bit you could do it at that. I understand you wanting to do something instead of stewing, but pulling a thing like this off..."

"I've got to know what happened to my brother. The police won't do anything. Please, help me."

For a long moment, Misty studied Brooke and then nodded. "Okay, you show up tonight about six-thirty, and I'll see what I can do, but Topaz may not go for it, and, if she doesn't, that's it." She opened her purse and put her gum pack away.

Blinking, Paul stared at Misty dumfounded. He'd expected her to refuse. The thought of Brooke in the Lido with the amorous men and all the sleaze repelled him. "Brooke, I don't think this will work. It's too dangerous." He crossed his fingers Topaz would say no.

Brooke ignored him and grinned at Misty. "It's a deal; I really appreciate your help."

"The only reason I'm only doing this is 'cause I had a friend who OD'd, and, if I knew who gave 'im the stuff, I'd 'a told the cops." She slid out of the booth. "I don't like Harley, but I owe Topaz, so I won't do more than tell her I know you and you need a job."

"That's all I need. And, thanks."

"You'll need a name." Misty surveyed her for a moment. "Umm, Candy Marsh, and you better be from out of town, maybe Indy. You'll also need some ID. Topaz always checks those. She doesn't want any trouble with the cops for underage kids. I gotta go. See ya at the Lido."

She started to leave then suddenly stopped and turned around. "Oh, if I were you, Paul, I'd stay away. Topaz thinks you're either an undercover cop or an enforcer for the big boys."

As the image of a hulking enforcer ala TV appeared in his mind, Paul laughed. "Thanks for the advice, Misty."

He and Brooke watched in silence as Misty sauntered toward the entrance and left.

Setting down his glass, he focused on Brooke. "I don't like this. If Harley is dealing, who knows what else is going on there. Drug dealers don't like stoolies or competition. Didn't you listen to Misty?"

"Yes, I heard her. I can't see how Topaz could think of you as an enforcer." Her teasing tone and grin took the sting from her comment. "Do you have any criminal ties?"

"You could get hurt, even killed."

"Paul, you've hit a stone wall." She turned her empty water glass around on the table, widening the wet mark it had made. "There's more to learn, but like Misty said, if Topaz doesn't trust you, you can't do any more. Stan was my brother. I owe it to him and my parents to clear his name. He wasn't a drug addict."

She pinned him with a steely stare; her blue eyes demanding his cooperation. "I have to try. If I don't succeed, we'll think of something else."

Impaled by those intense eyes, he saw no way to convince her. He shook his head. "This is all a sham. You just want a chance to step out of character and live a shady life."

"Yeah, maybe you're right." She grinned, a gamine now. "Just like you wanted to see the inside of the Lido." The grin faded. "I have to know who set up my brother. We haven't anything else to go on. I've got to do something." Her clenched fingers made her determination clear.

Paul sighed, wanting another solution. "I haven't finished checking out Stan's routines yet. Maybe I'll find something there, and you won't have to do the Lido."

"Sure, but then what? That won't tell us anything about the woman who left with Stan the night he died."

Admitting he didn't know where to look next fueled anger and frustration. He sensed he'd failed Brooke, and he didn't like it. "Promise me you'll be careful, and, if things look risky, you'll get out or call me." He reached for her hand and held it wanting to keep her there.

"I'm no fool, Paul, and all I'm going to do is watch and listen." She withdrew her hand with gentle firmness.

As a freelance writer, Brooke kept research files on a variety of local issues including those dealing with so-called adult clubs. Once home, she dug into her files for anything on the Lido and clubs like it. Most of the stuff dealt with zoning battles and complaints from people living nearby. She also pulled the article she'd written about fake IDs and how kids and illegals could get them. When researching that piece, she had interviewed Saul Kominisky. He owed her a favor. She keyed in his number, let it ring three times and disconnected. She hit *Redial* and waited for his gravelly response.

"Saul, Brooke Beldon here. I need a favor. I'm doing an undercover story on an adult club and need an ID with the name Candy Marsh, just arrived from Indianapolis. I need it ASAP, ideally by mid-afternoon. Can you do it?"

"Sure, but this clears us, right?"

"Yes." Brooke sighed. Saul owed her because she'd kept his identity secret. "Shall I stop by?"

"Better I drop it off. Say maybe 3 or so?"

"Great, see you then."

She replaced the phone and returned her attention to the articles on clubs. To her surprise, none of them mentioned the Lido. Maybe she ought to search the court records or the real estate deeds files. Extensive searches took a lot of time, even with a high-speed link.

At three, the doorbell rang. Brooke went to answer it, but when she opened the door she found only a white business envelope on the step. The muffled roar of a souped-up car filled the air. Down the street, a black car zoomed around the corner. It looked like Saul had gotten shy or scared of something.

She ripped his gift open and a driver's license fell out. Picking it up, she studied his handiwork. He'd used a picture that could have been almost any female, but the name read *Candy Marsh*. At least he got the physical data right. Satisfied, she closed the door.

Brooke ransacked her closet for clothing suitable for the Lido's clientele and that would pass muster with Topaz. She finally settled on a draped cocktail top that plunged more than usual and an old mini side-wrapped skirt she had always had to sit in with care because it exposed too much thigh. She applied heavy make-up, especially the eye shadow and the mascara, and swept her hair to the left leaving her neck bare. A pair of large, dangling earrings added extra glitz.

"Well I hope this is sexy enough," she muttered as she slipped on her highest heels and tottered toward the door. High heels looked good on models and dancers, but she'd rather wear running shoes.

Driving the short distance to the Lido, she fought to calm her churning stomach. This had to work for Stan's sake. Topaz and her jaded crew had to believe she could do the job.

Sandwiched between a freeway and a four-lane road, the Lido

looked almost abandoned. Perhaps its former life as a coffee shop explained the location. A high peaked roof and large front windows painted a matte black hid the nature of the business. The adjoining parking lot contained just two cars—a battered Buick and an elderly Cadillac. Brooke assumed the hour too early for customers yet. The *Adults Only* sign and a neon female figure gave obvious hints to what the inside held.

After circling past, Brooke parked in a nearby 24-hour supermarket parking lot. She took out two sticks of gum and started chewing them as she walked over to the Lido. Inhaling, she tried to calm her jitters before opening the exterior door to a small entry area. The stench of stale cigarettes, perhaps even a cigar, and spilled beer engulfed and almost gagged her.

She straightened her shoulders and whispered Stan's name before continuing through another door into the dim interior. It took a moment for her eyes to adjust to the dim light. The black walls absorbed rather than reflected light.

A peroxide blonde lounged behind the bar, probably Topaz, and two women occupied bar stools. Brooke looked twice, but it wasn't until one of them waved that she recognized Misty.

"Candy, right on time," Misty said as she patted the stool next to her. "Come on and meet the boss. Topaz, this is Candy Marsh, that friend I told you about. She just blew in from Indy and really needs a job. I thought maybe we could use another girl."

"Pleased to meet 'cha, I'm sure." Brooke took a deep breath and the warning look from Misty made her slow down. "I ran into Misty here, and like heard you might need girls. I'm kinda short, and like need a steady gig, you know." She popped her gum as she gazed around. "Nice place."

Topaz studied Brooke with narrowed eyes and nodded. "Well at least you're not a kid. I have to watch those or the police are on my case. You got some ID?"

Brooke pulled out the fake ID Saul had given her and flashed it at Topaz. For a long moment, she waited as Topaz squinted at the ID, looked from it to her, and back at the ID.

"Don't look much you," she said at last.

"A bad hair day. Like, you know how it is. Damn thing adds ten years to my face." Brooke waited, her stomach cramping. She willed

Topaz to accept the ID.

"You're right about that." Topaz grinned at her and returned the license. "The regulars like a new face now and then; you'll do. We open at seven and close at two; the cops stop by to make sure we close. You get a percentage on every drink, yours and his. You get three breaks a night, two short ones, and one longer one. We work around our customers and who's busy. I pay in cash after we close. You pole dance?"

"Not my gig. A pole and stripping don't interest me." Brooke cracked her gum,

"The shy type, eh? Won't get you far here. The dancers get the best tips." Topaz grinned at Misty. "We have enough for now, but if we lose one, you'll fill in."

Brooke hoped her raised eyebrow said enough. As to the dancing, she couldn't imagine stripping even for Stan.

"Well, since you're Misty's pal, you can start tonight. If you do okay, you stay, but your job is to sell more liquor and keep 'em coming back." Topaz gave her a hard look. "What you do on your own time and who you go home with is your business, but no tricks during working hours, get me?"

Brooke held up both hands, palm out. "Hey, I got ya, but I keep the tips right?" Relief seeped its way through her tensed muscles.

"If you earn 'em, sure." Topaz continued to straighten up her working area behind the bar and to slide clean glasses into the overhead racks.

"Candy." Misty touched her arm. "Meet Suzy, one of us, and probably, next to me, your stiffest competition. She's pretty good, so if you want a few pointers watch how she works."

"Glad you're joining us, Candy. The more the merrier I always say." Suzy, in shiny chartreuse satin, slouched onto the stool next to Misty. She displayed both generous cleavage and plenty of satiny thigh.

Brooke watched with Misty and Suzy as a few men drifted into the bar, and observed how the two approached them. It didn't look difficult.

Keeping the men drinking and talking didn't take much effort. That most of them only wanted to talk surprised her. They sought a sympathetic ear, preferably in an attractive body. A few wanted to feel the merchandise, but Brooke made sure she kept a certain distance from those. If that didn't work, she made a break for the john, leaving the hot ones to cool down. For the insistent ones, she suggested dancing, but made sure to avoid direct contact, or directed their attention to the stage dancers or even to Suzy or Misty. She managed, but the strain of having to be so alert, yet appear interested and relaxed, wore her out.

She had taken her break and just returned to a small table by the dance floor. The men had thinned out, but a prospect lounged at the bar talking to Topaz. Pear-shaped with fairish hair, he wore a polo shirt, dress slacks, and Topsiders. Somehow, he made her think of boats. He acted as if he knew Topaz well.

* * * *

"Who's the new girl?" Harley slouched against bar and surveyed the dim room.

"Name's Candy. From Indy Misty said. Pretty enough, if you like blue-eyed blondes."

"Not bad. Maybe I'll talk to her later."

"Do that," Topaz said, touching his arm. "But not too friendly, eh?"

"Don't worry, baby; you know me." He squeezed her hand. "I love you best, but I want to make sure the merchandise is top grade." Harley leered.

"Top grade? Here?" Her laughter annoyed him and he glared at her

Topaz looked at Brooke and then at him. "All she has to do is hustle drinks; I told her no tricks on my time."

"Our time," Harley snarled. "This is my place and you work for me. Besides, we don't need a soliciting bust from the cops." He stood up, sucking in his gut. "I'll just say hi."

He left Topaz watching the blonde, as he strutted over to the small table where she sat.

"Hello, doll baby. How ya doing?" Harley pulled out a chair and sat almost on top of the new girl.

* * * *

Brooke gazed up at the beefy guy. Another one to fend off. "Fine, buy me a drink?" The odor of his cologne mixed with male sweat almost knocked her out.

"Why not? I own the place." His burly arm snaked around her.

"Uh...that so?" She pulled back to study him, moving away from his arm. Her brain worked at a furious pace trying to identify him. "Harley? Like Topaz warned me to stay away from you."

"Aw, she works for me and does what I tell her, like all the rest." He hitched his chair closer and pulled her toward him.

Just what she needed, an amorous owner and a jealous boss. "Like maybe when you're here, but I gotta work with her when you're not." She struggled to scoot her chair farther away.

"I'll worry about Topaz. For now, let's just get to know each other a little better." He captured her hand. "Topaz sez you're from Indy, so what brings ya here?"

Trying to appear icy, Brooke withdrew her hand and picked up her almost empty glass. "Got tired of the scenery; needed a change."

Harley moved closer. "Steady boyfriend?"

Desperate, she wondered how to turn off Harley. Having a boyfriend probably wouldn't worry him at all. "No...a girlfriend."

"Oh, one of those." Harley paused and stared at her, but then he smiled and started to move closer again. "Maybe I could change your mind. AC/DCs have a lot of fun."

"Not me." She made her voice as bitter as she knew how. "The man who raped me left me HIV. Would you like some of it?"

Harley eased back a bit. "So what're ya doing here?"

"Like I gotta eat. Meds cost, so if some john like gets his kicks out pawing me and buying drinks, so what?" Brooke shrugged, a bitter smile on her face. Misty's words from their first meeting came to her aid. "Like I don't have to go home with him."

Harley frowned. "Kind of sour, aren't ya? Better not pull that with the customers. They want sweet talk, not sass, gal."

She shook her head. "Like I didn't know that. I'm just realistic. Suzy likes you. She enjoys a good time, and no sense my making Topaz mad, not like just starting and all. Like...Topaz is staring at you." Brooke pushed back her chair and ambled toward a man at the bar.

###

Harley shook his head. "Waste of good equipment that." He followed the blonde to the bar, but turned and sat opposite Topaz.

He watched for a moment and then swallowed most of the drink Topaz placed in front of him in one long gulp. "You hired another lesbo. She's gotta be a dyke."

"Oh? It doesn't interfere with her work, and that's what counts." Topaz smiled as she leaned over her small sink washing a few glasses. Harley only grunted.

* * * *

The evening had drifted slowly away, and it neared closing time. The cops had been in, and most of the customers had left. Brooke sat at one of the small tables resting her feet, and wondering if maybe she should have stayed home.

"Nice to sit down." Suzy chewed a wad of gum as she pulled out the other chair. "Say, Candy, you turned Harley off. Why?"

"Told him I had a girlfriend…and HIV. He didn't like it."

"You, too? Most of the dancers have it. So far, I've avoided it." Suzy appraised her from head to foot. "You gotta a girlie?"

"That's my business." Brooke sighed. "My feet hurt."

"Mine too. You'll get used to it, and we sit more than we stand. You sure you want to turn Harley off?"

Brooke slipped off her right shoe. "Topaz wouldn't like it."

"Harley can show you a good time, and, if you like to get a little high, he has the stuff."

"Like what'd ya mean?" Brooke rubbed her foot and slowly eased on her shoe.

"Well…" Suzy lowered her voice. "He can get you rocks wholesale or free for good friends. Cheapest high around. Topaz knows he picks up a little on the side, and, as long you don't try to make it permanent, so what? We all need a little fun. Harley can give you a good time, a real good time. He's a ladies' man and knows what we like."

Suzy leaned forward and smiled archly, "I'm betting he can even turn you on."

"Maybe, but like I need money, not a man. Okay, Suzy?" Brooke worked on the other foot.

"Hey, no skin off my nose. That leaves more of Harley for me. Only trying to share the wealth. My philosophy's take what I can and enjoy it. At least he gives for what he gets, not like some I've had." Standing, Suzy smoothed her short dress over her thighs. "Guess that's it. See you tomorrow, Candy." She sauntered toward the bar.

Topaz counted out the money and gave each girl her wages. Brooke tallied hers, surprised. With the tips, she had a hundred dollars. Not too bad for a beginner. Maybe it would pay for some new clothes.

So far she had learned nothing about the woman who had left with Stan. Worse, she began to wonder whether she could keep up the charade. Tension, the smells, the amorous men, the late hours, and even the weak drinks sapped her energy. Used to early to bed and early to rise, the Lido hours complicated things. Now she knew why surveys found shift workers irritable.

Limping slowly to her car, Brooke couldn't wait to get out of these killer shoes. She drove home barefooted. After removing her makeup and taking a quick shower, she crawled gratefully into bed. Her entire body ached. She closed her eyes and hoped sleep would bring peace

In a deep sleep, she almost missed the ringing noise. Opening one eye, she glanced at the clock. Eleven-thirty, time to rise or something. She reached over and lifted the persistent phone.

"Hello, Beldon residence." She yawned.

"Brooke, that you?" Paul's voice came over the phone.

"Yes, I'm just getting up."

"Late night, eh?'

The humor in his voice annoyed her, damn him. Sleep fogged her brain. "Yes, and my feet hurt."

"Did you learn anything?"

"About Stan? No. Columbus has a lot of lonely men whose wives don't understand them." She sighed. "I met Harley."

"Really? How was he?"

"Persistent, but I told him I had a girlfriend, hated men since I'd been raped, and had HIV."

A slight pause followed. "You did? Is any of that true?"

She almost laughed at the uncertainty in his tone. "What do you think?"

He sighed. "That you have a great sense of humor and tried to let him down nicely without saying no."

"Clever, aren't you? I'm not sure it turned him off, but the HIV got him and he backed away. Suzy said he gives the girls crack and maybe I should change my mind."

"That's a lousy idea." Paul's tone expressed his distaste.

"Yeah, I'm there to find that woman anyway, and the farther away Harley stays, the happier I am. I've managed so far, but Misty's right. I hope this doesn't last long."

"So do I. It could get dangerous, especially if Harley deals drugs." Another slight pause followed. "Brooke, why don't you drop the whole thing?"

"I'll make a deal with you; let me have two weeks. If the woman doesn't show by then, I'll quit, okay?"

"Fine." Paul paused a moment "Make it a week."

She shook her head. "Not long enough, but I don't want to keep this sham up for long. It's hard on my feet, makes my hair stink, and interferes with my sleep. How's your end going?" She played with the phone cord, wondering what Paul really did.

"Slow, but when I finish sorting through these funny little subroutines, I'll know what Stan was doing. At least I now know which ones are actually used. I'll call if anything strikes. Well, get some beauty sleep and contact me if there's any sign of trouble. I'll worry about you until this is over."

"That's nice of you, Paul. Thanks for calling." She hung up the phone.

Looking at the clock, she supposed she should get up. Maybe a little shopping would help. She didn't exactly have the right wardrobe for the Lido. Ochman's ought to have a few gems that would fit right in and they might also have some new Anne Klein's or Liz Claiborne's. The Lido clothes could go to the Salvation Army thrift store once she finished at the club.

Ochman's, a popular local retailer, dealt in manufacturers' closeouts, fire sales, last years' fashions, and anything they could sell at a reduced price. The merchandise contained a mixture of designer labels, seconds, and oddments. Intelligent shoppers could find some incredible bargains, and, the unwary, some pricey mistakes. The shoppers had to examine what they bought, but the low prices made the effort worthwhile.

Brooke found several sale dresses perfect for the Lido—plunging necklines, slit skirts, and figure-hugging fits in polyester satins, fake gold lame, and even a black velour. She also indulged in several pairs of party shoes with rhinestone clips and satin bows at the heels. Among the sale pantyhose, she found a couple of black lace pairs. At least no one would be likely to recognize her in such clothing. Add the heavy make-up and the wild hair and her own mother wouldn't recognize her.

The fancy dresses reminded her of a costume party for hookers. She'd always enjoyed the school plays, but she had never had as much at stake before. Paul had one thing right. The longer the masquerade continued, the greater the chances Topaz or Harley would grow suspicious.

Thinking about the Lido and its denizens, she wondered what to do besides observe. The itch to ask questions pestered her like a mosquito bite, but caution said no. At first just getting used to the routine took all her attention. She needed information, but Topaz and Harley had reasons to hide it. Suzy offered advice, but had told Paul she didn't know Stan.

So far, Brooke hadn't even considered the repeat customers. A list of questions to ask them might help her work them into casual conversation. To start with, she could find out how often they came to the Lido and whether they knew any of the other customers. If any did, then maybe she could slip Stan's name into the conversation and gauge their reactions. At least it offered a strategy and a focus.

As a freelance writer and consultant, she had been able to free up enough time so no one would miss her. Still sleeping in late and working nights, didn't leave much time for her writing. A morning person, she found the adjustment to the Lido's hours a hassle, but it offered the only lead to that 9-1-1 woman. The police had given up, and the coroner had ruled Stan's death an accident, leaving the implication that as a drug user, he had been careless. The only hope to prove otherwise lay in her efforts and Paul's. If they didn't find anything, she would fail Stan and her parents. This Lido thing had to work.

* * * *

Business at the Lido didn't vary much, except for brisker business on the weekends. Topaz had also hired a bouncer, Mike Fender, for the weekends. At 6'3" with broad shoulders and at least 300 pounds, he had no trouble with drunks. Men comprised most of the Lido's clientele, with only an occasional couple. So far, the regulars Brooke had spoken with said they didn't know and preferred not to know the other customers. After a deep laugh, one had replied he came for the girls, not the men.

Near the end of the first week, Brooke sat by the dance floor with Misty and watched a young girl enter. Pretty, in a petulant sort of way, she wore her dark hair cut close to her head and a pair of hoop earrings that dangled to her collarbones. Clad in a short, tight, black sleeveless sheath, she displayed plenty of thigh. Her high-heeled boots made a sharp tattoo as she strutted to the bar and stopped in front of Topaz.

"Who's the kid?" Brooke whispered to Misty. "She doesn't look old enough to drink." Brooke expected Topaz to eject her as underage.

"A friend of Harley's, but Topaz don't like her. Some rich kid from the Northwest. She comes in now and then and picks up Harley. Suzy can probably tell you more about her since she's gone with them a couple of times."

53

Misty looked around and spotted a new arrival. "Guess I'd better get back to business. See ya." She sauntered over to the man in ironed jeans with a tailored black leather jacket and began to talk to him.

Brooke worked her way over to the bar. Topaz had just motioned the girl toward the back. She nodded and strode in the direction of Harley's office.

"Looks kinda young, I'd say," Brooke said as she slid onto a bar stool in front of Topaz.

Topaz watched until the girl closed the door behind her. "Yeah, but she doesn't drink here; just comes to see Harley."

"Pretty girl, I didn't know Harley liked 'em so young."

"Like my old man, he likes anything in skirts; age don't matter." Topaz collected the few glasses from the bar and began washing them.

"Humph, like how do you put up with it?"

"I know Harley, that's how. My ma went through the same thing, but she celebrated thirty-five years last week."

"Maybe so, but like what about the cops? You said to watch it."

Topaz stopped washing the empties and glared at Brooke. "It's Harley's business, and the cops got nothing to do with it. He isn't going to marry her, just fuck her. It's none of your business anyway, get me?" The fierce look in Topaz's agate eyes gave Brooke chills.

"Okay, okay, like I'm sorry." She turned away to survey the room and, seeing a new customer, moved off before she angered Topaz more. The girl still puzzled her.

A little later, Harley walked out with his arm around the girl. Topaz glared at their backs from the bar. For a moment, Brooke wondered what Harley would say if he could see Topaz's murderous look.

Later in the john, while Brooke fixed her make-up, Suzy came in for a smoke.

"Slow night out there," Brooke said as she tucked her comb away.

"Yeah, I expected a bit better. Gotta pay my rent the end of the week, and, if it doesn't get better soon, I may have trouble. I need a big tipper or two." Suzy tossed a match into the toilet.

From the mirror, Brooke watched her. "Like we need competition from the kids. Who was that chick with Harley?"

"Her? Oh, that's Brenda. Her dad's a big shot in some bank or other. She comes in now and then 'cause she knows Harley'll give her some crack for a bit o' young skin. He likes 'em young; says he can teach 'em to do things right 'cause they haven't learned to do 'em wrong yet."

"Yeah, like so long as they're old enough." Brooke sniffed as she patted her hair.

"She is, don't worry." Suzy grinned. "You want some of Harley too?"

Shaking her head emphatically, Brooke gave her hair one last pat. "Like no way, I told you that before. It's the cops, I worry about."

Exhaling slowly, Suzy nodded. "That's why Harley gets her out of here. Only one has to worry about her is Topaz."

"Good. Like I'd better get back."

"Yeah, see ya' later." Suzy put out her cigarette and went into the one cubicle, locking the door behind her.

In the club, things hadn't changed much. Misty talked with the lone customer. Sighing, Brooke sat at one of the tables bordering the dance floor. She looked up hopefully as the door opened and a well-dressed, older man marched to the bar. Gray haired, but not flabby, he looked like he might be able to speak in more than monosyllables. He stopped in front of Topaz. Brooke got up and approached them at the bar.

"Where is he?" His voice had a sort of controlled fury, but control was slipping fast.

"Where's who?" Topaz snapped back.

"You know who I mean, that cradle-snatching boss of yours." His hands gripped the bar, showing white around the knuckles.

"Harley? He left a bit ago." Topaz wiped the bar in front of him.

"And not alone I'll bet. He had my daughter with him, didn't he?"

She sighed and gave him a sympathetic look. "Look, mister, I'm not his keeper. How should I know who he had with him?"

"You tell him for me to leave her alone. If he doesn't, I'll..." He sputtered and hit the bar. An empty glass jumped.

Grabbing it, Topaz placed it in the sink. "I'll tell him what you said, but I don't expect him back." To Brooke's surprise, Topaz looked at him with compassion. "Why don't you go home? You'll probably find your kid already there. Do you want a drink?"

"NO, no." He shook his head violently, clenching and unclenching his fingers. "I don't want a drink. I just want my daughter." He stared at Topaz with narrowed eyes. "Someday...someday..." He spun on his heel and stalked toward the door.

Topaz shook her head and continued to clean the bar.

"Who's the guy? Didn't seem too happy, did he?" Brooke observed.

"No, and Harley had better watch it. There's nothing worse than a fond father who wants to protect his little girl. They never seem to realize once kids get into sex, they aren't children any more. The barn door's been open on this one for a long time. It's way too late to change things.

"If it weren't Harley, it would be someone else. At least he won't do anything bad to her; just play around a little. Besides, he don't chase her. She comes after him, begs him, she does, too. The only reason he gets her out of here is to shut her up, and keep the cops out of it. That man doesn't know how lucky he is his kid latched on to Harley. Some of 'em are bad news, real bad news."

Topaz stared at the door and then eyed Brooke. "Say, shouldn't you be working the floor?"

"Yeah, but not much to work. Saw this dude like the best prospect." Anxious to let Topaz cool down, Brooke slid off the stool and sauntered toward the john.

* * * *

Boredom, booze, and bozos. Into the second week of playing a bimbo, Brooke detested the life and it only got worse. She hated washing her hair every night; it took so long to dry, but she couldn't stand the stink. Not much had happened yet, and she'd caught no sign of that mysterious woman. Maybe Stan's death had scared her off. Paul had it right; this stint as a hostess looked like wasted time. At least the ice in the drinks diluted the weak alcohol.

On top of everything else, the new bouncer Mike kept a close watch on Harley and Topaz. He didn't pay much attention to the dancers or the hostesses. His icy eyes make Brooke nervous. Misty said she knew nothing about him and Harley had told Topaz to hire him. At least he only came in on weekends. Just one more thing to worry her.

"Candy," Misty whispered in her ear, "that's the woman, over at the bar talking to Harley." She continued toward the johns.

Brooke looked toward the bar and spied a reddish-haired woman speaking with Harley. Picking up her half-finished drink, she sauntered toward them and took a stool one away from the woman. Up close, her red hair looked less natural. Fading into some indeterminate age beyond thirty, she carried an extra twenty pounds, but some men would find that attractive. She twisted something in her hand.

"Okay, Harley, I'm not happy about the price, but I'll take it."

Harley glanced around with a casual air. "All right, come into the office and we'll settle."

The woman dropped what she had been holding and slid off the stool. Brooke watched as they walked toward the manager's tiny office. Then she reached over and picked up the cylindrical object, recognizing it as a ballpoint pen. She opened her purse, checked her lipstick in her hand mirror, and dropped in the pen. Topaz polished the middle of the bar, but kept watch on Harley and the woman.

"Harley got a new girl friend?" Brooke slid onto a stool in front of Topaz.

"You gotta be kidding." Topaz laughed. "Not that one; she's just a customer."

Brooke gazed toward the office and then back at Topaz. "Like she's not bad, and some men like 'em well padded. Some customers become very good friends. Like she looks kinda sexy, you know." Brooke winked at Topaz.

"Her? You interested?" Topaz stared at her, a calculated look on her face.

"Umm, maybe. Any idea where she works?"

Topaz shook her head. "How should I know? She may not be your type anyway; she had some guy last time I saw her."

"Oh, one of ours?" Brooke's pulse accelerated.

"Used to be…." A long pause followed. "Uh, he had an accident."

"An accident?"

"Skip it, Candy. She's Harley business, and, if you're as clever as you seem, leave her alone."

Brooke shrugged as if to dismiss the matter. "If you say so."

"I do. You hustle drinks, not date the customers." Gazing up at Brooke, Topaz stared at her with narrowed eyes. "Why you asking so many questions? What Harley does and who he talks to is his business, not yours, get me? You'd better stick to yours."

"Okay." Brooke held up her hands. "Like I'm passing time. It's kinda slow."

"Yeah, you better hope it picks up, or you'll be on the street again." Topaz looked around the almost empty club. "At this rate, I only need two girls hustling, and we have plenty of dancers right now. I don't keep nosy people; remember that." She glared at Brooke.

"Like okay." Brooke slid off the stool. "I need this gig."

She put her half-empty glass down. Rousing Topaz's suspicions would only bring her trouble. After surveying the room, she made her way over to a middle-aged man sitting by himself.

"Lonesome?" she asked as she pulled out a chair.

"Not any more. Buy you a drink, beautiful?" Paunchy and balding, he smelled of one too many whiskies. At least he wouldn't be much trouble to confuse a bit.

"Sure, a Margarita would be great." Only another hour to go. At least the woman had showed, but Brooke had no idea who she was.

Brooke's partner grew maudlin, and tears flowed as he talked about his ex-wife and pulled out snapshots of his kids at Christmas. Sorry for him, she could only listen; small comfort at best. At the same time, Brooke watched for the red-haired woman. An hour later, she still hadn't reappeared, and Brooke began to wonder is she had missed seeing her leave. Asking Topaz didn't seem like a good idea.

"Candy," Misty whispered in her ear. "I gotta talk with ya. Meet me in the can in five." She sashayed off toward the back of the club.

Brooke made her excuses and followed Misty to the john. The cramped, dirty place was empty except for the two of them and the paper litter on the floor. "What's up?"

"Topaz's been asking about you. Says you're nosy. She wondered if you were an undercover cop. I said no way. Besides, if you were, you'd latch onto Harley, and you'd left him strictly alone. She wanted to know if you really are gay. I said you weren't when I knew you, but people change, so how was I to know. You'd better split before we both get into trouble."

Shoulders slumping, Brooke sighed. "If I could only identify that woman I saw tonight, but Topaz won't say anything."

"She left with Stan the night he died, but she hasn't come around since. I don't know her name. I've only ever seen her talking to Stan or to Harley. She must be Harley's customer. I know you want to find out what happened to your brother, but I gotta worry about my little girl, so either you split, or I spill to Topaz." Misty skewered her with icy eyes.

"Won't Topaz be angry with you for setting her up?" Brooke looked in the mirror, pulling and twisting the long strands of hair at either side of her face into long corkscrew curls and watching Misty's image.

"Not the way I tell it. I'm giving you time, so clear out like a good little girl. I've got my own skin to think about, okay?" Misty sounded hard-edged and brittle. "Playtime is over, gal."

"All right." Brooke nodded. "I'll have to try something else. This place is getting to me anyway, and so are the men."

Heels clicked on the hard floor of the hall outside, alerting them to Suzy's entrance.

"Well, it's a job, isn't?" Misty turned to Suzy. "Our little princess here doesn't like to be pawed."

"Tough shit; it goes with the territory. If you don't like it, get out." Suzy checked her make-up.

"That's what I told her." Misty sighed.

"One of you better get back, or Topaz'll send Harley in looking for us. I gotta pee."

Brooke and Misty walked out together as Suzy latched the cubicle door.

The men had gone, leaving the place empty. With Misty, Brooke sauntered over to the bar and watched Topaz as she finished cleaning the area.

"Business is slow," Topaz muttered. "Candy, I'm thinking of cutting back for a few weeks. I'll call you if things pick up, but don't come in 'til I do."

"Come on, Topaz, like what about my rent?" Brooke said, faking annoyance.

"Girl, I'm sorry, but I can't carry you, and Misty and Suzy have been with me almost since I opened. I'll give you the name of some other places. Maybe one of them can use you, or maybe you should go back to Indy."

"Yeah, like go home to ma, huh? No way! Like give me the names and I'll try 'em. I gotta eat."

At least Topaz gave her a way out. She'd never make it as an undercover operative. Anyway, she'd seen the woman, and she had the pen. With luck, it might lead to the woman. If not, she and Paul would find some other way to identify her, even if they had to set up a private stakeout and wait for her to come back to the Lido. Right now exhaustion sapped her energy, and not having to face Topaz, the sad stories, the unhappy men, or Mike's gimlet eyes again raised her spirits.

Chapter Five

Paul hadn't touched the bell at Brooke's when the door opened on her smiling face. He hoped at least part of her bubbling excitement came from his arrival, but guessed most came from her news about the woman at the Lido. He couldn't blame her, yet he hoped he had some part in it.

"Thanks for coming. I figured a home-cooked meal might tempt you, and we need to talk about the Lido." She took his windbreaker and hung it in the entry closet.

"No one could refuse an offer like that." He smiled, pleased at her mood.

The smooth fit of her tailored beige slacks reminded him how attractive men would consider her. He hoped she hadn't enjoyed the Lido. The idea of her in scanty clothing ogled and pawed by half-drunken men made his stomach churn. Selfishly, he hoped she'd hated every minute of it.

"So how did things go there?"

"Mixed, mostly boring." She led the way into the living room, and he followed, appreciating her graceful movements. "Have a seat." She motioned to the wide leather sofa. "Could I get you something to drink before dinner?"

"A glass of wine would be fine. Did you learn anything useful," he called as she retreated to the dining room to pour his wine.

"I'm not sure." Returning, she handed him a glass of Chardonnay.

He sipped the wine slowly, enjoying the smooth bouquet. Brooke perched on one of the chairs flanking the sofa.

"Last night, that woman, the one who left with Stan the night he died, came to see Harley. Misty pointed her out at the bar talking to him. I went over, but they left almost immediately for his office. I didn't get her name. Misty didn't know it, and Topaz clammed up when I asked about her. The woman left this on the bar." Brooke handed him the white ballpoint pen.

Turning it over, he noted the familiar blue logo. "First Bank. Maybe she got it from Stan." He a paused a moment, realizing other options might also apply. "Or she could work at the bank, be a customer, or..." He looked up at Brooke and she frowned.

"Or got it from someone who is, if we're unlucky. So how do we find out?" She sipped her own wine and sighed. "Topaz fired me, so the Lido's out for me."

Relief washed over Paul, but then he worried Topaz suspected something. The thought of danger to Brooke spooked him. "Did she say why?"

Brooke made a face. "Not really, but Misty's nervous too. Just before Topaz axed me, Misty told me to get out or she'd tell Topaz I was Stan's sister. They worry big-time about the cops there—probably because of Harley's little drug sideline, and the bad guys frighten them as much as the cops."

"Umm, yeah, Misty said something about an enforcer. Does the mob run Harley?"

"I don't know, but he must buy his stuff from someone. I've never seen any rough stuff or anyone dressed in black with sunglasses." Brooke grinned at him, but then sobered. "That weekend bouncer Mike might fit. He reminds me of Saul, my fake ID man. Maybe his job is to keep Harley in line."

"Saul? Saul who?"

"A guy I interviewed once who makes fake IDs. He owed me a favor."

"Yewouch! I'll bet he has mob ties. If he does, they know about you."

Blinking, Brooke stared at him, eyes wide. "I never thought of that. Saul's the grandfatherly type, not dangerous."

"Mike and Saul up the ante. We can't fight the Mob. Please, don't tell me they had something to do with your brother's death. If so, we've got real problems. Did this Mike say anything?"

"No, he never bothered with me or the other hostesses, but he sure watched Topaz and Harley like a rattlesnake looking for a meal. He did his job, but the regulars never cause any trouble. He gave me the willies." She rubbed her arms.

"Brooke, we might have hit deep water. Maybe we should drop this."

"No!" The rebellious look on her face made her determination clear. "I'll find that woman with or without you."

"Look, the sooner we dump this on the police, the better. We're in over our heads. We can't deal with organized crime." The more he considered the possibilities, the worse they looked. Somehow he had to get her to see reason.

"Paul, I…I can't let this go. We still have the woman; she might buy from Harley. She said something about not liking the price. Just get him to tell us who buys drugs from him or at least her name."

"Brooke, you can't mean that. Drug dealers would kill their best friend rather than share that kind of information."

"What else can we do? She's our only lead."

"Yeah." Paul rubbed his chin and considered what might work. If he could convince Harley, twist his arm some way, maybe, just maybe Harley would give them a name. "I'll try to figure a way to pressure him. If this Mike is associated with Harley's supplier, he must make him nervous. A little chat with Harley might jar something loose."

Grinning at her, Paul pushed thoughts of Harley away. "I'll work something out, okay? Let's not let him and his cronies spoil our dinner. I'm relieved you're not working at the Lido any more. I stopped by the Lido parking lot a few nights and considered night duty, but I knew you'd be all over me, and it might have created more suspicion."

Brooke laughed, amused he supposed, at the idea of him as watchdog. "Hey, weren't your daily phone calls enough? I'm flattered you thought a bodyguard might be necessary, but you would only have made Topaz more suspicious."

"Yeah, I considered that. The Lido just isn't the right place for someone like you."

"Well, Stan went there, and I have to find out why. Let's eat; I'm hungry."

He followed as she led the way into a gray room where a black, vaguely oriental dining room set occupied the center. The table could easily sit six, but only two chairs sat on either side.

She pointed to one of the black chairs. "Sit down and I'll get the food."

He nodded and did so. At home, he settled for functional, but this elegant table setting told him a lot about Brooke. A gray table runner crossed the rectangular black table between the two place settings, and a white one ran at right angles across the center. The sweet scent from the bowl of yellow, white, and purple hyacinths at one end of the white runner filled the air. Tall white tapers flanked the bowl. The flowers, the table setting, and the shiny black dinner plates all pointed to a woman who preferred quality with simplicity. All in all, the setting might suit Architectural Digest or one of those fancy decorator magazines.

Brooke's excellent dinner started with a crisp green salad dressed with a sharp vinaigrette dressing. Broiled snapper—moist and flaky—accompanied by crisp snow peas and rice pilaf with mushrooms. For dessert, she served a marvelous white chocolate mousse that slid down the throat too quickly and left him eager for the next bite. Gorgeous, smart, and a fabulous cook, too—his kind of woman. Why hadn't he noticed that when Stan had introduced her? Last Christmas, yeah, he'd been caught with a system crash and left the party early. Damn! Talk about a lost opportunity.

Dinner finished, Brooke removed the plates to the kitchen and returned with a tray bearing a teapot, cups, and the fixings. "I thought we'd have this in the living room."

"Here, let me carry that. Just tell me where to put it." Paul took the tray and followed her into the living room.

Once there, she pointed to the glass table in front of the sofa, and he set the tray there. She poured him a cup of fragrant smelling tea and one for herself.

After a sip of the tea, she gave him an apologetic smile. "It suddenly hit me we don't know much about each other. Like a downing woman, I grabbed at you when Stan died."

Shrugging, he grinned. "Hey, you needed help. How could I refuse a lady in distress, especially such a gorgeous one? And…I liked Stan."

"I'm glad you didn't refuse." She grinned back. "Since we're in this mess together, it might help if we knew more about each other."

"Not much to tell about me. I'm one of the techies—the guy they call when the system falls apart at three in the morning."

"Doesn't sound like much fun, but as a writer I've leaned what people do outside work tells me more about them. How about you?" She set her cup on the coffee table and leaned back.

"You mean in the occasional spare hour the bank leaves me?"

She nodded at his wry expression.

"I read, watch the odd television special or old movie, and I fence for exercise. Not very exciting I'm afraid"

Brooke raised an eyebrow at that. "Hasn't the Lido supplied enough excitement? Do you want more? Did you say fence as in foil?"

"Yeah, I took it up in college. It's a great sport, makes you quick on your feet, and you watch your opponent for the slightest hint to his next thrust so tricky feints don't sneak up on you."

"Sounds interesting."

"It's my weekly exercise, unless something interferes. Sometimes I referee the club matches for the beginning players."

"Say, that might make a great article what with all the fitness craze."

"We have our tournaments on Saturdays. Would you'd like to come sometime?" He watched to see how she responded, and, when she smiled, a spike of pleasure hit dead center.

"Sure, I've never seen a fencing match. I'll be your cheering section."

"That's great. I'll call you when the next tournament comes up." Paul sipped the last of his tea and set his cup down, grinning. "Now it's your turn. You never really told me how you managed to work and do the Lido too. Did you take vacation?"

Eyes gleaming, Brooke shook her head. "No, I write and consult, with the emphasis on the writing. Freelance stuff for local magazines and a couple of suburban papers keeps the paychecks coming. My schedule's pretty flexible, so the Lido job didn't present a problem. Actually, I'm thinking of doing a piece on the place. A couple of groups would like to see it closed." She raised the teapot offering him more, and Paul held out his cup.

"Thanks, as in exposé?"

Nodding, Brooke filled his cup. "Yes, but it's less exciting than most of them would like to think. Newspapers worry about libel and all those scandals about making up situations, so you have to document what you write. I thought maybe a piece from the viewpoint of a hostess, hustling for drinks, sort of 'as told by,' but make sure it isn't assumed to be me. No way do I want Harley to come looking for me." She shuddered, but a wry smile followed. "I doubt he reads much anyway."

The thought of the hazards of working at the Lido made Paul frown. "What did you tell Topaz? Didn't she want an address?"

"I told her I moved around a lot to avoid some unwanted friends and bill collectors. I gave her a number where she could reach me. Actually, it's a commercial answering service. I figured it would be safer than using my voice mail. They answer as instructed, in this case saying they're friends of mine and that I'm not there, but they'll give me the message."

"Darn, I sort of hoped you were independently wealthy or maybe a lottery winner." Paul sighed, hoping she got the joke.

Her grin said she did. "I consider this research for a couple of articles. One editor said he'd be interested, so I won't risk losing income. Actually, with the Lido tips, I may be making money, but I'm not sure how to report bimbo income on my taxes."

Her humor made Paul smile. The more he learned about Brooke, the more he discovered to like. He had started out feeling sorry for her, but now he hoped, once they sorted out the business about Stan, they might consider other things.

Rubbing her arms, Brooke frowned. "We've got to find that woman."

"Hey, I've got a few ideas. Let me work on it, and I'll let you know what I learn. Just stay away from the Lido."

"No worry, I will. I don't want any more to do with that place." She began to place the cups back on the tray and yawned. "It's getting late, and I have to call my editor first thing in the morning." Her smile took the sting away and gave him a glow.

"Yeah, time for me to go." With regret, Paul followed her into the entry hall. "Thanks for a great dinner. I don't often get to eat so well. I'll call you after I've talked to Harley."

Brooke took his jacket from the closet and held it for him. As he shrugged into it, she released the shoulders and then opened the door. "Thanks for coming. Maybe we can do dinner again when you learn something more from Harley."

"I'll remember that." He stared at her for a moment and then leaned forward to brush her cheek lightly with his lips. A pleasant floral scent rose from her soft skin. Reminding himself not to come on too strong, he pulled back and grinned at her. Anticipation only made the future sweeter.

"Now I have a good reason to twist Harley's arm." He turned before the temptation to kiss her overpowered him and walked at a brisk pace to his car without looking back.

As Brooke closed the door behind him, she leaned against it a moment remembering the feel of his lips on her cheek. She liked Paul, and, the more she saw of him, the better he got. Somehow thinking of him that way triggered guilt. She needed to stay focused on ferreting out the truth about Stan's death, not thinking about his buddy.

* * * *

Despite letting Brooke believe he'd have little trouble with Harley, Paul had doubts about getting anything out of him. While he kept himself physically fit, he didn't see himself as an intimidating hulk. Without some leverage or knowing more about Harley, he'd find himself in a situation he couldn't handle. The problem remained where to get that kind of help. After mulling over the situation, he realized Misty might have the answers. Paul sighed. Just what he needed, another trip to the Lido.

The next evening Paul sat in his car in a parking lot just across the street from the Lido near closing time. He rubbed his arms for warmth. A cold breeze blew through the open window—down a bit to keep the windshield from fogging. Only an occasional car passed; most people were long asleep. The parking lot of the Lido held just three cars.

A cab pulled into the Lido's parking area and stopped in front of the entrance. Topaz came out struggling with a man; his arm hung over her shoulder as he stumbled forward. The cabby jumped out of the cab and opened the rear door. He helped Topaz manhandle the drunk into the vehicle. She spoke briefly to the cabby and then reentered the club. The cabby shook his head and got back in the taxi. He pulled away and drove off.

The bright neon lights of the Lido with its outline of gyrating dancers blinked once more and then faded as someone turned out the lights. Soon Suzy, Misty, Topaz, and a portly man came out. Topaz locked the doors as the others walked toward the three parked cars. Suzy drove off first followed by the man who stopped his car at the club door for Topaz. She waved to Misty just grinding out a cigarette as she unlocked her car door. Misty waved back.

Once the car with Topaz drove away, Paul started his engine and pulled across the street into the Lido lot. He parked next to Misty's car. Startled by the lights, she reached up and locked her car door. Paul got out and stood for a moment, clearly visible in the glare of his headlights.

He approached the driver's side. "Misty, it's me, Paul Counts. Can I talk to you for a minute?"

Inky eyes surveyed him and a hint of fear on her face made Paul's heart tumble. He hadn't meant to frighten her.

Then, she recognized him and lowered the window a crack. "What in the hell do you want this time of night?"

He rested his arm on the top of her car. "To ask you a question or two about Harley. Remember, you told me to stay out of the Lido."

"Yeah, but you could 'a warned me. I thought you were some creep trying to cause trouble. What do you want to know?"

"Is Harley really a drug dealer?"

"Yeah…" She hesitated a moment. "But not in a big way. He's pretty choosy who he sells to. Some broad who works at a bank checks credit references for him."

"You're kidding!" Eyes wide, Paul stared at her. The very idea startled him.

"No." She shook her head, grinning at his shocked surprise. "She comes in now and then with a list for him of where they work, car loans, the like. Topaz showed me one last week. That way he told her, his customers have more to lose than he does, and they're more afraid of the cops than he is."

It sounded like Harley believed in hedging his bets. Maybe the same woman Brooke had seen did the checks. "The woman who left with Stan?"

Black curls brushed her shoulders when Misty shook her head. "Nah, this is another one, a tall woman who looks down her nose at us every time she comes in. No time for anything, just talks with Harley, usually in his office. Look, it's getting late and I have to get home." She started to close the window.

"Wait." Paul lowered his hand to the window. "Is Harley tough?"

Her loud laughter surprised him. It took a moment for her to catch her breath. "You're kidding, right? Only with weak sisters and his customers, Harley's a marshmallow for hard cases. He traded drugs for sex and then one of the kids told him she'd give him money, too. She passed the word to someone else about him, and his business just grew, word of mouth. The biggies don't care 'cause Harley buys from them and stays off the street. He doesn't compete for customers. He keeps a gun in his office. Protection he says, but I don't think he even knows how to use it. I gotta go, Paul. My sitter'll be furious."

"Sorry, Misty. Thanks for the info." Paul stood back and watched her back up and then drive away. At least talking with Harley took on a more positive light. Paul strolled to his car considering how he could pressure Harley into giving him the names of people from the bank who bought drugs from him. The problem occupied him all the way home.

A tall woman who checked credit references Misty had said. Did she work at First Bank, too? Someone with access to the customer files could do it. If she checked on people outside the bank clientele, she'd have to tap into one of the big credit bureaus, so that meant she had to have a position to access both. Maybe it also provided a motive for Stan's murder. The bank wouldn't look kindly on any employee helping a drug dealer. If anyone reported her, she'd lose her job. Fascinating possibilities, but he needed names first and only Harley could provide those.

Paul parked his car in its usual spot in the apartment parking area and sighed as he locked the doors. Good thing the bank had flextime and that he had an understanding boss, because he wasn't going to be on time tomorrow. He detested late nights.

Shadow would be upset with him, too. Poor cat, tomorrow would be another late one when he confronted Harley at the Lido. He'd have to give her a special treat and some catnip.

* * * *

The next evening having given Shadow a can of gourmet cat food and a liberal sprinkle of catnip around her scratching post, Paul changed into a leather bomber jacket, a black tee shirt, and sweats instead of his usual jeans and western shirt. He scratched Shadow's ears before leaving and she purred.

At the Lido, a couple of hours passed as he waited for Harley to show. Busy at the bar, Topaz hadn't even looked at him when he ordered a beer. Suzy had picked him as an easy mark and hung onto him like a burr, but he dislodged her by not buying her drinks.

Nursing his beer, he puzzled over whether to give up or stay a bit longer. He had just decided he might as well call it a night, when a portly man in polo shirt and dress pants leaned on the bar in front of Topaz. He looked like the guy Paul had seen driving off with Topaz last night. Beer in hand, Paul drifted closer to them.

"Harley, where've you been? I figured you weren't coming in tonight." Topaz filled a glass and set it in front of him.

"Things to do tonight. How's business?" Harley sipped his drink.

"Slow, but okay."

"Excuse me," Paul interrupted. "Are you Harley Donovan?"

"What's it to ya?" Harley eyed him with suspicion.

"Friend of mine said if I ever needed to get high I should see you." Paul grinned despite sweaty palms.

"What's your name?"

"Paul Counts."

Grunting, Harley studied Paul with narrowed eyes. "And who's this uh friend?"

"He works at First Bank, a programmer there. I don't know him well, but at a party several weeks ago he said I'd find you at the Lido. Said you could be trusted, that it was a lot safer than dealing with the street scene, and you even take credit cards."

"Is that so? Maybe your friend got it wrong. I run a clean business here, drinks and a girlie show, that's all we offer. Right, Topaz?" Harley gave her a hard look.

"Right, Harley." Topaz nodded and her eyes widened when she recognized Paul. "Say, you're the guy who asked about Stan Beldon."

"Yeah, a few weeks back, I told you he owed me."

"Stan Beldon?" Harley frowned and blinked. "Uh ...maybe we should go to my office."

Paul followed Harley to the tiny office at the back. Inside the dingy cramped room, a wooden chair with its back to the door faced a metal desk with a worn leather chair behind it. Papers and magazines—issues of *Hustler* judging by the cover of the one on top—cluttered the desktop. Harley slid behind the desk, leaving Paul to slouch in the wooden chair.

"This friend of your, what d'ya say he's called?" Harley rested his crossed arms on his budding paunch and leaned back.

"Like I said, Stan Beldon."

"Heard he died recently. So what d' he tell you?" The club owner surveyed him with suspicious eyes.

Anxious to get what he came for and leave, Paul leaned forward and rested his arms on the desk. "Cut the crap, Harley. I know about your little game here, and, if you don't cooperate, the cops might like to know what I can tell them about you." Eyes narrowed, Paul skewered him with an intent glare, trying to imitate those movie and TV hard guys.

"Yeah, you and who else? A dead man?" Harley sneered.

"One of your dancers will testify."

"Who?" Harley's eyes widened briefly, but then he grinned. "Nobody'd believe one of those bitches. Besides, they'd never make it to the witness stand."

Two could play rough. "This one would. Hey, Harley, you're no big time dealer." Time for bigger guns. "The bad guys are watching you—Mike keeps tabs on you." Paul straightened and paused for effect. "The heat's on drug dealers, and if you try to play hardball, there's a murder charge pending I'll see hung on you."

"Murder charge?" Harley bolted upright. "What the hell're you talking about?" Sweat beaded his forehead.

Rising, Paul edged past the desk to lean on the wall behind Harley. He lounged in a relaxed way, but used his position to force Harley to look up at him. Having gotten the initiative, he wanted to finish this before Harley had time to think.

"Remember Stan Beldon? He's currently listed as an OD, but we both know where he got his stash, and a little whisper to the police is all it would take. They're just itching to get something on you. I can see it now 'Local night club owner is tried on Murder One.' The prosecuting attorney can't wait."

Harley swiped at his forehead. "I didn't have nothing to do with Beldon's death."

Paul shrugged. "Maybe not, but you supplied the drugs, and they just sent a dealer up for that when his customer died. The jury didn't see it as any different from giving a man a loaded gun. The lawyers can cite plenty of precedents, and, anyway, it would hurt business. Those who get scared won't buy and the others will find another dealer, afraid the police might catch them buying from you."

Pausing a moment, Paul let that threat sink in, and, when Harley didn't say anything, he decided to up the stakes a bit. "Don't you think your supplier might get a little antsy and arrange to get rid of any link to them? Whatever, you lose."

"What d' you want?" Harley snapped and glared up at Paul.

Taking his time before responding, Paul used the delay to add to Harley's nervousness. Mentally, he crossed his fingers. "Just give me a list of people working at First Bank who buy from you."

"How the hell do I know where people work?" Harley sputtered. "So long as they have the dough, I don't care."

"Yeah, but you're a careful business man and don't deal with someone you don't know and whose credit rating you haven't checked." He emphasized each word.

"You know where they work, who they owe, how much they make. You only deal with the ones who still have something to lose, because you have a hold over them. I'm not asking for all your customers, just those who work at the First Bank." Paul leaned closer to Harley. "Now give, or I take what I have to the prosecutor and let him make it hot for you."

Harley sweated and fiddled with his signet ring. Lowering one hand slowly, he started to ease open the top drawer.

Remembering Misty's warning about a gun, Paul guessed Harley kept it there. He raised his foot and straightened his leg in one swift explosive move, shoving the desk hard. It knocked over the chair on the other side. "Uh, uh, Harley, none of that. A gun will only get you in trouble, especially if you use it. What were you going to do with it anyway, threaten me?" He laughed in Harley's face.

"'Cause," he continued with a harder tone, determined to play the tough guy to the hilt, "I don't threaten, and if you kill me, you'll get life. At your age, even with parole, you'd might make it out in time for a nursing home."

Harley slumped in his chair, still saying nothing.

"Harley, Harley, a few names cost you nothing and get rid of me. Tell me what I want to know and I'll forget about the link between you and Stan. If you don't..." Paul paused. "The police can get nasty, and they have to make an example of any drug dealer they get the goods on. I'll help them nail you. Think about it."

Turning his signet ring, Harley shifted in his chair.

"All I want is Stan's killer. I know you didn't kill him—you just supplied the goods—but believe me, I can make your life unpleasant. I'm only asking for First Bank people, that has to be a small number, right?"

Looking up at Paul looming over him, Harley sank even lower in his chair. He licked his lips and eyed him again. "Okay, okay, let me think...Stan Beldon wasn't a steady customer. There's John uh...Pierce, Ken...no, Kent Carpenter..." Harley stopped for a moment.

"Two, that's not all."

Harley's tongue flicked his lips, and he looked away from Paul. "Uh, Jimmy Jones, Mike Thompson, David Striker." The names came out in a rapid string.

"Is that all?" Five names and no women.

"All?" Harley stared up at him. "All, umm…and Walter Vavor. Yeah, that's all." He continued to twist the ring on his hand back and forth, refusing to meet Paul's eyes.

"You're lying, Harley. Now come on, give." Paul pulled him upright by his open shirt collar and thrust his face close to Harley's. The acrid smell of stale sweat filled the air, but he held on.

"What d' ya mean?" Harley squinted up at him.

"Because, Harley,"—Paul spaced each word, speaking slowly and distinctly—"you haven't mentioned any women, and there are some. The names, Harley, the names."

The worm tried to squirm, but Paul held him tighter and shook him like a yappy dog.

Glancing around, the overweight man maybe hoped for help from Topaz, but the office door remained shut. He looked again at Paul and shuddered.

"All right already, ease off, huh, pal. I'll…I'll tell you what you want to know." Harley pushed at Paul's hand, and Paul slowly let the fabric slip through his fingers. Harley slumped back into his chair.

"Women, okay, women. There was this broad, Pat Jensen. She works there I think."

Paul leaned forward. "You think, Harley, only think?"

He stared up at Paul and then at the door. "Yeah, yeah she works there."

"But she's not the only one. Give, Harley, or do I use violence on you?" Paul raised his fist as if to strike him.

Harley licked his lips. "Another…another woman?"

Paul glared at him and pulled his arm back.

Harley flinched. "Her name? Oh yeah…Donna…Sands, that was it."

"You sure?"

Staring at Paul's raised fist, Harley nodded.

"Those are the only ones?" Paul leaned forward, eyes narrowed.

Sighing, Harley slumped in his chair. "Yeah, those are the ones I deal with."

Paul straightened and eased the tension in his muscles. "Right, I hope for your sake one of them owns up. I won't say anything to the police…or the prosecuting attorney for now."

With relief foremost, Paul walked to the office door. Sometimes bravado worked, especially with guilty people. He stopped, looked back at Harley, and sighed. He felt sorry for the worm; the man had gotten in over his head.

"You ought to stick with the girlie show. This business has too many risks. Another death and, who knows, the police or your supplier may come after you anyway." Paul opened the door and left.

He had what he'd come for, and he found the list interesting. If he remembered correctly, Vavor was a Vice President and wasn't Kent the one taking over Stan's work? He wasn't sure about the others, but he would find out soon enough and maybe which of the women had been with Stan. At least he'd kept his promise to Brooke, and she had no reason to come back here.

Once he learned more about these people, he could work out some way to proceed. A look in the bank directory tomorrow would at least place them. With a jaunty step, Paul strolled through the club and left.

Harley followed Counts back into the club and mopped his face as he watched him leave. Straightening his shirt, he threw his shoulders back. He stalked over to the bar and stopped in front of Topaz.

"If that bastard ever shows his face in here again, don't serve 'im. Kick 'im out. I need a drink, a strong one."

"What's up?" Topaz stared at Harley, surprise on her face.

"He wanted a list of my customers." He took a long swig from the double Topaz set before him. "I gave him some names of people I never heard of. For the hell of it, I threw in that snooty fellow's name, that banker big-shot who's always looking for his daughter."

"He a cop or another dealer?"

"He ain't neither, but trouble for us. I don't want him here, and don't let any of the girls talk to him, you hear me?" Harley glared at her.

"You want I should tell Mike?"

"NO!"

Several customers looked toward the bar, and Topaz placed a finger on her lips.

"Un, no," he continued in a lower voice. "We don't want the big guys involved. They'll ask too many questions and make trouble. If Mike's here, maybe act like the guy's giving you hard time and have Mike hustle him out, but nothin' else, get me?"

She gave him a puzzled frown, but nodded. "Yeah, I hear you. No drinks, no talk, and boot 'im out. I can manage that."

* * * *

When Paul reached his car, he sat for a few moments to still his shaking legs. At least his talk with Misty had clued him in to Harley's bluster, but when the guy started to reach for his gun, at least Paul assumed it was the gun, fear struck hard. His bluff had worked and pushing the desk away had startled Harley. His fencing practice on that showy leap, the ballestra, had paid off. The exercises had strengthened his leg muscles. Just like TV, a little tough talk for a slob like Harley was all it took.

Paul didn't consider himself a coward, but hell, why look for trouble, and he knew better than to get into a brawl where he was outclassed. Intimidating Harley had come easier than he'd expected. With Harley's list of names he could start investigating the people tomorrow. He crossed his fingers that Harley had included the woman who had called 9-1-1.

Chapter Six

At work the next day, Paul pulled out the bank employee directory and began checking for the names on Harley's list. Kent Carpenter? Cramer had said Kent was taking over Stan's work, so, as expected, he found the name in the same section as Stan. Did Kent know about those special routines of Stan's? By now, he should have identified most of them, so what had he done about them? If he had deleted them, he might have considered them inconsequential or wanted to eliminate any links to Stan.

According to the directory, John Pierce worked in the Accounting Section several levels below Walter Vavor, an interesting connection with both of them on Harley's list. However, he found no Jimmy Jones, Mike Thompson, or David Striker. He tried variant spellings of the last names, but none appeared close to any of the three. Then he remembered Harley hesitating before reeling off these names. Having expected reluctance from Harley, Paul assumed he might have given him some red herrings or they were new employees not yet added to the directory. He'd recheck those names later.

Paul paused for a moment reviewing the list. Harley couldn't know the names of bank employees unless he sold to them. The thought gave Paul some confidence that any people he found in the bank directory from Harley's list had some relationship to drug use and possibly to Stan. The paunchy man impressed him as an unreliable source looking out for himself, so he might pull a swift one by slipping in false names as well. Anyone Paul couldn't link to the bank could belong to that category. Reassured, he turned to the two women's names.

Pat Jensen worked in the Human Resources Department. No Donna Sands, but a Donna Sanders in the Customer Support Section might fit. None of this told him much, but at least it provided a start. Pat would have access to the personnel files, and Donna could access both the customer files and the TRW service, making her a strong candidate for the woman who checked credit histories for Harley. If so, that left Pat as the woman with Stan, but his encounter with Harley emphasized the value of understanding motives and whether or how someone might respond. He needed all the advantages he could muster.

Starting with the men, Paul figured Cramer knew Kent and could tell him the kind of person he was. Paul drummed his fingers as he keyed in Cramer's number and waited for him to answer.

"Hi, Cramer, Paul Counts. What can you tell me about Kent Carpenter?"

"I assigned Stan Beldon's work to him. He's a good programmer, but not as good as Stan. What's up?" Suspicion tinged his words.

"Uh, nothing immediate." Paul scrambled for an acceptable reason. "A project may come up next year. If it does, I'll call you and we can talk in more detail. With Stan gone, I'll have to find someone else. Don't worry, I'm not going to steal your staff." Uncertain what to ask, he hesitated a moment. If he let Cramer think it was job-related he might get a little more. "He's reliable, on time, all the usual?"

"Oh sure, almost never sick either. He works the occasional odd hours when we're testing, but that's all. Oh, he's a baseball and a hunting nut, so he takes time for some special events, but he's a good worker, and most of his projects come in on schedule. Anything else you want?"

"No, not at the moment. If this project gets approved, I'll get back to you."

"Right now I need him to finish up Stan's stuff and wouldn't approve a transfer. I recruit good people, but you have to watch out for predators. Good programmers are in short supply."

Cramer's warning hit home. "I know. You can relax for now, and thanks, Cramer." He disconnected, glad for any information, but Cramer's reaction warned him he better plan ahead on how to get information without generating suspicion. If people didn't see an obvious reason, they made up one. Paul sighed, all too aware playing detective didn't sit well on his shoulders. He liked problem solving, but figuring out people drove him nuts. Too often they acted in crazy ways. As for asking direct questions, that generated suspicion or outright refusal. He needed leverage.

Other than Kent's assignment to work on Stan's programs, Cramer hadn't given him much. So far, he only had Harley's claim Kent bought from him. Confronting Kent about that might produce a response. Paul picked up a pencil and put a check mark against Carpenter's name.

John Pierce came next. Paul hadn't worked much with the Accounting Section. He dredged his memory for anyone he knew who did. The organization chart showed Kincaid as the section manager, but after Cramer's leery response and not knowing whether Pierce really had anything to do with Stan, Paul hesitated to call him. It wouldn't help Pierce to start with his boss just yet, and mentioning the Lido wouldn't help either. He didn't want to give Pierce time to make up a story until he had figured out how to pressure him and knew where Pierce fit.

Considering his next move, Paul stared at the Delacroix sketch and focused on the sharp contrast of the figures against the white background. If only this situation were black and white instead of all these messy grays.

Paul sighed and considered where to get information on Pierce. He needed someone who worked with Accounting. He frowned for a moment and then it hit home, Sharon Belling, one of the systems programmers, worked with that section. He'd try her first. They'd worked together, and he'd dated her a few times. A nice girl, but he had a thing against office romances, especially with someone in his own section. Too many of them ended in nasty messes with hurt feelings. He preferred to stay on friendly, but not intimate terms with his co-workers.

Sharon answered on the third ring.

"Hello, Sharon, Paul Counts. You've worked with John Pierce. What can you tell me about the guy?"

"John Pierce, the yuppie accountant?" Sharon's voice retained a slight touch of the broad Northeastern 'ah', faded, but recognizable. "Snazzy dressah, must spend a lot on clothes, and I think he lives in that ritzy downtown development on the riveah, The Pines? No, The Oaks it's called." Sharon sighed deeply. "Guess they pay accountants well these days or he has rich relatives or won the lottery."

"Hmm, we should talk with Human Resources about pay inequities."

Sharon laughed. "Yeah, why not? I could do with a raise."

Extravagant life styles might fit with Stan's little programs, but what else would tie in Pierce. "You've worked with him; what's he like?"

"A bit of a know-it-all, snooty with his nose in the air, but he knows his numbers and gets them right." She sighed.

Helpful, but not much he could use. "Gave you a hard time, eh? What's he like to work with?"

Sharon said nothing for a moment. "Not a good ol' boy, if you know what I mean, and no interest in us ladies." Her voice carried a bitter tang.

Did she mean Pierce was gay? "Reliable?"

Paul could almost see her shrug. "So far as I know, but his boss, Jim Kincaid, could probably tell you more about that."

"Did he date anyone or hang around with any people from the bank?"

Sharon sniffed. "I wouldn't know what he does outside of work. We move in different circles."

"Any tie-in with Stan Beldon, Pat Jensen, or Donna Sanders?"

"Stan and he worked on the customer account programs I think. I seem to remembah John as part of the test team. Never heard anything about him and Pat or Donna." She sounded surprised.

From the sound of her voice, he had piqued her curiosity. He'd better cut things short. "Well thanks for the info, I appreciate it."

"Okay, Paul. Say, what are you up to now? Why so many questions? What's up with Pierce?"

"Nothing." He tried to sound innocent. "Just helping Stan's sister track down a few loose ends left when he died. I'd heard he and Pierce were friends, that's all. I owe you, so let me know if you need anything from me."

"Don't worry, I will." She paused, and the slight click of the beads she always wore and flicked whenever nervous came over the line. "How about lunch soon? I haven't seen you for some time."

"Yeah, it has been awhile, but I'm snowed with work just now, Sharon. How about in a week or so, okay? I'll call you. Thanks for the info." A pretty girl and their few dates had been fun, but nothing serious. Now he'd rather think about Brooke instead, but a lunch would be okay.

"Just don't forget. Ta ta for now."

Based on what Sharon said, John Pierce had to know about the programming changes Stan did. He'd have to check the test results and notify Documentation. Paul underlined his name. As to Pierce being gay, Paul shrugged. That probably had no bearing on Stan's death.

Paul's email alarm beeped, and he checked the monitor. Operations wanted him to contact them as soon as possible. He sighed, almost relieved. Work came first. Playing detective would have to wait, and, anyway, he dreaded tackling the women.

* * * *

Paul had never met Donna Sanders, and Pat Jensen's name didn't ring any bells. He couldn't imagine any connection of either of them with Stan. However, unless Harley had lied on him, one of the two women on the list must be the woman Brooke saw talking to Harley at the Lido.

The office grapevine usually knew more about most people than their own managers. He might learn something about Donna and Pat there. His best contact would be Cramer's secretary, Marilyn Johnson. She always knew what was happening and who slept with whom. It wouldn't hurt to stroll by and chat with her. Marilyn liked to gossip, and how she responded might tell him even more than what she actually said.

When he reached Cramer's office, Marilyn sat peering at her terminal screen. He slouched onto the chair next to her desk. She looked up, smiling her Whooppi Goldberg smile at him. "Hi, Paul, what's up?"

"I'd like to pick your brains." He gave her a broad grin. "You know more about what goes around here than anybody."

Marilyn nodded, looking pleased at his compliment. "I keep my eyes and ears open. Who are you interested in?"

Uncertain where to start, Paul picked up a company issue pen from the desk with the bank logo and turned it, studying the design while searching for a way to begin. None occurred to him. "What can you tell me about Donna Sanders and Pat Jensen?"

Pursing her mouth, Marilyn sat for a moment, thinking. "Let's see, Donna's moved up fairly rapidly. She interned as a part-time teller in college. When she graduated, they promoted her to head of the Customer Support Section. She's as tough as they come, and no one in her section gets any leeway. It's all by the book there—do it right the first time or get out. Glad I don't work for her!" Marilyn grimaced.

A sharp electronic beep interrupted.

"My email. Wait a second while I check." She depressed a function key and focused on the terminal screen as the message came up. "Nothing important," she muttered as she deleted the message and looked up again at Paul.

"And Pat?" Paul prompted, fiddling with the pen.

"Pat Jensen..." Marilyn paused, looking off into space. "Umm...Yeah, she used to be up in the organization, worked as an Administrative Assistant for Walter Vavor, and then for Morgan Jones."

Looking around, Marilyn leaned closer.. "I don't know what happened,—she lowered her voice—"but rumor has it she and Morgan had something going, until he tired of her. Then, to make matters worse, her husband divorced her. He's a nice guy too, one of the branch managers, Sam Stephanowsky."

Marilyn shook her head and looked like she pitied both Sam and Pat. "Pat should've stuck with Sam even if he isn't a ball of fire. Let's see...after that she moved into Human Resources to look after clerical staff. Still, she's an exempt, so it couldn't be all bad. They say she's on the ball, which is why she's still here, or maybe she has something on someone, who knows."

Paul rubbed his chin. "I don't remember Pat so she must have worked for Morgan before he took over the Systems group. Ever hear about Donna or Pat outside of work?"

Marilyn shook her head. "Not really, everyone says they're both gung-ho work-a-holics. Donna keeps to herself, no close friends, no boyfriends. Like I said, Pat had a thing for Morgan for a bit. I haven't heard of anyone else since."

Sighing, Paul put the pen down. So far Marilyn hadn't given him much. If only he could tie one of them to drug use or Stan. "How about drugs or alcohol?"

Jerking upright, Marilyn raised an eyebrow. "What? I never heard. Do you really think so?" Her eyes lighted at the thought.

Ouch! Paul mentally kicked himself. He'd done it again. He grappled for a diversion and shrugged. "Hey, I don't know. Stan Beldon's sister asked me to help investigate how he died. I asked because someone told me one of them dated Stan."

Disappointment showed on Marilyn's face. Paul suspected she'd hoped he might know something juicy. "Yeah, too bad about Stan. If you think he dated one of them, just ask them."

"Good idea, Marilyn." Paul gave her an ingratiating smile. "Go to the source, but I'm lousy at dealing with women. Besides, I don't know which one dated Stan. Then with him dying...well, I, ah...sort of hesitate to say anything. I didn't want to start the water works. I hate tears; never know how to deal with them."

Kicking himself mentally, he regretted falling prey to the Marilyn's insatiable curiosity. Stirring up gossip wouldn't solve Stan's murder. He'd better change the topic and fast. "His sister would be a better one to talk to them anyway. Oh, by the way, has Kent started working on Stan's programs yet?"

"Yeah, he's been at it for a couple of weeks now. Hasn't said much though, except to complain we need to get in a replacement. He says he already had enough to do and Cramer had better get a new man or offload some of his old work to someone else."

Marilyn sighed. "You know how it is—always more work and never any new staff."

Nodding, Paul unkinked his legs and got to his feet. "Yeah, guess I do. It's always tough picking up the slack when schedules slip. My work has piled up too. See you later" He smiled at her and strolled off.

Playing detective required more tact and discretion than he possessed. First Cramer, then Sharon, and now Marilyn wanting to know why he asked so many questions, and, on top of that, he'd added to Marilyn's gossip store. Their reactions only reinforced his hesitation to approach the women. He'd concentrate on the men first and leave the women for last or better yet let Brooke deal with them.

Paul sighed. He'd rather deal with a system crash or the best fencer in Columbus instead of struggling to ferret out information on his fellow workers. How in the hell did undercover cops and private investigators do their jobs? It took more gall and savvy than he possessed.

At least Marilyn had given him some useful information. Pat worked for Morgan so Paul might as well ask him about her or maybe even talk to her ex-husband Sam Stephenow—whatever his name was. Meanwhile, he'd listen for any gossip on all of them. Marilyn always knew the juiciest morsels, if he could just figure out how to tap her or others without being so obvious or having to explain his interest. Asking questions only led others to ask them, too.

Chapter Seven

Determined to talk to the people on Harley's list, Paul settled on Kent Carpenter first. According to Marilyn, Kent often stopped by Chiquita's after work for a drink before going home. Its fake Mexican cantina décor featured dark rustic wooden tables and wicker seat chairs that contrasted with cream-colored stucco walls and the rust ceramic tile floor. At least the gaudy serapes, brightly decorated ceramic pots, and occasional piñatas provided color. The peasant blouses and full ruffled skirts of the female staff flattered most of the women, but a few of the too well-padded ones didn't need the ruffles.

Despite stopping there several nights in a row, Paul had failed to find an opportunity to catch Kent alone. This evening Kent and his buddies congregated around a table across from the long wooden bar. From a chair across the lounge, Paul watched the buddies drift out and leave Kent with his attention focused on the television set over the bar and the spring batting practice displayed there. Sharon's description of the programmer as a good ol' boy suited him like a well-worn catcher's mitt. Dressed in a plaid sports shirt barely covering a growing beer-gut, tight jeans, a wide leather belt with a large silver cowboy buckle, and a Reds baseball cap, Kent ignored everything but the action on the TV. By five-forty, he sat alone. Paul picked up his beer and walked over to him.

"Mind if I join you?"

"Suit yourself." Kent's eyes didn't leave the television set.

Taking a ladder-backed wooden chair, Paul placed his beer on the table. "Aren't you the dude who's taken over for Stan Beldon?"

"Yeah, that's me, picking up the pieces." Kent lifted his beer and drank, but his gaze remained riveted on the screen.

"I'm Paul Counts, a friend of Stan's sister. Bad news about Stan."

"Yeah, real sorry to hear about it, especially since it means extra work for me." Kent set his mug on the table with a thud.

"Were you close friends?"

"Nah, we worked for the same boss. I never saw him much." Kent ignored Paul. "Yea, team," he yelled when a batter hit a home run.

The man's rapt attention to the TV annoyed Paul and he wanted to get up and shut it off. Maybe shock tactics might get his attention. "Does your boss know about your drug habit?"

"What drug habit?" Kent swiveled to glare at Paul. His eyes widened and then narrowed, as he recovered himself.

Amused, Paul sipped his beer, but at least he'd gotten a reaction. "Your supplier, Harley Donovan at the Lido, told me. I'd be careful. Stan Beldon got his there, and he's dead."

"Those guys'll say anything. Sure I went to the Lido now and then, so what?" Kent twisted his glass on the coaster, leaving a wet ring.

Paul waited. Some people couldn't stand silence.

After a moment, Kent stared across at Paul. "Just who in the hell do you think you are anyway? What do you want?"

"Stan's sister says he didn't do drugs and wants to know what really happened to him. You can help me find who left the Lido with Stan the night he died."

"Not me. I never hung around with him. We worked on different projects. Hell, I wasn't even at the Lido that night." Kent pushed his words out in a rapid jumble. He picked up his mug of beer and drank almost half of it.

None of this helped at all. Stymied, Paul struggled for what to ask next. "Ever see other bank people at the Lido?"

Kent eased his grip on his mug and shook his head slowly. "Not so's I remember. The beer's too pricey for me and no sports feed." He set the half-empty glass down.

"Ever see Stan there with a woman?"

Staring at Paul for a moment, he frowned before answering. "Just the manager at the bar. He never talked to me, so I left him alone."

Defeated, Paul sighed. He'd hit a blank wall and couldn't think of anything except Harley's list and the Lido to link Kent to Stan's death. "If you remember anything else about him, particularly any women he talked to at the Lido, call me. I'm in the bank directory under Counts, Paul Counts."

Kent appeared to weigh his options and eyed Paul. He nodded. "All right, but there won't be. I barely knew him." He glanced down at his mug, twisting it again before looking up at Paul and studying him like a fencer assessing an opponent.

Draining the last of his own beer, Paul pushed back his chair, and got to his feet. For a moment, he stared down at Kent wanting more, but uncertain the man knew anything or how to get it if he did.

"Thanks for talking to me, and good luck with the customer programs."

After one quick glance at him, Kent returned to staring at the TV screen, mesmerized. Paul hadn't learned anything except to confirm Kent had been at the Lido and seen Stan there. He hadn't admitted to buying drugs from Harley, but then who knew. If Kent told the truth and, Paul hadn't any reason to doubt him, he knew nothing of the mysterious woman.

John Pierce came next on Harley's list. Paul would call him tomorrow and see what the 'snazzy' accountant had to say. Too, when he finished checking Stan's data, he might find something to use with Pierce.

The next day Paul cleared his in-tray, and, after reading his email, decided, even if Pierce arrived late, he'd be at his desk by now. Finding the number in the bank directory, he punched the extension, wondering what to make of the fact Pierce, an accountant, worked for Walter Vavor, the Finance VP. He speculated whether the two had any drug-related or other connection besides Harley Donovan. Someone picked up the receiver.

"Hel-lo?" The light tenor voice dragged out the syllables.

"John Pierce?"

"Ye-es?"

"Paul Counts, I'd like to speak to you after work if possible."

"Have we met?" This time Pierce clipped his words, as if to say 'who the hell is Paul Counts?'

Paul grinned. He'd anticipated Pierce's reaction. "No, but we have friends in common, Stan Beldon and...Harley Donovan." He waited for Pierce to react.

"Oh...ye-es, perhaps after work would be better." A brief pause followed. "Panera's is close; how about there at five?

"All right, I'll see you there." He'd upset Pierce all right. His initial hesitation and then quick agreement made him sound like a good candidate for a little judicious pressure. The voice reminded Paul of

Sharon's comments: 'no interest in us ladies.'

Most of the day remained for the cleanup on the user codes. Then he could dig a little deeper into Stan's subroutines. A sixth sense nagged him about those changes, but for now he had to finish up his own work.

Deep into the user code changes, the phone interrupted around ten thirty.

"Hello, Counts here," Paul answered.

"Hi, Paul, Brooke Beldon. I hadn't heard from you and wondered if you had confronted Harley yet. I...I've been having second thoughts. If you're right about Mike, maybe you shouldn't."

Pleased at her concern, Paul chuckled. "Too late. I've already had a chat with Harley. I forced a list out of him, but it may not be complete or even accurate. So far I've checked the names against the bank directory and found most of them except for three."

"How many did he give you?"

"Eight total. Not many, but it included two women. I've only talked with one man, and he doesn't appear to know much. I have more hopes for one I'm seeing this afternoon."

"What about the women?"

"I'm looking for more information before confronting them. I can't imagine accusing them of calling 9-1-1 without knowing a little more about them."

"Can I do anything?"

"Not yet. I'll let you know how things go."

"I'm glad you've made progress. I hope one of the women will tell us how Stan died."

"Don't get your hopes too high. Playing detective doesn't come easy. We need a strategy."

"When you're ready, call me and we can work it out together."

"Now that's a great idea. After I talk with this guy this afternoon and dig up a bit more on the women, we can meet and sort things out." The thought of seeing Brooke again provided ample reward for his efforts.

"I'd like that. Oops, call waiting is beeping. I've got to go. Bye."

At the disconnect, Paul grinned. Right now he had no idea how she could help, but once he had a clearer understanding of what Stan had done and how the others might relate to that, he and Brooke could brainstorm.

The user code changes took him most of the day. With email, lunch, and the code changes, he had no time to consider Pierce until late afternoon and, by the time he glanced at the clock, it read almost five. Sighing, he signed off the system and then the locator board.

Paul arrived at the nearby Panera's a few minutes early. A far cry from Chiquita's, he wondered what that indicated about Pierce. The booths along the side offered some privacy. A cozy fireplace occupied the middle of the floor. Scanning the large room, he saw no one matching Sharon's description of Pierce. A few people sat by the fire and at tables near the order area. Most of the booths remained empty. Paul picked one with a good view of the entrance and watched for Pierce.

Promptly at five, a prepie type wearing wire-rimmed glasses entered and gave the place a nervous survey. Attired in a well-cut, fitted gray suit with a silky sheen and a pale green shirt with a pink and gray paisley tie, Pierce matched Sharon's description of 'snazzy' indeed. He had combed several long strands of thinning blonde hair over the center of his receding hairline.

"Mr. Pierce?" Paul called from his booth.

Pierce gave the room a hurried glance before approaching Paul. "Yes, Mr. Counts?" He looked at him for confirmation as he slid onto the booth across from him. A second covert scan of the room followed.

Grinning, Paul nodded. "Would you like a latte or something? We might as well be comfortable."

Pierce nodded and Paul ordered a chai for himself and a latte for Pierce. Carrying the two cups, he returned to the booth. Paul eased back and sipped his chai, allowing the silence to work for him.

Perching rather than sitting on his seat, Pierce circled his cup with well-manicured hands before looking at Paul. "What did you want to see me about, Mr. Counts?"

"Paul will do. You go to the Lido now and then?"

"I've been there once or twice. I'm not a habitué of such places."

"Oh?" Paul looked at him, one eyebrow raised, and waited.

"Well…" Pierce stared down at the table. "Not really. Mostly, it would be because a friend wanted to go. I find such places so depressing." Pierce picked up his latte and took a delicate sip.

"Interesting, I'm not sure Harley would agree with that."

Pierce's hand jerked, and, eyes wide, he stared at Paul. "Harley?"

"Yes. Harley Donovan, owner of the Lido, remember him?"

Pulling out a pink handkerchief, Pierce mopped his brow. "I go to the Lido now and then, but this Donovan isn't a friend of mine." His lip curled in distaste, and, straightening, he picked up his latte. His hand trembled.

Paul swallowed some of his chai, amused at Pierce's reaction. "Friend isn't the right word. It's more like supplier, isn't it?"

"Uh…" Pierce focused on the far corner of the room. "You did say something about Mr. Donovan when you called, didn't you?"

"I did, and Harley says you're a regular buyer." Watching for reactions, he saw Pierce flinch and a muscle jumped at the corner of his left eye.

"Well, hardly." He licked his lips. "Why would I buy from Harley…uh, Mr. Donovan? I'm not a drug user."

"No?" Paul gave him a crooked grin, and Pierce glanced away. "You ever see Stan Beldon at the Lido?"

Blinking, Pierce stared at him. Paul could almost hear wheels turning as the accountant hesitated. He licked his lips. "Stan? No, we move in different circles."

"But you both went to the Lido."

"Uh, ye-es, I saw Stan there once or twice, but we never spoke."

Paul picked up his cup, savored a little of his chai, and then set it down before looking at Pierce. "Does your boss know you do drugs?"

A hint of panic filled Pierce's eyes as he again studied Paul's face. "No, of course not." He straightened his shoulders. "I told you, I don't use drugs."

His air of righteous indignation struck Paul as ironic. The guy visited the Lido, knew Harley, and worked with Stan, so he knew something. Considering his nervousness and Sharon's comments, Paul couldn't imagine any other reason for him visiting the Lido. Harley had given Pierce's name at the start and the accountant's reaction fit with a guilty conscience.

Viper-like, Pearce's tongue flicked out moistening his lips before continuing. "What's your game, blackmail?"

Smiling at him, Paul waited a moment before responding, and, to ratchet the tension another notch, decided to try another approach. "Interesting idea. You helped Stan test the programs he worked on for the new customer accounts system." He lounged, relaxed, sitting well back in the booth, one arm resting on the table, the other holding his chai.

Pierce stared at the fireplace and the play of light on its surface, and then shook his head as if he wanted to clear his thoughts. "Our unit uses the reports, so I talked to Stan now and then about the conversion and helped with the testing." He perched forward on his seat, alert and ready to flee.

"Did you notice anything unusual about the reports or what Stan had been doing?"

"Unusual?" Raising his latte, Pierce swallowed a little before replying. "Nooo... I'm not sure I know what you mean."

The hesitancy in his response made Paul smile and further convinced him Piece knew something. "It looks like Stan modified other routines not directly related to the conversion."

A choking fit shook Pierce. He coughed and sputtered. Concerned, Paul reached over to slap him on the back, but Pierce shrank away and put down his cup.

"I wouldn't know anything about that." The viper tongue flicked out again as he licked his lips. "I'm not a programmer you know, just an accountant."

Keeping his face impassive, Paul sought to dig deeper. "So far as you know the conversion programs produced the expected results?"

Pierce's vigorous nod increased Paul's suspicions. "Why of course. Everything we reviewed checked out. We found no discrepancies." He clasped and unclasped his hands, picked up his cup, and then put it down untasted.

Pleased to have rattled him, Paul pressed ahead. "Would you swear to that in a court of law?"

"Court of law?" Pierce face looked ashen.

"Someone's bound to ask questions about Stan's programs, and it may end up a criminal matter." He paused for emphasis. "It's possible someone murdered him."

"Murdered?" Pierce's eyebrows almost reached his receding hairline. "The paper said he died from a drug overdose."

"Yes, but according to his sister Stan wasn't a drug user."

"Well, I never knew him socially." Pierce licked his lips again and looked away.

"The real issue isn't that, but whether you had anything to with his death and with his program modifications. I'm keeping an open mind about murder, but..." Paul leaned forward slightly. "You're in a perfect position to know about the modifications."

Eyes wide, Pierce stared at him. He pulled out his pink silk handkerchief again, dabbed at his face with it, and folded it. Putting it away, he took a deep breath. "Don't threaten me, Counts," he snapped and jumped to his feet. "I...have another appointment."

He started toward the exit and then stopped. "Don't ask to meet me again. You've...spoiled my appetite, and I had a special dinner planned. Don't...don't call me." He hurried toward the exit.

Paul stared after him and smiled. Judging from Pierce's reactions, he knew something—too uncomfortable, too nervous not to be hiding it. These days drug use might merit a yawn, and, even with the bank's anti-drug policy, his boss would warn him first and urge rehabilitation. Pierce's response at the mention of the modified programs suggested he either had some involvement or at least knew about the modifications. Did that mean others were involved too? And if so, who? Vavor? It could be.

Paul shook his head; he'd have to find a way to broach the matter without pushing too hard. Vavor was a vice president. Morgan would know about him.

Common sense said to keep an eye on Pierce. If a few questions bothered him this much, a few more might produce some interesting results. For once, he began to hope he might have found an approach to answer Brooke's questions. After polishing off his beer, Paul strolled to his car in a thoughtful mood.

The next day at work, he called Sally Morris, Morgan's secretary, and made an appointment to see Morgan later that morning. He still had his own work to do. With all the distractions, he'd gotten a little behind. Paul logged on to the system and called up the program file he had been modifying for the new user codes.

At ten-thirty, he stored his code changes and signed off, clearing the screen. He wrote his initials on the locator board and left his cubicle for Morgan's office.

On Paul's entry, Morgan looked up and smiled. "Good morning, Paul."

"Morning, Morgan," he responded as he folded himself onto the chair facing the desk, or rather the large table that served as Morgan's desk. "What can you tell me about Walter Vavor?"

"Vavor? Why?"

"He may have a tie to Stan."

"Stan? I don't see how. He's Vice President of Finance, a family man, and active in community affairs. Fair, but tough with his employees." Morgan leaned forward, resting his forearms on his table.

"His name came up as a drug buyer."

"Walter?" Morgan raised one eyebrow. "That surprises me. He's so straight, a ruler looks crooked next to him."

"I'd always thought so, but now I'm running out of suspects, and I'm left with Vavor, Donna Sanders, John Pierce, and Pat Jensen."

Morgan leaned back in his chair, considering the names. "Of the four, I probably know Walter and Pat best. I think highly of them both. Walter, of course, is a bank officer. Pat worked for him and I think Pierce does." He paused a moment. "I don't know anything about a Donna Sanders."

Paul nodded. So far, everything tallied with what Marilyn had said. "I talked to Pierce yesterday, and he acted anxious and nervous. I haven't talked to Vavor yet, Donna Sanders, or to Pat Jensen."

"Hmm, I don't think you need to talk with Walter." Morgan paused for emphasis, leaning forward. "He's a senior officer of the bank. Besides, he'd never do anything crooked." He leaned back in his chair and picked up a letter opener.

"Maybe not, but he's linked to the Lido and Pierce works for him"

Morgan fingered the sharp edge of the opener. "Anything on Stan's program changes yet?"

"No, not really." Paul grimaced. "So far, I've concentrated on Stan's link to the Lido and it's where I got Vavor's name and all the others."

Putting the letter opener down, Morgan raised an eyebrow. "The Lido? Isn't that one of those sleazy night clubs?"

"Yeah."

Morgan frowned, puzzled or surprised. "Somehow I can't see what connection Walter would have with such a place, or for that matter Pat either."

"That's part of my problem and why I'm need to talk with them."

Studying him with intense scrutiny, Morgan leaned back in his chair, steepling his fingers. "Hmm…well I'd let Walter go. Unless you find something to embarrass the bank, I don't see this Lido thing as very important. Stan's work on the accounts relates to the bank. You promised to update me on your progress." The accusatory note came through loud and clear.

"Yeah, and I will, Morgan, but I don't have anything right now. Talking with Pierce again might tell me more. He signed off on all of Stan's changes." Paul got to his feet, relieved to have informed Morgan of Vavor's possible connection. "If I learn anything, I'll tell you at once."

"See you do. This entire situation could pose problems. You need to resolve it as fast as possible. Make it priority one."

"After any System crashes, but you could make it a formal assignment."

"Yes, you have a point. I'll consider it, but the fewer people involved, the better. We don't want any more rumors."

Paul nodded and left. Strolling deep in thought back to his office, he knew he had little on Vavor except for Pierce working for him and his name on Harley's list of drug buyers. The last sounded out of character according to Morgan. What else might be out of character and would any of the others react in the same way?

Chapter Eight

Given Morgan's warning about Vavor, Paul debated what to do next. He'd shied off talking with the women so far, but he'd have to speak with them eventually. Because of Pat Jensen's links to Morgan and Vavor, he decided to leave her for last, hoping to learn more first. Morgan claimed to know nothing about Donna Sanders. Marilyn had given him what little information he had on her.

Marshalling his scattered thoughts, when Paul reached his office he pulled out the directory to locate Donna Sanders's extension. He keyed it and waited as the phone rang three times.

"Hello, Sanders here." A woman's voice, crisp and quick, answered.

"I'm Paul Counts, Information Systems. We need to speak about a confidential matter."

"Confidential?"

"Yes, about Harley Donovan. We could meet at five-fifteen at Waldo's."

"Harley Donovan?"

"Yeah. He owns the Lido and gave me your name."

"Oh? I can't imagine why." A pause followed and Paul began to wonder what else to say.

"Waldo's? The bar near Main and Third?"

"Yes."

"All right, five-fifteen. See you there."

* * * *

Paul left work promptly at five and arrived at Waldo's at ten after. Small candles on the low tables opposite the bar eased the darkness of the tunnel-like lounge only a little. A purple banquette lined one wall with small tables at intervals and low matching ottomans clustered around the tables. The bar occupied the other long wall. Paul chose a place near the back with a view of the door. As his eyes adjusted, he saw only one other person, a middle-aged man seated at the bar and talking in low tones with the balding bartender.

At five-fifteen the lounge door opened and a tall woman entered. That tallied with Misty's description. She wore a severe, dark gray suit, a tailored white blouse, and no jewelry. Paul noted her straight hair cut very short in a mannish style. As usual, Marilyn had pegged her right—nothing soft about this one. He rose as she strode purposefully up to the table.

"Mr. Counts?"

"Yes. Miss Sanders? Won't you sit down?" Paul motioned to the ottoman next to his. "Can I buy you a drink?"

"Scotch, neat, please." She set her briefcase on the floor and sat on the ottoman indicated, her back lamppost straight and her feet together. She watched as Paul rose and walked to the bar to order her Scotch.

He returned, placed the drink in front of her, and then resumed his seat. She picked up the glass and sipped the amber liquid as she studied him.

"What do you want, Mr. Counts?"

Deciding the direct approach would serve best, he took a deep breath before starting. "Harley Donovan gave me a list of people who work at the bank and buy drugs from him. Your name appeared on the list."

"So?" She showed no surprise or even much interest.

A tough hide all right, she displayed none of Pierce's nervousness or even Kent's surprise. "So you buy and use drugs."

"Nonsense." She laughed and then drank her Scotch before saying more. "It means I may have stopped in from time to time, but it doesn't identify me as a user."

He needed to crack that smooth surface. What had Marilyn said about Donna? No friends and not much else, so what did that leave? Her job?

"The bank disapproves of drug use, especially for someone in Customer Services."

"Are you trying to blackmail me?" She appraised him with a dismissive glint in her eyes. "Because, if so, find another patsy. It's only your word against mine. You have no real proof do you, Mr. Counts?" She fixed him with a belligerent stare, challenging him to produce it.

"No, I don't, but I don't need any. I'm not interested in drug use."

"Then why would this Donovan give you a list of his customers?"

Running a hand through his hair, Paul sighed in frustration. "The recent death of a friend of mine, Stan Beldon, from a drug overdose raised some questions. His sister and I don't believe he died by accident. Someone helped that happen. We're talking to anyone at the bank who might have known Stan or who frequented the Lido and may have seen him there."

"I didn't know Mr. Beldon. I don't think I've even met him, so I fail to see how I can help you." She raised her Scotch and swallowed some.

"When Stan died, a woman called 9-1-1"

She looked straight at Paul, an amused gleam in her eyes. "It wasn't me."

"But you've been to the Lido. Did you ever see this man?" Paul pulled out the snapshot of Stan and passed it to her.

Holding it close to the candle, she then shook her head. "I don't recognize him." She returned the snapshot.

Paul replaced it in his shirt pocket. "Do you know anything about anyone else at the bank who frequents the Lido?"

Looking him in the eyes, she gave him a crooked grin. "Mr. Counts, even if I did, I have no reason to tell you. As it happens, I don't. I seldom go there. The Lido offers me nothing."

Donna finished her drink and put the glass down. "Now, if you'll excuse me, I have other business. Good evening, Mr. Counts."

Paul watched as she marched out. He knew of no ties to Stan or anything he might have been doing. However, she appeared the one most likely to be Harley's contact at the bank. Tomorrow he would check on those system traces he'd put in to track Stan's routine. So far, Pierce came across as the weak link in the scam, but he needed facts to force anything more out of him.

* * * *

The following morning before starting his own work, Paul mulled over his encounter with Donna Sanders. She had told him nothing. He still had Vavor and Pat Jensen from the Harley's list. Despite Morgan's caution, Paul wanted to know just where Vavor fit. His connections to Pierce and Pat made him a prime candidate. Paul turned to the directory, looked up Vavor's number, and entered it.

"Mr. Vavor's Office, Wilma Princeton."

"Paul Counts, Information Systems, I'd like to speak to Mr. Vavor, please."

"Can I tell him what it's about?"

"It's a personal matter." The line went quiet as she placed him on hold.

"Hello, Vavor here," a deep, pleasant voice answered.

"Mr. Vavor, I'm Paul Counts. I'd like to talk to you briefly, if I may, on a somewhat confidential matter."

"Confidential?"

"Yes, it's concerns Harley Donovan, owner of Club Lido."

For a moment Vavor said nothing. "I haven't anything to do with either one."

"That's not what Harley says, and everyone else he mentioned checked out. I'm keeping an open mind, but considering your position..." Paul let his words trail off.

Silence followed. Paul assumed Vavor was considering what Harley might have told him.

A deep sigh came over the line. "Oh...perhaps you'd better meet me, say Saturday morning about eleven." Vavor's voice reflected icy distaste. "I'll be at the Antrim Park parking lot just off Olentangy near the walkway under 270."

"That'll be fine, sir, I'll see you then."

Tomorrow was Saturday. Hopefully he would be able to cross Vavor off the list after they talked. Morgan had insisted Vavor would not be involved in any questionable scheme, but any association with Harley or the Lido required checking.

In the meantime he should see what his trace program had recorded. Paul logged onto to the system and called up the program. He hadn't wanted to make any changes to Stan's routine because it might alert others using it, and he would've had to go through Documentation. By using a trace in the operating system debugging code he could avoid all that and even another systems programmer would only see it as a routine matter. With luck, he could find the information he needed and delete the trace without leaving any record it had ever existed.

According to the log, Stan's routine had stored all the rounding sums into a separate account numbered 529999999. The 529 represented the branch code and the nines the account number. Paul nodded at that. Usually all nines represented garbage and the bank never used them for real accounts. No one would bother to check anything consisting of all nines.

He keyed in the account number and whistled as he read the balance. A hundred thousand give or take a few cents. Not bad. The name on the account read Jovanoski, Sandy. No street address, just General Delivery for the Central Post Office. Somebody had messed up there. The question remained whether this Jovanoski represented a real or a fake name. If real, he had another suspect for his list.

Paul deleted the trace and added another routine to track the activity on the Jovanoski account. He'd have to monitor that and see what else he could learn. He debated whether to tell Morgan and decided to wait until he saw if the new trace found anything.

* * * *

Saturday, a warm, clear day, chided Paul for not taking advantage of the excellent weather as he drove toward the park. It made a nice change from the rain of the preceding week. He saw several families strolling along the river.

The Metro Park System had set aside strips of land along the various rivers passing through Columbus and the surrounding area. Biking paths and walks in these places proved popular with many people. Antrim also allowed fishing in its small lake. Paul parked and approached the tunnel walkway.

A tall, gray-haired man stood at the entrance. "Counts?" With his open face and trim appearance, he could easily have been used as the model for 'your personal banker' ads, a face you could trust. He looked suitably casual in a navy windbreaker over a white open necked polo shirt and tan slacks.

"I'm Paul Counts. Mr. Vavor?"

"Why don't we walk a bit, Mr. Counts?" Vavor turned and led the way through the tunnel. "We can talk by the lake."

When they reached the path around the lake Vavor turned left and Paul followed. "Now, what did you want to see me about?"

"It's a long story really, but I'm here because Harley Donovan gave me you name as a drug buyer."

Vavor stopped cold and stared at him. "Drugs? Donovan? Are you a policeman, Mr. Counts?"

Paul shook his head. "No, I'm not. I'm a friend of Stan Beldon, and I'm trying to find out who killed him."

"Beldon?" Vavor paused a moment. "Oh, yes that programmer from the bank. Killed him?" He blinked and resumed walking. "The newspaper reported he died of a drug overdose."

"He did, but Stan wasn't an addict, and I don't think his death was an accident. With a little persuasion, Donovan gave me the names of his customers from the bank for his drug sideline and included your name."

"Mr. Counts, anything that slime tells anyone is suspect. I thought when you phoned you had something on that criminal. "

"What made you think that?"

"It's none of your business." The arctic edge in Vavor's voice chilled Paul. Vavor picked up his pace almost to a jog. "I've nothing more to say to you, Mr. Counts."

"Hey, a man who worked on the new customer account programs is dead, and Donovan gave me his name and yours." He paused to let Vavor absorb what he had said. "Are you the one behind murder and embezzlement?"

"What," Vavor snapped, his face flushed.

"First Stan Beldon dies, then John Pierce who works for you acts scared witless when I asked him about Stan and the customer account changes, and a review of Stan's files revealed some interesting money transfers going on. Did you engineer all this?"

"I had enough. You...you've gone too far. My personal integrity is above reproach."

"Wait a moment, Mr. Vavor. I'm focusing on Pierce, not you. The bank should check his accounts to find out what he's doing."

Vavor slowed his pace a bit. "We audit all accounts on a regular schedule, but you've raised serious allegations with negative implications for the bank. I'll have Pierce's accounts reviewed."

"Thank you, sir." Paul sighed. What would Vavor do when he learned about Jovanoski or did he already know?

"Don't contact me again or I'll see you regret it. Goodbye, Counts."

Paul watched with a twisted smile as Vavor hurried off. The man had only talked with him because of Harley's name. Why? Somehow Paul couldn't see him as a drug user. It seemed unlikely, but stranger things happened all the time. His refusal to discuss Harley left him open to suspicion; he was hiding something, something associated with Harley. His outrage when Paul as much as accused him of knowing about a scam appeared genuine as did his surprise about Pierce.

Sighing, Paul hoped a review of Pierce's account revealed

something. Meanwhile, upping the pressure on Pierce might produce results. Paul debated the options as he walked toward his car.

Chapter Nine

The preemptive buzz of the intercom line shattered Morgan's thoughts. Only senior executives used this line, so he picked up the receiver with haste.

"Morgan, what in the hell is going on?" Walter Vavor greeted him, his anger clear. "A member of your staff accused one of mine of fudging the accounts. On top of that, he asked me personal questions."

Morgan sighed, annoyed and ready to throttle Counts. What in the hell had he said to Vavor? "That must have been Paul Counts."

"Yes, that's the name. Now, what are you pulling?"

"Me? Nothing, nothing at all. Counts said he thought someone from the bank murdered Stan Beldon, one of my programmers."

"And you agree?" Vavor sounded incredulous.

"Not necessarily. The police treated Beldon's death as accidental." Morgan tried to keep his voice calm and suppress his annoyance at Counts for ignoring his warning about Walter. Apparently, he hadn't made himself clear to that idiot.

"To protect the bank's interests, I encouraged Counts to review Stan's recent work and his friends to see if he found anything odd. So far, he's only linked some bank people to a sleazy nightclub. He's talked to some of them. What did he say to you?"

"He accused me of…never mind that. He hinted I had some scheme to skim the books underway." Walter stopped for breath. "I want him off my back and out of my personal affairs." Cold and steely, his adamant voice brooked no excuses.

"I told him," Morgan responded at his conciliatory best, "you were a straight arrow, and he'd gain nothing by talking to you, but, if I'd stopped him, he had mentioned going to the police. None of us wants that. It would look bad for the bank just having any suspicions raised."

"Whatever, you'd better muzzle him. I won't have him or anyone else asking questions about my personal life. He has no right."

Walter paused, as if struck by a sudden thought. "You don't think there's really anything to his story?"

Morgan laughed. "No, of course not. You can't fool our system of checks and balances that easily; you know that. I'll talk to him, Walter; I promise. Now don't worry, everything will work out. I'll see to it."

"It had better. I'll see you at the meeting this afternoon." Mollified, but not satisfied, Vavor disconnected.

He wondered if Morgan could manage this Counts. He supposed he had to trust him to take care of it. Then a repellent thought struck him. Had Morgan initiated this stunt to undermine Finance or him? Turning that thought over, a tiny doubt nudged Vavor. He might have to take action against Counts himself, but what? He'd never heard of him before. Maybe a few questions about the man would help.

Not for the first time, he wished he had never gotten involved with Donovan, but he had had no choice, had he? If only things could have been different.

As for Pierce, he considered him a good man who did his job well, always had—never a thing wrong with any of his work. What did Counts want anyway? Experience told him whenever one man accused another, he ought to look first at the accuser before investigating the accused. Morgan better take care of the matter and soon, or he'd take care of both Morgan and Counts.

* * * *

Paul arrived at work Monday buoyed by the bright sunshine and milder weather. He hadn't made much progress on Stan's murder, but he had begun to understand the people on Harley's list, and, because Pierce showed distinct promise, he had someone with whom to start.

The fluorescent pink message slip sitting in the center of his desk caught his attention when he entered his office. Morgan wanted to see him ASAP, according to the message left by Sally Morris, Morgan's assistant. Interesting. He'd better find out what Morgan wanted. Never a good idea to rile the boss.

Still wondering, he sauntered up to Sally's desk where she sat opening the morning mail. "Hi, what's with Morgan?"

She shrugged. "No idea. He said to get you here first thing, so you'd better go on in."

"Okay, wish me luck." He strolled on into Morgan's office.

"Good morning, Paul," Morgan greeted him as he entered. "Have a nice weekend?"

"Not bad, and you?" Paul sank onto the chair facing the desk. Morgan never indulged in small talk, so something or someone had gotten to him. Vavor?

Face solemn, Morgan steepled his fingers and rocked back in his chair. "Walter Vavor called this morning. He's a mite upset over your weekend chat."

Paul grinned wryly. "He told me his dealings at the Lido were none of my business, and he's right, but until I've worked out what Stan was doing and how it ties in with that place, I won't know for sure. Right now with John Pierce and Vavor, both on Harley's list, it makes for interesting possibilities."

Frowning, Morgan nodded. "Yes, I see that, but Walter is a senior officer and has never had a hint of scandal associated with him. How do you know this Harley character told you the truth? You're placing too much reliance on gossip from a strip club."

Paul shifted slightly on the chair. "I hear you. As for Vavor, there's always a first time. Look at all the corporate scandals. I told him I'd wait until he reviews Pierce's accounts, so I won't bother him for a while anyway."

Leaning forward, Morgan placed both hands on his desk and skewered Paul with a steely glance. "Talk to me first and I'll decide whether to do that. Don't anger Walter. He's one of the most powerful men in this bank."

"Right." Paul nodded. "Anything else?" He inched forward to the edge the chair, ready to rise.

"No, but so far you've told me little about this entire matter. The bank doesn't need more bad press right now." Morgan leaned back, but didn't relax. "Have you made any progress on Stan's routines?"

Paul grimaced. "A little. I've tried to track the activity on some dummy accounts. They may only be test files, but I'm not sure yet."

Morgan snapped upright. "You told Vavor you suspected some sort of scam. Look, Paul, either there is or there isn't, and I want to know. If you can't find out, I'll ask Cramer to look."

"That's up to you, Morgan, but since Vavor agreed to review Pierce's accounts we'll know by next week at the latest. I still have my regular work to do, and I can't spend all my time on this. As it is, I've spent my evenings and weekends trying to sort things out."

Studying Paul for a moment, Morgan apparently weighed what options to pursue. "Hmm...we have to protect the bank, and the fewer people involved the better." He paused for a moment. "I don't want to involve the auditors or the police."

Chewing over Morgan's implied warnings and threats, Paul pursed his lips. "I can't promise that. If someone murdered Stan and works for the bank, the police will be involved."

Morgan waved a hand to dismiss all that. "Yes, yes, but we still don't know that for sure. My major concern is whether Stan participated in a swindle. I want you concentrate on that. Let the police deal with Stan's death—that's their job. You just focus on the bank's interests and keep me in the loop."

Sighing, Paul nodded. "That's what I'm doing." He pushed back his chair, and, standing, unkinked his legs.

"All right, see that you do." Morgan picked up a report from his desk as Paul left the office.

Grinning, Paul descended the stairs on the return to his office. Vavor hadn't wasted any time calling Morgan and had obviously put the heat on him. He must have really gotten to him, but Vavor could wait for now. Anyway, the review of Pierce's accounts would provide a few answers, and Paul still had the nervous accountant to pressure.

Morgan hadn't mentioned Pierce. Antsy and frightened, he might respond to a little more persuasion. Talking to him again could do it. The man acted as if he had something to hide, but the question of what remained unanswered.

Back in his office, Paul sat and debated for a moment. He hadn't talked to Brooke since she'd called last week. He'd put off phoning her because he'd hoped to have more to tell her. She would want to know what he learned, and he owed her. A movie and dinner would give them time to chat. He dialed her number with a pleasant sense of anticipation.

"Hello, Brooke Beldon." As always, he liked her confident voice.

"Hi, Brooke, it's Paul Counts. How are you?"

"Fine, and you?" Her voice held a warm welcome. "I debated calling you. Did you learn anything from the people on Harley's list?"

"A little. I'll tell you what I've learned, that is, if you'll let me take you to a movie and buy you a dinner after. I still owe you a meal, but I'm not much of a cook."

"When?"

"Well, are you free tonight?"

"As it happens I am, and I've love to. What time?"

"I'll pick you up at five-thirty so we can get the twilight show and have dinner afterwards. That sound okay?"

"Fine, I'll look for you then."

"Great, it'll be good to see you. Until this evening." He disconnected. The thought of seeing her again left him with a pleasant glow.

He'd review things with Brooke and settle what to do next. With luck, she could add to what he'd learned about Stan and people on Harley's list. Having upset Vavor, he now had Morgan angry with him, too. The sooner he settled this mess, the sooner he could get on with more pleasant things, especially with seeing more of Brooke.

Pierce remained the obvious weak link.

Staring at his monitor, Paul gave himself a shake, remembering all the work piling up while he played detective. He'd better get moving, if he wanted to leave at five. His e-mail file overflowed with unanswered messages. Sighing, he began the process of reading, replying, or deleting messages. Morgan had pegged the mess right—most of them shouldn't have been sent. CYAs generated useless clutter.

At five, Paul left work filled with anticipation and arrived at Brooke's just at five-thirty. He parked in front of her house and, after a quick glance in the rearview mirror, walked up the walk with brisk strides. The door opened before he rang the bell, a good sign.

Brooke's soft green jersey dress clung in all the right places and ended in a flowing skirt. She looked regal with her hair wound into a crown atop her head. Tinkling earrings of turquoise and silver framed her oval face. He couldn't imagine how he had missed her beauty at their first meeting and chided himself for letting work control his life.

"Lovely as always," Paul greeted her. "I like your dress. Ready?"

"Of course. I'll get my purse and shawl."

They reached the theater in a little over thirty minutes. Bexley residents and university students patronized it, and it showed an odd mixture of films with an occasional art film and some retrospectives. A small shopping center had taken root nearby.

Tonight's film, part of a festival honoring Tom Hanks, featured "Joe Versus the Volcano," a silly film with a ridiculous ending. Paul enjoyed fairy tales now and then, and they kept away more serious thoughts like murder. He and Brooke laughed in all the right places as they shared a tub of buttery popcorn. Tom Hanks, a natural comic, didn't have to do much to get a laugh.

As they left the theater, Paul reached for Brooke's hand and she squeezed his. Relieved and willing to chance more, he took her arm and slipped it though his own. He savored her nearness and the gentle floral scent she wore. Jasmine?

"Where would you like to go for dinner?"

"Somewhere close and quiet, so we can talk without shouting."

"There's a small Chinese restaurant over there." Paul pointed across the parking lot. "They don't play music. How would that be?"

"Fine." She smiled at him as they walked arm and arm across the lot.

The restaurant décor, subdued for a Chinese restaurant, featured cream walls with a few Oriental drawings, but in pale pastels and charcoal. For Paul, the absence of brilliant reds and golds made a pleasant change from most oriental eateries.

The Monday evening dinner patrons had come and gone, so the place contained only a few diners, including one large group and several couples. They had no problem getting an isolated booth. Brooke restrained her questions until the waiter had taken their order and left a large pot of Chinese tea.

She poured tea into each of the small cups. "Well? What have you learned?"

"Not much yet, but I've managed to annoy some people. Kent Carpenter—he's the programmer who's taken over Stan's work—doesn't look likely, but at this stage it's impossible to tell." Paul reached for his tea and almost dropped it.

He rubbed his fingers gingerly and picked the cup up by its rim. "That'll teach me—you always sip Chinese tea and hold it by top, not the sides. I guess the pleasure of your company proved too distracting." He smiled at her and enjoyed the fleeting surprise crossing her face. "Did I tell you I like blue eyes?"

"Umm, I can't remember." She grinned for a long moment, and then gazed down at her tea. "Uh, who besides Carpenter?"

"Let's see, besides Kent, there's John Pierce, an accountant who worked with Stan, and shows the most promise. He knows something, but doesn't want to talk."

"What do you mean?" Brooke studied him, a slight frown creasing her brow.

"When I suggested someone might be siphoning off bank funds, he almost choked on his wine."

"What?" She stared at him "Are you serious?" The surprised look on her face amused him.

Paul nodded. "I'm pretty sure, but have to do more digging to be certain. So far, I've only turned up an account for a Sandy Jovanoski. If this account is active, someone in Accounting should know and might be helping with a cover-up. I plan to talk with Pierce again. A little pressure might make him respond."

The waiter arrived with their order, so they sat in silence until he had served the food—oval platters of mild Moo Goo Gai Pan, Beef with Snowpeas, and spicy Mala Beans accompanied by a large lacquered container of steamed rice. For a few minutes, they concentrated on the food.

"Umm, good." Paul sighed as he settled back and poured tea for both of them.

Brooke smiled at him. "I love Chinese food. All those healthy vegetables make me feel virtuous." She paused a moment and tasted her tea. "What about Jovanoski?"

Considering how he little knew, Paul frowned. "I haven't decided about Jovanoski yet and of course that name doesn't appear in either the bank directory or the Columbus area one. As for the eight names Harley gave me, I couldn't find three in the bank directory. Maybe he wanted to confuse us." He grinned to show his doubts.

"Besides that, he included a Donna Sands, but I found a Donna Sanders in Customer Services. When I talked with her, she admitted going to the Lido and knowing Harley. She said she'd never met Stan and dared me to say anything to anyone at all, but I found no connection to Stan or to any of the funds transfers, although I suspect she's the one giving Harley the credit reports." He drank a little of his tea.

"The others included Walter Vavor, a bank vice president; and Pat Jensen from Human Resources. I spoke with Vavor on Saturday, and he's hiding something, but I'm not sure what. He has a squeaky-clean reputation at the bank, but Harley's name upset him. He refused to say why and complained to my VP, Morgan Jones, who laid into me about

Vavor. He told me to leave him alone." Paul sighed.

Her brow wrinkled, Brooke stared off in to space for a moment and then at him. "The first week I worked at the Lido, a young girl came in one night and then left with Harley. When I asked about her, Suzy said her name was Barbara…" Pausing, Brooke shook her head. "No, Brenda, and that her dad's a big shot at some bank. A short while later, a well dressed, middle-aged man came in looking for his daughter. He was in one of those quiet, but dangerous rages, but Harley had gone. I didn't see him again."

"Umm, it could have been Vavor. He has a daughter, but I've not seen her." Paul held his cup for a moment pondering the possible connection and how it might relate to everything else, then sighed in frustration. "That still doesn't tie him to Stan though. Pierce works for Vavor, and if Pierce is in on some scam, maybe Vavor is too."

"What about Pat Jensen? We're looking for the woman who called 9-1-1, and you said this Donna Sanders has no connection with Stan. Doesn't that leave Pat Jensen as the most likely person? What's she look like?"

"I've no idea yet. Stan's section secretary Marilyn said Pat was romantically involved with Morgan a few years ago. Her husband divorced her shortly after. Nobody I've talked with so far has mentioned anything about Pat and Stan or even any other man."

Sighing, Paul stared down at his empty plate. "I'm going to dig more into what Stan did with those programs at the bank, and I've made Pierce edgy. I'll bug him a bit and then try the Jensen woman. Truthfully, I'm not sure just how to deal with her. Donna Sanders stopped me cold."

"I could try, if you think that would be better."

"I'm stumped. We need some way to force these people to tell us what they know. Let me think about it first, and see what Pierce has to say."

"What about this ex-husband? Who is he?"

"Marilyn said his name is Sam Stephenow…Stephanowsky and that he's a branch manager for the bank."

Brooke grinned. "Quite a mouthful, that name. What about talking to him?"

"I'm not sure." Paul grimaced. "I don't think you say 'tell me more about your ex-wife and the men she dates.'"

"No, but maybe I could do something. As a free-lancer, I talk to and interview many people. Maybe I could interview him for a story on the bank or some such."

"It has possibilities, but let me try Pierce first."

"Paul, do you think Stan had anything to do with this…this scam?"

Her question hit hard, and he struggled with what to say. "I can't say, but his code would make that likely." He stopped, unwilling to add to her worries and accuse her brother, but also wanting to be honest with her. "I'm sorry, Brooke, but it provides a possible motive for someone to murder him." He reached for her hand and squeezed it.

"I can't believe Stan would do that. He's not a thief."

"I didn't say he was. Right now, I can't tell you much. Why not wait until I find out more?" He wanted to reassure her, but his instincts told him Stan had written the code. Right now, he had no idea how far the scheme reached.

Brooke looked unsatisfied, but nodded. They skipped dessert and settled for a fortune cookie apiece. The fresh cookies cracked sharply as they opened them. Brooke smiled as she read hers.

"All right, what is it," Paul asked, his curiosity sparked.

"It says, You will find your heart's desire."

"Hmm, have you?"

"It says 'will,' not have." She grinned at him, eyes sparkling. "I'm not sure, let's just say things look promising. What's yours?"

"All things come to those with patience, a hopeful sign in this mess."

"But not necessarily true," she reminded him, a faint smile edging her lips.

"Please, let me have what hope I can find," he joked, "even if it's only a Chinese fortune. Ready?" Paul picked up the check and left a tip.

She slid out of the booth, and they walked to the cashier's counter at the entrance to the restaurant where Paul paid for their meal. Silence reigned on the drive to her house. Paul walked her to the door and watched while she unlocked it.

Finished, she turned to him. "It's been a lovely evening, Paul. I've really enjoyed it."

"Me too, we'll do it again, if you're game."

"That depends on my writing schedule, but if we work around that, yes."

"Good, I'll call you." He kissed her cheek and then his lips brushed hers. "Umm, I could get to like this."

"Oh?" Brooke gazed at him, a challenge in her eyes.

He pulled her closer and kissed her again, this time nuzzling her lips until she responded. He explored her soft mouth, tasting a mixture of tea and sweet fortune cookie. She fit his embrace so well; he eased back with reluctance.

"I'm not sure this is the time or place for what I'd like to do."

"Which is?" She stepped back and gazed up at him.

"You want it sweet or straight?" He grinned to take the edge off his words.

Staring up at him a moment, she nodded. "Paul...I..."

The lost look on her face made him wish Stan's death didn't still hang between them "Sssh, it's fine. I understand, really I do."

A large sigh escaped her "Later...after we settle all this." She gave him a small smile that edged into a frown. "I hate uncertainty."

"Yeah, I know what you mean. I'll call you after I talk with Pierce, okay?"

"Please do. We've got to find out who killed my brother."

Paul grimaced. "Yes, I haven't forgotten that, but I'm not sure that's all."

"What do you mean by that?"

"What I mean is this business with the bank could also be serious, and, then of course, there's you." He touched a loose strand of hair near her face.

"Me? What's that to do with anything?"

"You're a beautiful woman; one I like a lot. Once we clean up this mess, I want us to spend time together and get to know each other better, much better."

She drew back and studied his face. "We have to sort this mess out first, okay?"

"All right, I'll call you when I learn anything else." He paused a moment, wanting more and yet hesitant to seek it "Good night, Brooke."

"Good night, Paul." She opened the door and slipped inside.

For a moment, he stared at the closed door and then shrugged. He'd find some way to speed up things

* * * *

The next day in his office, Paul stared at the Delacroix lithograph. Maybe fate should give Mr. Pierce a slight nudge. He punched Pierce's number while trying to work out exactly what to say. He still hadn't decided when the phone stopped ringing and Pierce answered.

"Pierce, this is Paul Counts. We met a week or so ago in Panera's, remember?"

"I remember all too well, Mr. Counts, and I told you then I have nothing to say to you."

His tone made Paul's ears feel frostbitten. "Yes, you did, but since then, I've talked to senior bank officials."

"You what?"

He could imagine Pierce staring at phone as if it were suddenly a poisonous snake. "I talked with senior bank officials." He hoped Pierce's discomfort would lead to some hard evidence.

"What did you tell them? Did you tell them about Harley and me?" The man sounded on the edge of panic.

"About you and Harley?" Paul paused for effect. "No, although I suggested a review of your accounts might be timely."

"What?" A clatter and thud sounded as if Pierce had dropped the phone. "Why did you do that?"

"Well, when someone acts like you, it raises questions. You might find it better if you talked to me—much better than talking to the police. If the account review should turn up anything, I'll be able to prove shortly that Stan Beldon siphoned off customer funds. When I do, it's a police matter. I warned you of that last time."

"Look, I can't talk now. Let me think about it and get back to you. I'm really not sure there's anything I can tell you."

"I think you can. You tested Stan's routines, and signed off on them. You had to check the results, so you knew exactly what he was doing."

"I don't remember any discrepancies; I really don't." A pause followed. "When did you talk to these...senior officials?"

"Last Saturday. I'm sure the review won't take very long, so you probably don't have much time left. It would be in your interest to talk with me, Mr. Pierce."

"I said I'd think about it, okay? I have work to do, Mr. Counts. Good-bye."

The receiver clicked as Pierce disconnected. Well that should get his temperature up a bit. Paul hoped, putting a thorn in Pierce's hide would spur him to confirm what he suspected about Stan's money transfers. 'Patience' his fortune had counseled. Now, let's see if it would work for him and against Pierce.

Chapter Ten

John Pierce punched the familiar number and almost miskeyed in his haste. His fingers tapped a ragged staccato beat as he waited for the ringing to stop. Sandy had to be there. He had to talk Sandy.

"Hello?"

He gasped, relieved as the expected voice answered. "Pierce here, we have a problem, a big problem. Paul Counts is getting nosy. He thinks he's on to something in Stan's work. If he finds out what we've done, he'll hang us." He wiped his brow and worried the anxiety and nervous tension in his voice would annoy Sandy, but he needed reassurance.

"You worry too much." The calm voice dismissed his concerns as unimportant. "I know about Counts and have taken steps to see he leaves us alone. Just don't panic."

"Yeah, but he wants to know about the Lido. He got a list of drug buyers from Harley Donovan." John mopped his forehead with his crumpled silk handkerchief.

"That won't help him much."

"But my name's on that list."

"And so are several others. I don't control your private life, but maybe you'd better stay away from there for a while. Counts can't touch us, so don't sweat it." A brief pause followed. "Just sit tight and keep your mouth shut."

John twisted the phone cord back and forth. "You don't have to worry—he probably doesn't know about you—but he has my name."

"A name doesn't prove anything. I said I'd take care of it; just relax. I'll tell you when to worry, okay?"

"All right, but I'm not taking a fall for you or anyone else."

"You won't. I'll let you know if we have a problem, but we won't unless you slip, remember that." A click sounded as Sandy disconnected.

Sunk in thought, Sandy pondered the options. John had always represented a weak link. Maybe something should be done about him. A nervous type and a weakling anyway; sooner or later his drug habit would cause a problem. Maybe sooner, especially, if it also solved another problem. Counts had become altogether too nosy and troublesome.

* * * *

At home after work, Paul's phone rang and interrupted the evening newscast.

"Hello, Mr. Counts?" The low whisper made the words hard to hear.

"Yes, who is this? Can you speak louder?"

"It's me, John Pierce. We talked earlier."

"Yes?" Hope rose that Pierce had decided to tell what he knew. "Do you want to talk to me?"

"Uh, yes, I do," the hoarse whisper continued, "but not over the phone. Come to my apartment, The Oaks, apartment Five B. Come right away. I'm finishing some work at home, so I'll be in my study. I'll leave the front door unlocked."

"It'll take me about twenty minutes."

Replacing the handset, Paul mulled over the call. So Pierce wanted to talk. As for the whisper, he probably didn't want anyone to hear him. Paul, phoned Brooke because of her disappointment over his delay in calling after his visit to Harley. He keyed in her number in a hurry.

"Beldon residence."

"Brooke, Paul here. John Pierce just called. He wants to talk to me; so maybe we're getting somewhere. I'll fill you in you when I get back and tell you what he has to say."

"Better than that, why not stop here on your way home? I'll make us some popcorn."

"Sounds great. I'm don't know how long I'll be, but it shouldn't take long. I'll come as soon as I can." He hung up the phone and shut off the television. "Guard duty, Shadow." He scratched her ears and then put a bit of catnip on her scratching post

He hoped he remembered how to get into The Oaks. He thought he recalled only one entrance into the apartment complex.

Within twenty minutes, he reached the elegant, but discreet sign for the Oaks. A trendy new development, it consisted of remodeled Victorian homes divided into large airy apartments—so the commercials insisted—on the river, many with views across it of the downtown. A lot of young business people, lawyers, and insurance executives rented the remodeled units with large windows and rooms with high ceilings. It amazed him a bank accountant could afford such luxurious quarters. Systems staff made good money, but not enough for The Oaks, and he thought accountants did less well than the programming staff. Maybe he'd chosen the wrong profession.

Paul discovered Five B on the second floor of one of the houses. He rang the bell still speculating on what Pierce would tell him. He hoped he'd get the information on the account changes and the names of any others involved. A scam like this took several people and any of them might want Stan out of the way.

No one answered. Strange, Pierce had asked him to come straight over. Maybe he had his head buried in work

Debating what to do next, Paul then remembered Pierce had said the door would be unlocked. He turned the handle and pushed. The door swung inward. Cautious, he poked his head inside and, seeing nothing, stepped into the entryway.

"John," he called. "John Pierce? It's Paul Counts. Are you here?"

No one answered.

Walking into the living room, he observed with pleasure the lovely river view framed by the large front window. On the sidewall, a high-mantled fireplace with a basket of logs to the side offered promises of comfortable evening fires. The white leather sofa with matching side chairs and the rug, a deep, uneven shag of mixed shades of brown and green, showed Pierce favored Scandinavian modern. The pictures on the wall looked like original oils of indeterminate subjects, but attractive in a formless swirl of colors. It all added up to money. If Piece didn't come from a wealthy family, he had to get it from somewhere—like a bank scam.

Pierce had said he would be in his study so maybe he hadn't heard the doorbell. Where in the hell would the study be? Paul followed the hall toward the back, passing an elegant dining room, and coming to an open door at the end. He looked into a decorator's bedroom with a round bed and wall of mirrored closets to the right. Inside, he glimpsed another door. Perhaps it led to the study.

Paul walked over the soft fawn-colored carpet toward the half-open door. As he reached it, he hardly saw the round spa tub and modern fixtures. His eyes focused instead on the figure crumpled at the edge of tub and half submerged in the bubbling water.

Instinctively, he ran forward and pulled the body from the water. He turned it face up. John Pierce, his hazel eyes wide, stared at the ceiling. His thin blond hair dripped water. Paul loosened Pierce's tie and tried CPR, knowing it was too late and inwardly cursing himself.

Breathe in, blow, take a breath in, blow.

"Stop, right there."

"What?" Paul looked up see two uniformed police officers and a paramedic standing in the doorway. "I think he's dead. I was trying CPR, but he isn't responding."

"Let the paramedics deal with him. You come with me." The taller of the two police officers motioned Paul to follow him.

The officer returned through the hall to the living room. "This will do. Have a seat. My partner is calling Homicide, and someone will come shortly to talk to you."

The police officer occupied one of the side chairs and Paul sat on the sofa. The officer studied him as if he were a prime suspect. Maybe he was. The police had come and found him alone with a dead man. Paul slumped, uncertain what had happened, or who had called the police.

It all looked too pat. Had John Pierce really phoned him? The voice had been a hoarse whisper; it could have been anyone. At least he didn't have a motive. You had to have a motive for murder and he had none. John Pierce was dead, of that he was certain.

The doorbell rang, and the police officer got up to answer it. After several minutes, he returned to the living room with a neatly dressed, fair-haired man.

"I'm Detective Milton Meyers of the Homicide Squad. Suppose you tell me who you are, and the name of the man in the bathroom." Meyers sat down on the chair next to Paul, took out a pencil and small pad, and began making notes.

"I'm Paul Counts and he is ...er, was John Pierce."

Meyers wrote something down. "You live here, Mr. Counts?"

Paul shook his head. "No, this is Mr. Pierce's apartment. He phoned me about a half hour ago and asked me to come by. He said he wanted to tell me something."

"He let you in?"

"No..." Paul frowned. "No one answered when I rang the bell. When he called me, Pierce said he might be in his study and that he'd leave the door unlooked. When he didn't answer the bell, I tried the door and it opened." He looked at Meyers who nodded. "I assumed he was probably in his study. I entered, but didn't see him, and walked toward the back. I saw the open bedroom door, and thought the other door might lead to the study, but it didn't." Paul paused a moment, wondering what Meyers made of all this.

"And then?"

"Then I walked into the bathroom and found him lying half in the tub with his head underwater, so I pulled him out and tried CPR. Then the police arrived."

Meyers nodded. "Why did he call you?"

"Well…" Paul paused, uncertain just how much to tell him. "It's sort of complicated. We both work for First Bank, so did Stan Beldon."

At Stan's name, Meyers' intense scrutiny worried Paul. "Stan Beldon? That fellow who OD'd last month? What does he have to do with Pierce?"

Taking a deep breath, Paul debated how much to say. The police had labeled Stan's death as accidental. "Stan's sister, Brooke Beldon, said he never used drugs, and she asked me to help her prove the police view wrong."

Meyers shook his head, a look of disgust on his face. "Didn't she talk to the police?"

"Yes, but…" Paul's words tumbled out in a rush. "She said they were satisfied it was an accidental death. Anyway, in going through Stan's stuff at work, I found he spent time at the Lido and later learned John Pierce had too. I talked to Pierce about Stan and the Lido. He got angry and acted nervous, and, despite working with Stan, he said they didn't see each other outside work."

"So?"

"Tonight he called me and said he wanted to tell me something. At least, the caller identified himself as Pierce He asked me to stop by."

"Have you any idea what he wanted to tell you?"

"No, he refused to say over the phone." Suddenly the entire situation struck Paul as all too pat, too convenient. "Say, why did the police arrive when they did?"

"An hysterical elderly man called 9-1-1 about two men fighting in this apartment. He worried someone was getting hurt." Meyers looked at

Paul. "He was right about that."

Frowning, Paul shook his head. "But there was no fight, at least not when I arrived."

"So you say, but it's also possible that someone was here before you, or…" Meyers paused. "You fought with the victim and then killed him."

His forehead wrinkled in concentration, Paul stared at Meyers, all too aware how bad this all looked and grabbed at Meyers' suggestion. "Someone might have been here first. Maybe whoever it was heard me ring the bell and left. I didn't fight with Pierce, and I certainly had more to gain from him alive than dead." He paused, wondering about two phone calls—too convenient to be accidental. "Are you sure the caller was an elderly man? Did he give his name?"

Meyers shook his head. "No, he called from a payphone, but that's not unusual, particularly when someone is scared. He'll probably turn up when we canvass the neighbors. In any event, we found you with the victim. We'll need an official statement from you."

"Of course, any way I can help. I'm sure this relates to Stan's death. Pierce knew something. I don't know what, but maybe it implicated someone in that death." He focused on Meyers to emphasize his next point. "You know they didn't find that woman with Beldon who called 9-1-1."

"Yeah, but we'll take care of that, that's our job. Private citizens should stay out of police business, unless we ask for their assistance. Now, if you'll give the officer your address and phone number, home and work, we'll take you to the station so you can make a formal statement. After that you can go home, but you should remain available in case we need you." Meyers closed his notepad and put it and his pen in his jacket pocket.

Paul gave the uniformed officer his addresses as requested and then followed the detective's car to the downtown police station where he repeated his story for a police stenographer. She gave him a printed copy of his statement and he signed it. Finished at last, he returned to his car and drove to Brooke's. He hoped she hadn't gone to bed yet. Most likely, she would have given up on him.

This puzzle with the bank staff had grown Byzantine. Maybe he should have told Meyers about his suspicions, but that would mean an investigation of the bank, and he wasn't sure he knew enough yet to pursue that. Besides, Morgan would have his hide for sure if he said anything to the police without talking to him first. Vavor still hadn't called about Pierce's accounts unless he'd spoken with Morgan. Let Morgan take the responsibility for dealing with the police.

So far, he'd had one hell of a night, and he wasn't happy about his own position. Still, he had nothing to worry about, unless Meyers could establish a motive, and he didn't have one, so he could relax. But who set him up? He hadn't told anyone about Pierce's call except Brooke.

Who would want Pierce dead and why? It had to be connected with Stan or the bank. The questions about the customer conversion programs had bothered Pierce. There must be something fishy in those changes and Pierce knew it. The question was, who else knew?

The only people he had told about Pierce were Brooke, Vavor, and Morgan. Except for Stan, Brooke had no connection with the bank. While he had asked Vavor to have Pierce's accounts checked, he hadn't told Morgan what he suspected, and neither Morgan nor Vavor knew he planned to meet Pierce this evening, unless one of them had set him up. Maybe Pierce had talked to someone, but to whom?

No answer had surfaced by the time he reached Brooke's. He wished he didn't have a death to report. He'd much rather talk about something else. He rang the bell with mixed feelings.

"I wondered where you'd gotten to, and debated whether to go to bed or wait." Brooke, in jeans and a shaggy sweater, greeted him as she opened the door. "I thought something must have happened."

"It did. Someone killed John Pierce." He hung his windbreaker on the hall tree.

"What?" Her face mirrored his earlier shocked surprise.

"And set me up as the fall guy."

"I think we both need a drink. Come and sit down." She led the way into the living room and took a decanter from a tall cabinet on the far wall. She poured them both a glass of single malt whiskey.

"What happened?"

Paul sipped his whiskey, grateful for its warmth, but too bothered to appreciate its smooth smoky flavor. "I phoned you, after Pierce called me." She nodded.

"Well, I reached his place in about twenty minutes, rang the bell, and no one answered. He'd said he'd leave the door unlocked and to come in, which foolishly I did, thinking since he expected me, he had left it open. The apartment appeared empty. I went through to the back, and found Pierce half submerged in his spa tub with his head under water. I tried CPR and the police arrived." He took another sip of his whisky.

"What did they say?" Brooke held her glass with both hands, warming the contents, and watching Paul intently.

"Not much. They said some old man called 9-1-1 about a fight, and there I was with a dead man." He shook his head, bewildered by the sudden events of the evening.

"At least they didn't arrest you." She sipped some of her whiskey and then set the glass down.

Paul grimaced. "Not yet, but don't count on it. If they can establish it was murder and find a motive, they will. Lucky for me, I don't think they can. It's possible they'll want to talk to you, since I told them about the tie-in with Stan. I forgot to tell them I'd called you before going to Pierce's place, but that probably doesn't make any difference anyway." He sighed.

"Since I'm here now, they would probably say we cooked it up afterwards, and it wouldn't prove I didn't kill him. I also didn't tell them about Harley or the list of drug buyers. I'd rather follow up on that myself first."

"Paul, I'm sorry. I had no idea when I asked for your help, that anything like this would happen. I want to know who was responsible for Stan's death, but I didn't expect anyone else to die." She rubbed her arms as if suddenly cold.

"Look, this isn't your fault, any more than it's mine. There's nothing to apologize for. I'm helping because I like you and considered Stan a good programmer. On top of that, it also looks like the bank may be involved in some way. Something stinks about Stan's death. Maybe now, the police will believe that."

He set his empty glass down and got to his feet. "It's late, and we both have to get up in the morning. I only came by, because I promised. Right now, I think we could both do with a good night's sleep. I'll be in touch if anything happens."

They walked side by side to the front door. He stopped and picked up his jacket from the hall coat tree. He faced Brooke as he shrugged on the windbreaker.

"Brooke, don't let this bother you. It has nothing to do with you. A person who stoops to one murder has nothing to lose by a second."

"That's exactly what worries me, and, if Pierce was working with someone, he probably told them about you. Please, Paul, you will be careful, won't you?" She looked at him with concern and fear.

"Hey, don't worry, I'll be fine." He touched her face gently. "Besides, I'm likely to have a police escort for a while anyway. At least until they figure out I had nothing to do with Pierce's death."

"Well, that's something." She stood on tiptoe and kissed him briefly. "Now take care of yourself, or I will feel guilty."

"Hmm, how about another of those?" He pulled her close and kissed her lightly, wanting more, but weighed down by the evening's events.

"Multi-talented are you, Mr. Counts?" She hadn't resisted his embrace.

"Well, that depends on a lot of things, but I can concentrate better if we clean up this mess first. I prefer not to have a lot of distractions. It cramps my performance." He grinned down at her. "I'll call you, Brooke; sleep well."

He kissed her forehead and released her. Turning, he opened the door. It closed softly behind him.

After shutting the door, Brooke leaned against it, thinking about the evening's events. John Pierce's death raised the stakes, as well as eliminating one suspect. They hadn't yet talked with Pat Jensen and knew little about her. Maybe she should explore that avenue before things got worse. That ex-husband, Sam Stephanowski, must know something about Pat and maybe Stan. It wouldn't hurt to ask him, and she had plenty of practice asking awkward questions. Maybe the time had come to do another series of interviews of rising young executives.

Chapter Eleven

The phone rang, waking Paul from a strange, tangled nightmare in which he struggled to free himself from the embrace of a muscular python. He pushed one coil off, only to be engulfed by another. With concerted effort, he managed to stretch out an arm and reach the phone.

"Hello, Paul Counts," he muttered, not yet fully awake and still partially entangled with his comforter.

"So you think you got away with it, Counts," the voice rasped. The whispered words jolted him awake.

His hackles rose. "Got away with what? What the hell are you talking about?"

"Pierce, John Pierce. You killed him, and the police will nail you for it. I'll see to that," the hoarse whisper promised.

"Pierce? I didn't kill him; I only found the body. Who is this anyway?"

"Yeah, that's what you told the police, but we know better don't we?"

"I didn't kill him, and if you think you know who did, tell the police. Goodbye." Paul dropped the handset none too gently. It was too early for cranks. He pulled up the covers and tried to settle down.

Suddenly, he sat bolt upright, dislodging Shadow from the pillow. A loud meow signified her displeasure. He scratched her ears, and she settled down

"Sorry about that," Paul muttered.

With Shadow mollified, his thoughts reverted to the phone call. The voice accused him of killing Pierce. What possible reason could anyone have for believing he might have killed him? No, the call made no sense. He should phone that detective…Meyer? No, Meyers, that was it, Detective Milton Meyers.

Shadow's quiet purr soothed Paul and in a short while he drifted off to sleep.

Monday Paul tried to contact Meyers, but failed and had to leave his name and number. The clock read almost three before Meyers called him back.

"Hello, Mr. Counts? Milton Meyers here. I understand you wanted to speak to me."

"Yes, yesterday morning I had a crank call I thought I should tell you about. Some screwball accused me of killing John Pierce. I told him he should call the police and hung up on him."

"Did he say anything else?" Meyers' tone revealed nothing.

"No, just that he'd nail me."

"I received a note in the mail today that said something similar: 'Ask Counts about Pierce's murder'."

Sighing, Paul ran a hand through his hair. "I've already told you all I know about that. Could it have been the person who killed Pierce?"

"I doubt that; murders often bring out crank notes. I suggest we wait and see what develops. Meanwhile, we'll continue our investigation. I presume I don't have to remind you not to make any travel plans without contacting us first."

"Meaning I'm still a suspect?"

"You were found at the scene, Mr. Counts."

"Yes, I was, but I didn't kill him; I had no reason to. Well, I hope you'll let me know how things progress. I still believe Pierce's murder is tied in with Stan Beldon's death."

"So you said the other night. Could you be more specific about how?"

"No, but I'm sure they're related. Good-bye, Detective Meyers."

"Good-bye, Mr. Counts."

Paul replaced the phone. Somewhere he had gone wrong. He took out his lists of suspects to review: Kent Carpenter, John Pierce—scratch him, Donna Sanders, Walter Vavor, Pat Jensen.

What had he missed? Kent still seemed unlikely. He really hadn't known Stan, except for having the same boss, and Paul couldn't identify any motive. No link between Donna Sanders and Stan or Pierce, but she had said so little. Vavor puzzled Paul. His sincerity rang true, but John Pierce had worked for him. Better leave him on the list.

Pat Jensen? He hadn't talked with her yet. Unless she was the woman who had called 9-1-1, she had no motive or connection with

Stan. Maybe she met Stan at the Lido or through work. Human Resources staff often had contact with others outside their department. He knew nothing about her except for what Marilyn had said—she worked for both Vavor and Morgan. Maybe he should talk to one of them. With Vavor so angry, Morgan would be the better choice. Marilyn said Morgan had once been linked to Pat romantically.

Paul phoned Sally Morris and arranged to see Morgan.

As usual, when Paul entered the office, Morgan faced his PC, checking his email. He finished and swung his chair around to face Paul.

"Sally said you wanted information on Pat Jensen." Morgan leaned back in his chair, looked upward, and began steepling his fingers as an aid to thought. "Let's see, she worked for me about...umm, two years ago. Very competent secretary as I remember. She worked for Walter Vavor before that."

"Why did she leave Vavor?"

"I guess she felt I was more of an up-and-comer and I'm single. Walter isn't." Morgan grinned as he straightened his tie.

"You still are." Paul grinned back.

"Right you are, and I intend to stay that way, something Pat didn't understand. She's a pretty enough girl, but beginning to show her age. She'd been around, and while she was okay to play with, that's as far as it went."

Morgan's frankness surprised Paul. "A little dangerous these days, what with sexual harassment and all."

"You're right there, one of the reasons I decided to end the thing before it caused trouble." Morgan leaned back in his chair again.

"I don't imagine she was happy about it."

"No, but she knew advancement mattered to me, I even Anglicized my name, and then I explained, if she was really serious about me, it would hurt my chances for the CEO slot, and we had best cool it. So I arranged a nice little transfer for her into one of the exempt positions, no loss of salary, and a few gains in leave, etc. So far as I hear, she's doing very well. I haven't seen much of her since."

None of that helped since it didn't involve any of the other suspects. Paul decided to try another tack. "How did Vavor get on with her?"

Studying Paul, Morgan matched the tips of his fingers together and leaned back. "Well...he recommended her for my position, and told me he hated to lose her. Do you think she had some link to Stan?"

Paul shrugged and looked toward the windows. He had nothing yet, and her relationship with Morgan didn't make Stan likely. If she wanted a V.P., why settle for a programmer? "I can't say, but the owner of the Lido included her name as a crack buyer."

"That's news." Morgan sat up straight, his eyebrows raised. "She wasn't into drugs when she worked for me. She smoked an occasional cigarette."

"Did she drink?"

"A bit, but not extreme, more wine with dinner than anything else. Smart and a climber, Pat never went into extremes on anything." Morgan leaned forward. "I'm not sure what you're looking for."

"Neither am I." Paul slumped deep in thought against his chair, discouragement etching a frown on his face. "Well, no sense taking up more of your time. If you think of anything that might help, let me know." He rose from his chair.

"Of course. Have you finished identifying all of Stan's changes?"

"What?" He stared at Morgan, wondering at the question. "No, not yet. Kent has taken over the main body of Stan's work. I'm following up on some subroutines. Like I said last time, I'm trying to determine if any of them are active and what they do. I should have worked it out shortly. Well, thanks again, Morgan."

Paul strolled out the door still puzzled. Pat had links to both Morgan and Vavor, but no one else. She looked like a dead end.

A sudden thought struck him. At least one person could link Pat with Stan. Why hadn't he thought of it before? Misty said she'd seen Stan leave with a woman, the same woman Brooke had seen talking to Harley, and who had left a pen with the bank logo at the Lido. He could ask Brooke, but if Misty identified Pat, they would have something to take to the police.

He needed a picture. Morgan might have one, or maybe one of the other staff would. Then he remembered whenever the bank promoted or transferred anyone, it printed his or her name and picture in its newsletter. He only had to find the right newsletter. When had Pat been promoted? Didn't Morgan say she had worked for him two years ago? That would be the time to start.

Paul took the elevator to the top floor and marched with jaunty steps toward the bank library. He smiled at the pretty, dark-haired girl seated behind the reception desk at the entrance. Beyond her loomed the tall gray shelving holding the books and journals.

"Hi, Nancy. Say, where do you stash the old newsletters?" He perched, half-sitting on the corner of her desk.

"Which newsletter? We get at least fifty." She smiled at his ignorance.

"Our bank newsletter; you know, the one with promotions and all that jazz."

"They're filed by date in the second row of shelving at this end. If you have trouble, let me know."

"I'm having trouble already." He backed playfully away as she frowned at his levity. "Okay, okay, I can find them myself."

Reading the shelf labels, he found the stack of newsletters almost at once. He thumbed rapidly through the last two years and found the notice and picture he wanted. Pat probably had been a pretty girl, but age had added a touch here and there and that petulant look didn't help. Then he had another thought, what about Donna Sanders? Maybe he should take pictures of both women. After a little more scanning, he found a picture of Donna, too. She wasn't smiling. She looked competent and the epitome of business-like. He walked back to Nancy's desk whistling.

"How do I get copies of these?" He waved the newsletters in front of her.

"Easy, all you do is go to that copy machine in the corner and press the right buttons." She pointed toward the far corner just beyond the range of stacks. "That is, if you can find them."

"What? You don't have any faith in my intelligence?" He made an exaggerated face.

"Oh, so now you're intelligent, too?" Nancy raised her eyebrows.

"Just watch me. If you can operate those machines, so can I." He walked off, newsletters in hand.

He made his copies and returned the originals. "You had better be nice to me, or I won't come back," he said as he passed Nancy's desk.

"I should be so lucky, I didn't even think you programmer types knew we have a library."

"We just look illiterate on the outside. Underneath, we not only develop software that requires reams of documentation, but we write all those lengthy company reports—you know the ones, four-inch binders and all."

Nancy groaned. "Just what I need, more software and manuals to catalog. I can't wait to get yours—the shortest manual on record."

Paul shook his head. "No, no, it's the only blank one, self-documenting, user intuitive. Seriously though, thanks for the help."

He had his pictures, and, lucky too, the bank used high quality photocopying machines because they were almost as good as the originals. All he had to do was show them to Misty.

When Paul arrived home that evening, he found a note in his mail. Individual words cut from the local newspaper had been pasted on yellow lined paper to make the message. It read: I'm watching, Counts, and so are the police. With Pierce gone, how much do you get?

It carried no signature. Perhaps Meyers would be interested enough to test it for fingerprints. He put the envelope and the note aside. Shadow meowed a welcome and followed him to the kitchen

* * * *

In her study cum home office, Brooke had located the telephone number for Sam Stephanowsky and punched in the number quickly.

"Hello, Stephanowsky." His warm tenor made her toes feel toasty.

"Hello, Mr. Stephanowsky, my name's Brooke Beldon, I'm a freelance writer doing a series of profiles on professional men in this area. Several people recommended you as a person to include in the series."

"What sort of an article?"

"A personality profile, something about you as a person, your job, your goals, that sort of thing. I have a list of questions I'd be happy to send you so you can think about them. We can arrange a time for the interview that suits your schedule and conduct the interview at your office, over lunch, or at a time and place convenient to you."

"I'd like to see the questions first. I'd also like to know the name of the magazine for which you're writing."

"The magazine is the monthly insert in *Business First*. I'll send you a copy of the questions today and call you next week to arrange a time."

"All right, I'll let you know after I've seen the questions whether I'm willing to be interviewed. Good-bye, Ms. Beldon."

Well, that was at least a start. The questions she planned to use came from a series of profiles she had done a year or so ago and could be easily adapted to fit this situation. She also picked out several articles she had written, including two profile pieces, to show Stephanowsky her writing credentials.

She and Paul knew too little about Pat Jensen, and she hoped Stephanowsky, Pat's former husband, could provide a vital clue or two useful in deciding how to approach her. All they really had at present was her connection with the Lido and the possibility she was the woman who had left with Stan the night he died. It wasn't a lot.

* * * *

To Paul, the Lido's dim atmosphere reeked of stale air, rancid beer, and cloying perfume. The few customers sitting at the small tables did nothing to diminish the feeling of sleaze and decay, as they languidly watched a dancer gyrate. One hostess in a tight green dress with almost no skirt sat alone at the bar. She exposed a shapely thigh with no visible cellulite.

Recognizing her, Paul slid onto the stool beside her. "Let's see, Vodka Collins, right?"

"Good memory, handsome, where've you been?" Suzy smiled a warm welcome.

"Around, how's business?" Paul surveyed the room.

"So, so, certainly not busy tonight. Maybe we can have a dance or two." Suzy placed red tipped fingers on the arm he rested on the bar.

"Not a bad idea." He picked up her hand and kissed it.

"Mister!" Topaz glared at him from behind the bar. "Harley told you, you aren't welcome here."

"He might have said something like that, but buying a drink can't hurt, can it?" Paul grinned at her.

"Harley said he don't want you around, so that means no drinks. Now, get your damned carcass out of here." Topaz frowned. She looked ready to hurl the glass in her right hand at his head.

Paul studied her, but decided not to push things. "Well, I guess that's that." He bowed to Suzy. "Sorry, little lady, maybe next time."

He turned to Topaz, smiling. "I'll hit the can before I leave. You wouldn't want me to piss here at the bar for you to clean up, now would you, Topaz?"

Strolling with a bit of a list toward the restroom, Paul spotted Misty at a table on the edge of the dance floor. His route would pass right by her. He managed to bump a few chairs on his way. As he neared Misty's table, he stumbled and knocked her chair sideways.

"Sorry, ma'am, just clumsy I guess." As he helped straighten her chair, he whispered in her ear. "I need to talk to you."

Righting himself, he lurched on across the floor to the john. When he came out, Misty stood leaning against the wall.

"Okay, make it fast. What d'ya want?"

"I have a couple of photos I need you to identify."

"Not here, the lights bad, and there's no time. Tomorrow, 11:45 at the Clock." She almost ran into the ladies' room.

He straightened up and nearly knocked Suzy down as he started forward. "Whoa, little lady. I didn't see you." He grinned at her.

"Topaz wanted to be sure you hadn't gotten lost. I'm sorry she won't let you stay. It would'a been fun. You're a good dancer and a gentleman, too. We don't get many of that kind."

"Thanks, kid. Here's a bit for the Collins she wouldn't let me buy." He slipped a twenty-dollar bill into the plunging vee of her dress. "See ya' around."

Paul half-walked, half-staggered toward the exit. He waved to Topaz as he passed the bar and made a half-bow. She glared back as he hurried out the door. It wouldn't do to stir her up or Harley. Once Misty identified the picture, he didn't care about them.

* * * *

Arriving at the Clock a little early, Paul took a booth with a view of the entrance. When Misty arrived, dressed in a sweater and pleated skirt, he stood up and signaled her. She walked rapidly toward him, her ponytail swinging saucily, and slid into booth opposite him.

"I appreciate your coming. We've about run out of suspects, and I need to know if this is the woman who left with Stan." He pulled out the copied newsletter pages with Pat's and Donna's pictures. Misty took them and studied them both for a minute or so.

"Yeah, I'd say this was the same woman, and she's also the one who comes to see Harley now and then." She handed the page with Pat Jensen's picture back to him.

"This one," she said, pointing to Donna Sanders's picture, "brings Harley those reports."

"That's exactly what I needed. That ties Ms. Jensen to Stan Beldon and settles Donna's role, too. Now that business is done, let's have lunch."

"Lunch for you, breakfast for me, remember? And please, stay way from the Lido."

"What ever you want, Misty, you've earned it."

A surge of satisfaction raised Paul's spirits. He now had the lever he needed to use with Pat Jensen. With a little judicious encouragement, she might provide some of the other missing links. God, he was glad he didn't do this for a living. Gathering all these tenuous bits and pieces and trying to make sense out of them wore him out. Soon the police could have it. Detective Meyers didn't appear convinced about his innocence in the Pierce death. Only his lack of a motive kept Meyers from arresting him, unless somehow he believed the crank that had called and sent that note.

* * * *

Paul dialed Homicide again. This time Meyers answered.

"Meyers here."

"Hello, Detective Meyers, this is Paul Counts."

"Yes, Mr. Counts, how can I help you?" Meyers' voice sounded cool and professional.

"Yesterday, I received a note in my mail on yellow lined paper with words cut from the newspaper. Would you test it for fingerprints?"

"We could do that. The note we received didn't have any." A short pause ensued. "Mr. Counts, how would you profit from Pierce's death?"

"No way I know of. I told you I hoped to get information out of him about Stan Beldon." Paul picked up a paper clip lying on the desk.

"All three of you—yourself, Mr. Pierce, and Mr. Beldon—work or worked at First Bank?"

"Yes, I mentioned that." He tossed the paper clip up in the air.

"Is something happening at the bank?"

Paul dropped the paper clip. "I'm not sure what you mean. It's a busy place. I didn't know Pierce until a few weeks ago. He and Stan worked together on a special project."

"I have the feeling you know more than you've told me. It might be useful if you could stop by, and review the statement you made the night Pierce died." Meyers paused a moment. "Maybe you might want to add something."

"I'll do that and leave this note for you at the same time."

"All right."

Paul said good-bye and replaced the receiver. It sounded like Meyers had begun to think he had a motive.

* * * *

Two days after Brooke had mailed the questions to Sam

128

Stephanowsky, she again called him, this time at the bank branch.

"Mr. Stephanowsky? Have you reviewed the material I sent?"

"Yes, Miss Beldon. I see no problem about the questions. Lunch might be the best time to do the interview, so it won't interfere with work. Why don't we go to the Windchimes, if that's all right with you?"

"Fine, what day would you prefer?"

"Why not today?"

"All right, I'll pick you up at the bank at 11:45."

Saying good-bye, Brooke then replaced the receiver, glad she would be able to learn a little more about Pat Jensen and have an excellent lunch at the same time. The *Columbus Dispatch* had cited the Windchimes as one of the best Chinese restaurants in the Northwest area.

Brooke dressed carefully in a deep claret-colored wool suit, a port wine silk blouse, and burgundy leather pumps. She wanted to set Stephanowsky at ease with her professional appearance and gain his confidence. She carried a slim, burgundy leather briefcase that matched her pumps.

Arriving promptly at the bank branch at 11:45, Brooke went to the receptionist's desk and asked for Mr. Stephanowsky. Soon a man of medium height dressed in a brown business suit approached her. His black hair had receded slightly and, while clean-shaven, he had compensated with long sideburns. Dark eyes, a strong jaw, and pleasant features combined to create an appearance most women would consider attractive.

"Miss Beldon? I'm Sam Stephanowsky." He held out his hand and shook hers with firmness, holding it trifle longer than necessary while his brown eyes gazed into hers. His mellow tenor voice sounded even better in person than on the telephone.

She returned his smile. "How do you do? It's a pleasure to meet you. Ready to go?"

He followed her out to her car, and they drove the short distance to the Windchimes, a one-room oriental restaurant in a small suburban shopping mall, but with a well-deserved reputation for excellent food as proven by the lunchtime crowd. They had to wait a few minutes for a table. Brooke admired the carved screen with white pearlescent lotus blossoms and long tailed birds standing behind the cashier's counter and separating it from the eating area. It would look well in her dining room.

The hostess soon seated them at a table in the far corner. The square white room had white-covered tables scattered about. The black chairs, oriental with tall, slender backs, offered comfortable seats. Stepanowsky held Brooke's chair for her.

After removing a burgundy leather portfolio from her briefcase, Brooke waited until they had ordered and the waiter brought the tea before asking any questions.

"How long have you lived in this area, Mr. Stephanowsky?"

"Call me Sam; it's a lot easier to say." He smiled at her. "I've been here about ten years. I'm originally from the Cleveland area."

"Oh? What brought you here?"

"The bank and my ex-wife. We dated in high school. She came to Columbus and found a job at the bank. I worked at a Cleveland bank, but when we got engaged, I applied for job here and got it."

The waiter arrived with the food, and as they ate, Brooke studied Sam. His smooth, confident manner and pleasant good looks would make him popular with the singles crowd. If it weren't for Paul, she might want to get to know him a lot better.

They had ordered Moo Goo Gai Pan, the pressed duck with a hoisan sauce, and a dish of mixed Chinese vegetables. The food presented an interesting mixture of textures and tastes. The Moo Goo Gai Pan—chicken chunks, bamboo shoots, celery, onions, and broccoli with light chicken gravy—while the crispy pressed duck had a pungent sauce with crunchy mixed vegetables. Brooke enjoyed the food and guessed Sam did too because he took seconds of everything. They left only a few smears of sauce on the serving dishes.

The meal finished, Brooke pushed her empty plate to the side and picked up the burgundy portfolio. Opening it, she took out a pen. With it poised, she looked up at Sam.

"You've had an opportunity to review the list of questions, so I'd like to get started. We can begin with your job. You're currently a branch manager for First Bank?"

"Yes, I was promoted about four years ago from the branch loans officer."

"What does a bank manager do?"

"Manage the branch business, hire and develop his staff, work with our larger accounts, and fill in for the loans officer or other senior staff. I also develop and implement, with central office support, our customer and community relations program." Sam sipped his tea.

Brooke made a few notes and then looked up at him. "What is the community relations program?"

"Oh, I belong to the local Chamber of Commerce and the Rotary, we sponsor a little league team, and allow certain activities to use our facilities. Last week we let the seniors use our parking lot for their annual car wash, that sort of thing. We want the community to think of the bank as a good neighbor."

"Have you had any robberies?"

Sam smiled. "I don't remember that as one of the interview questions."

Brooke blushed. "It wasn't, I'm just curious."

"No, we haven't, but we always worry about it, and we have a set of procedures staff would follow."

"Such as?"

Sam looked at her, one eyebrow raised. "Really, Miss Beldon, those aren't for public distribution."

"I'm sorry." She looked down at her list of questions. Might as well get on with it. She really wanted to steer him onto Pat somehow. "Do you have a set of career goals?"

Sam gave her wry smile. "I like branch work, but there isn't any room for promotion. I could move to branch operations at the head office or into some other management position there. I've been thinking about it, but not too hard."

First sipping her tea, Brooke then continued with profile questions on his job despite her impatience to turn to more personal matters such as his ex-wife. "You intend to stay in banking?"

"Yeah." He shrugged and grinned at her. "It's all I've ever worked at."

"What do you especially like about your job?"

"The people, interactions with the customers and staff; banking has become more customer oriented. In the past it we always focused on the big accounts. Now we're doing more with and for the small customer."

His earnestness appealed to her. "What don't you like?"

"Umm…" He paused a moment, considering the question or maybe his answer. "Too few people, too much to do, the emphasis on numbers. While we're working on customer service, salary increases still depend on the number of new accounts, not on how well satisfied your customers are. The new customer system should give the branches more information and the ability to control the accounts.

"In the old days, my father told me the branches kept their own records, but with the big computer systems, they all went to the central office. Updates took time, sometimes the system was down, it was a real pain. Glad those days are gone."

Brooke decided she could now depart from the prepared questions, ask a few personal questions, and perhaps slant things more toward Pat. "I'd like to know a little about you, Sam; what kind of person you are. What do you do in your spare time?"

He set his tea down. "Well, that sort of depends on free time, the season, and the weather. During the fall and winter, I take classes at Ohio State University in Russian Language and Literature, watch football, play a bit of racquetball. In the spring and summer, I play golf. More tea?"

Brooke nodded, and he refilled both their cups. Sam certainly had wide-ranging interests. "Russian? Why?"

"Well, I'm of Polish extraction and hope someday to visit Russia or Eastern Europe. The bank is developing relations with a number of foreign banks and, who knows, perhaps I could get into international banking."

Brooke raised her eyebrows at that. "Sounds ambitious, but wouldn't you have to go to New York or Washington?"

Smiling at her, Sam set his cup down. "Not necessarily, the banking industry in Ohio has changed, and international banks aren't limited to the East coast."

Interesting, but this hadn't gotten her closer to Pat, maybe sports or something more personal would do it. "You mentioned racquet ball and golf."

"Well, I play occasionally. I don't do it as much as I should. Banking isn't a physically active job, so a bit of exercise helps."

Brooke gave him an appraising look. "Yes, I can see it keeps you fit. How about your favorite foods?"

"Chinese, naturally." He smiled "That's why I suggested the Windchimes."

"Mine too, although from the number of pizza and Italian restaurants, I'm not sure how many others agree."

Sipping her tea, Brooke struggled with what to ask. Maybe she would have to be direct. "You said you were divorced."

"Yes." Sam grimaced. "My wife worked for a couple of Vice-Presidents and liked the glamour." He looked at Brooke as if assessing her. "To be honest about it, she had affairs with her bosses, and I walked out."

That confirmed what Paul had heard. Apparently it still rankled a bit. "I'm sorry"

"Don't be. It was all for the best. Pat's a very ambitious lady and money means a lot to her; more than it means to me." Brooke sensed a bitter note in his voice. "We're both much better off divorced."

She wondered what Pat's ambition and Sam's bitterness might mean as incentives for skimming bank funds. Somehow, she hoped it meant Pat, but not Sam, too. She looked down at her list of profile questions; she still hadn't didn't have much about his personal life.

"You're an attractive man. Do you date or have a steady?"

"I date occasionally, but no steady."

"How would you describe your ideal woman?"

"Umm, let's see." He cocked his head to one side as he surveyed Brooke. "I'd say a cool, elegant blonde, sophisticated, clever. Actually, someone like you."

"No, seriously,"

He smiled, leaning forward. "I am serious. Do you like jazz?"

"Yes, why do you ask?"

"Well, there's a combo playing at a club in the Short North this Friday. I wondered if you'd like to go."

Brooke hesitated. She hadn't learned a lot about Pat, except that her "ex" believed she'd slept with two vice presidents and she liked money. Paul had mentioned rumors about Pat and Morgan, but hadn't mentioned anyone else. Perhaps a date with Sam would give her an opportunity to learn about those affairs. Personable, he'd be good company, and she liked jazz.

"Does it take that much thought?" He looked into her eyes as if trying to read her thoughts.

"No, no, I was just trying to remember what I had on my calendar. I'd love to go." She paused again and grinned. "That is, so long as you realize it won't influence how I write the profile."

"I never thought it would and that's not why I asked. It does my reputation good to be seen with an attractive woman. Some people think of bankers as stodgy people only concerned with interest rates and points. I just want to show you we're real people and like other things, including jazz." His smile generated a warm, cozy sensation.

"Fair enough, and I'll include that in your profile."

Despite, Sam's attempt to pay the check, Brooke refused. "No, the magazine pays for our lunch."

"Ok, but Friday evening is on me. Agreed?"

Nodding, Brooke paid the bill and then returned Sam to the bank, arranging for him to pick her up at her home Friday at eight-thirty.

Chapter Twelve

The Homicide Squad room hadn't changed from Paul's last visit—rows of desks piled high with papers and folders. He had no trouble recognizing Meyers, who rose as he approached.

"Well, Mr. Counts, I'm glad you could come in." Detective Meyers extended his hand. "We've followed up some loose ends and thought you could assist us."

"Any news on the note fingerprints?" Paul settled on the chair next to Meyers' desk.

"Oh, yes, the note you brought in." Meyers opened the folder in front of him and read from the top page. "We found only your prints. The note had been mailed from a post office close to the bank."

"I guess that's not surprising, but I had hopes." Paul slouched a bit in disappointment.

Meyers studied him, one eyebrow raised. "You did? With your prints on the note, the place it was mailed, and the form of the note, we wondered if you might have sent it?"

"What?" The detective's words startled Paul. He jerked upright and stared at him. "Why?"

"You could want to direct our attention elsewhere. Too, the note resembles ones we received." Meyers scrutinized him for several moments with laser like eyes. "How well did you know John Pierce?"

"Like I told you, I met him only recently—after I heard he and Stan had spent time at the same bar, the Lido."

"Do you know any of his friends?"

Shaking his head, Paul sensed Meyers sought a tie between Pierce and himself. "No, we worked at the bank, so we must know some people in common—Stan anyway."

Meyers leaned forward slightly. "Would that include a Sandy Jovanoski?"

Struggling to maintain s poker face, Paul hoped his surprise at the name wasn't obvious. "No, I don't know any such person." How in the hell had Meyers found out about Jovanoski? What did he know?

"Do you know anything about Mr. Pierce's lifestyle?"

"Only what I saw from his apartment. I'd say he earned a good salary, but must have gotten in deep with his credit cards from his fancy apartment and clothes. He dressed well in a flashy way." Paul shifted a bit and rested one arm on Meyers' desk.

"Know anything about his sexual preferences?"

That made Paul blink. What did Meyers want? A motive? He could see the newspaper headline now: *Civil rights violated, gay man murdered.* In that case, maybe he should refer Meyers to Sharon instead. He discarded that idea at once. She'd really have it in for him if he did.

Wanting to make Meyers believe him, Paul looked him in the eyes. "No. I know little about Pierce except for his link to Stan."

Referring to the papers in his folder, Meyers turned over several pages and then looked up at Paul. "We believe Mr. Pierce preferred men. Does that surprise you?"

"Uh, I know nothing about him; we had no contact before Stan's death."

Staring at Paul, Meyers remained silent for a moment. "Was Stan Beldon gay?"

"Stan?" Stunned by the question, Paul knew his face mirrored his surprise. "He was a loner, but so far as I knew, he wasn't gay. You could ask his sister, but I doubt she'd know either."

Meyers sighed. "This puts a different light on Mr. Pierce's death."

"Why?" Edgy, but determined not to show it, Paul picked up a loose paperclip, and fiddled with it.

"A jealous lover might have killed him. It happens all too frequently in that community." Meyers turned over several more pages to expose a lined yellow sheet. "Mr. Counts, we received another note today. It suggested we ask you about Sandy Jovanoski."

"I told you, I don't know a Jovanoski and don't recall having heard anyone mention the name." Paul focused on the paperclip he tossed from hand to hand.

"We'd like to know who that person is and why this note-writer believes you know Jovanoski."

Paul set the paperclip back on the desk and stared hard at Meyers.

"Look, I've told you repeatedly I didn't kill Pierce, I don't know who's writing the notes, and I don't know who Jovanoski is. I'll sign a statement to that effect if it will help."

"I may ask you to do that, but we'll let it go for the present." Meyers closed the folder. "We're still investigating Pierce's death as a homicide."

Tired of parrying Meyers' questions and even more puzzled about the note-writer, Paul sighed. "I wish you luck. Catch the murderer and we can stop fencing with one another."

"Fencing?" Meyers raised an eyebrow.

"Look," Paul leaned forward, his voice earnest. "You found me with Pierce's body, but I didn't kill him. I had no reason to kill him."

Looking unconvinced, Meyers nodded. "So you've said. Hmm, that will be all for now, Mr. Counts. We may need to talk to you again, so please stay in town." He closed the folder.

"Yeah, I'll do that." Without looking at Meyers again, Paul rose and stalked out.

The entire interview puzzled and annoyed him. Someone wanted to frame him—the murderer or Pierce's lover? Either way, who had it in for him?

At home, Shadow greeted him with a loud meow.

"Glad to see me, eh, girl." He scratched her ears and went to the kitchen. Her feeder still had plenty of food and water. "Guess you missed me." She twined about his legs and purred.

Paul grabbed a frozen entry from the freezer and popped it in the microwave. "You know, Shadow, this mess bothers me. Do you think Meyers can find the real murderer, or will he take the easy way out like he did with Stan?"

The beep of the microwave signaled dinner was ready. Paul dumped the food onto a plate and turned on the small counter TV. "Knowledge, Shadow, knowledge. Looks like I'd better learn a lot more about Mr. Pierce and his friends."

Shadow washed her face and smoothed her whiskers. She gazed up at Paul.

"Okay, okay, I get the message." He put the empty food tray on the floor next to her feeder, and she sniffed at it before taking a lick of the gravy from the Swedish meatballs. "Glad you like it."

Paul chewed his own food and considered the problem of Pierce. Sharon Belling had told him the little he knew about Pierce. She had joked with him about lunch. He'd call her, ask her to lunch, and see what else she knew.

The next day at work, Paul phoned Sharon. They settled on the Clock for an early lunch. Since the restaurant was close to the data center, they walked the few blocks through the fine spring day. The rain had gone, and, even in the city, the scattered beds of flowers softened the angular concrete and steel lines of the major buildings. Office workers munched on sandwiches and enjoyed the warm sunshine from benches in the broad plazas surrounding some buildings. After the recycled data center environment, Paul found the cool air refreshing, with only a hint of auto exhaust.

When they reached the restaurant, he asked for a booth near the back for privacy. Over the top of his menu, Paul watched as Sharon smoothed her dark hair down where the slight breeze had disturbed it. Apparently satisfied the cap-like arrangement was again neat, she picked up her own menu and began scanning it.

After the waiter had taken their orders, Paul took a deep breath before beginning. "Sharon, you remember when I asked you about John Pierce?"

"Yeah, I wondered why. I can't believe he's dead." She shuddered.

"He phoned me just before he died, and I had the rotten luck to find the body. The police consider me the prime suspect, but so far they haven't found a motive. I need your help."

Frowning, Sharon began clicking her long chain of green wooden beads together. "That's heavy. What do you want from me?" She stared at him, uncertainty in her dark eyes.

"I hardly knew Pierce and wouldn't have met him if not for his connection to Stan Beldon. They worked together on some program changes. Now I'm after anything that might explain both deaths."

Sharon nodded. "Yeah, too bad about Stan. How can I help?"

"Tell me anything you know more about Pierce—who he hung out with, who he feuded with, in short anything that could lead to trouble. The police think Pierce had a lover. Have you have any idea who?"

Staring down at her cup, Sharon fiddled again with her green beads. "I told you he wasn't a ladies' man." She released the beads.

"Yeah, I remember that, but you also said you didn't think he was involved with anyone."

"I did?" She paused a moment, turning her cup in her hands and then gazed up at Paul. "I heard he and Kent Carpentah were...uh friends."

Paul smiled at the way her Northeastern accent mangled Kent's name. Then the importance of that name hit him. He couldn't suppress his surprise. "What? I thought Kent was a good ol' boy, baseball, hunting."

"So?" Sharon shrugged. "That doesn't mean anything."

"Yeah, you're right about that. That gives me something to think about."

The waiter arrived with their orders, and they stopped talking to eat. Paul's mind digested Sharon's comments about. Kent Carpenter. He'd taken over Stan's programs. He must know about the special subroutines. If so, that explained the note to the police about Sandy Jovanoski.

Finishing his hamburger, Paul signaled the waiter for more coffee. He sipped from the steaming cup, and then asked Sharon about her work, and that, along with the local Computer Society activities, occupied them until they returned to the bank.

Once back in the building, Paul decided Marilyn Johnson, the section secretary, would know about Kent. He strolled over to her area, hoping to find her free. As he approached, the rapid movement of her fingers across the keyboard of her PC and the steady rhythm of the keys indicated she was hard at work.

"Hi, Marilyn, how've you been?"

"Fine." She smiled as he eased onto the side chair next to her desk. "Haven't seen much of you lately."

"Been busy with work; lots of changes and testing underway. How's Kent doing with Stan's programs?" Paul picked up a pen from the desk and turned it as he talked.

"Seems to be okay; but he doesn't say much. Another quiet one, just like Stan."

"Oh?" Raising an eyebrow, Paul leaned forward. "I heard he favored...uh somewhat different tastes."

Marilyn blinked. "I meant in being quiet and not making waves. He isn't at all like Stan in other ways. He drinks more for one thing."

"And others?" Paul put the pen down and focused on Marilyn.

"Well," she lowered her voice and leaned closer. "I heard he and John Pierce were close."

"Close?"

She looked around before speaking. "You know, John is…uh, was gay, I guess that means Kent is too."

"Pierce's death must have hit Kent hard."

"You bet. 'I'll get the son-of-a-bitch,' he said, and he meant it. Real vindictive he sounded. Hate to be the one to make him angry." She shook her head.

"For some reason, someone seems to think I killed Pierce because I found his body."

"I didn't know that." Marilyn's voice showed her surprise and interest. "Were you really there?" She stared at him as if he had suddenly become a celebrity.

Paul nodded. "Yeah, I was there. Pierce had phoned me to say he wanted to talk about Stan, but when I arrived, he was already dead. I haven't any idea what he wanted to tell me."

Frowning, Marilyn looked thoughtful. "That might explain something else, too. Kent groused about you and your fussing with Stan's programs. Said he wouldn't accept any blame, if you made changes, and Cramer had better know it. He muttered something about first Stan and then John, and mentioned you too. You couldn't wait to get your fingers into some account."

"Really? Any idea what he meant?"

"No, he was just blowing off steam. He took John's death pretty hard. He even took off the days before and after the funeral. His eyes looked sort of red and puffy for a while. Claimed it was allergies, but we knew better. Still…" She shrugged. "What can you say when it wasn't an open relationship. It's always touchy, unless they've make it public."

"Yeah, I know what you mean. Well…" Paul got up and stretched. He'd gotten what he needed and told Marilyn almost too much "I'd better get back before they send out the scouts to see if I've lost my scalp. See you later." He sauntered off toward the elevators.

Now two sources linked Kent Carpenter and John Pierce, and, coupled with Marilyn's comments about Kent's anger, led to intriguing thoughts. It made Kent Carpenter a prime candidate for the sender of the notes. A little talk with him might confirm it.

As for other loose ends, he hadn't yet eliminated Pat Jensen and Walter Vavor. Either could be Jovanoski, but Jensen and Jovanoski both began with J and criminals often used similar names or ones beginning with the same letter. Pat had been the woman with Stan when he died.

Had she killed him?

As Paul entered his office, the telephone rang. "Hello, Counts here," he answered as he sat at his desk.

"Paul, Brooke. I thought we might talk about what I learned from Sam Stephanowsky."

"Stephanowsky?" Paul puzzled for a moment and then remembered it as the name of Pat's ex-husband. "When did you talk to him?"

"I interviewed him for an article—at least that's what I told him. He said some interesting things about Pat. According to him, she had affairs with two vice presidents."

Paul's eyebrows shot upward. "Two? I knew about Morgan, and, as far as I know, Vavor is the only other vice president for whom she worked."

"Sam, didn't name them, but he definitely said two vice presidents. I don't know whether Pat told him or he guessed, so I can't tell you for certain she did, but he thinks she did."

"Sam?" Paul wasn't sure he liked the way Brooke said that name.

"He asked me to call him Sam. After all, Stephanowsky is an awful mouthful."

"Yeah, it is," Paul admitted and then grasped at straws. "It's not that far from Jovanoski. Does that tie in Sam, or Pat, or both of them?"

"I don't know, but so far, other than Pat, Sam has no ties we know of to the Lido, to Stan, or to any of the others."

"But he works for the bank"

"I don't think Sam has anything to do with this, but he asked me to a jazz performance tonight, and I said I would go. Maybe I can learn more then."

Brooke's voice sounded a little cool to him. "Is that necessary?"

"No, but we still haven't settled things about Pat Jensen, and you haven't turned up anything more. Besides…" Brooke paused a moment. "After Pierce, I'm worried by digging so hard, you may have made yourself a target, Paul. I want to find out about my brother, but I don't want you or anyone else getting hurt. If Sam can tell us anything, we need to know it. This isn't a game; people get killed. We have to get to the bottom of it, or leave it to the police."

"Yeah, I've had a few thoughts about that myself. Since the Lido though, you haven't been directly involved, but this interview and date with Sam could make you a target. How do you know he isn't Jovanoski and just trying to find out what you know?"

"Frankly, the thought never occurred to me. Sam doesn't impress me as a crook—he's not the type—but I'll be careful, and I promise I won't see him again, at least not until we've found Stan's and Pierce's murderer."

Not entirely satisfied, Paul didn't like that 'at least.' It implied maybe Brooke had more of an interest in Sam Stephanowsky than the fact he was Pat Jensen's ex-husband.

"Promise me you'll be careful and won't stay out late."

"Paul, for heaven's sake, I'm over twenty-one and I know how to take care of myself. I managed the Lido, remember? If it'll make you happy, I'll phone you when we get back, but it may be late."

"All right, I'll be waiting. Take care, Brooke." Paul heard her soft good-bye and the click as she disconnected.

He didn't like this at all. Talking to Stephanowsky probably wasn't a bad idea; at least it might provide a bit more information to use with both Pat Jensen and Walter Vavor, but what more might Stephanowsky know? Besides, if somehow Pat and Sam had cooked up the scam and then involved Stan, Brooke could be in real trouble. He wanted to see this Sam and hear what he said, but Brooke would be furious. He contented himself with waiting for her to call.

He could still talk with Pat Jensen. Misty had confirmed Pat had left with Stan the night he died and that meant she had probably called 9-1-1. An eyewitness who could identify her provided leverage. Too, Harley had included her name as a customer. If involved in murder or a bank scam, she might trip and say or do something to unravel this Gordian knot.

* * * *

When Paul phoned Pat and mentioned Harley's name, she agreed to meet him after work at a small sidewalk cafe in a nearby hotel. The lack of patrons provided the privacy he sought. One couple sat near the door at one of the cast iron tables. Eight other empty tables provided plenty of seating and some privacy.

He waited for Pat at the entrance and, when she arrived, he suggested they sit at the far end of the outside area. Her pear-shaped figure pulled her features downward. In his view, she suffered the beginnings of middle-aged spread. Lines of petulance outlined both sides of her mouth and the pouches under her eyes made them appear puffy.

Five years and twenty pounds ago, she might have been attractive, but make-up, age, and flab fast overpowered what little beauty she had left. Paul found it hard to imagine either Morgan or Vavor attracted to her. He almost felt sorry for her.

They ordered drinks and Pat hastily lit a cigarette. Puffing away, she rapidly filled the ashtray in front of them with ashes. Her Irish coffee sat almost untouched. Paul relaxed, suspecting her smoking came from nerves and could work to his advantage.

After a few moments, he set his beer on the table. "I asked to talk with you because you knew Stan Beldon. Someone saw you leave the Lido with him the night he died. A woman called 9-1-1. You."

Eye wide, she stared at him and snubbed out her current cigarette. "Sure I knew Stan. We both work for the same bank. I was Morgan's administrative assistant and Stan worked for Morgan, but that was as far as it went. Stan and I didn't see each other outside of work." She pulled out another cigarette and lit it. The acrid smoke swirled about her head.

Paul tried a different tack. "You visit the Lido?"

"What does that have to do with anything?" She raised an eyebrow and stared at him.

"I said you were seen there with Stan the night he died and left with him."

"Who says so," she snapped, snubbing out the last of her cigarette and carelessly knocking ashes on the table.

"One of the women who works there."

"You believe her?" Pat's voice dripped sarcasm as she lit another cigarette.

"Yes, and so will a jury." He gave her a grim smile.

"Jury? What in the hell are you talking about?" She paused in the middle of a puff.

He leaned forward to press his advantage. "I'm talking about murder. Stan wasn't into crack. Someone forced it on him—you."

"Now just a minute." She tapped off the excess ash into the ashtray. "Aren't you jumping to a lot of conclusions?"

"I don't think so. You see, I also know Harley Donovan sold you drugs on a regular basis. He said Stan wasn't a customer."

"You can't take his word. Buying and using are different things." She leaned back and watched the cigarette smoke curl slowly upward.

"Someone else told me that, but in your case, I'm not so sure. If you don't use it, then who does?"

"It's none of your damn business." She ground out her half-smoked cigarette, almost snapping it in half.

"If I tell the police, they might think differently."

"Being at the Lido doesn't mean I left with him…" She paused to drink her Irish coffee.

To Paul, her hand appeared shaky.

"Even if I did, it doesn't follow I was with him when he died."

"Maybe not, but it adds to a strong circumstantial case, particularly if the police do a voiceprint on that 9-1-1 call." Paul watched her reactions as he sipped his beer.

"What?" She set her glass down abruptly. "What do you mean? Those calls come in all the time."

"True, but you remember last year, the controversy over a call for a man having a heart attack? They got so much flak over how long it took, having gone to the wrong address first, that they not only log the calls, automatically record the number calling, but now even record the calls themselves. Normally, they dump the tapes within six months, but if they have any questions or a felony's involved, the police can order them to keep those tapes indefinitely."

He set his beer down. "You didn't know that call was being recorded, did you?"

"I didn't make any call. I've had enough of your accusations. I'm leaving. Don't call me again and don't threaten me. The police don't like blackmailers." She grabbed her purse and almost ran to the exit.

Paul left a tip and enough to cover the bill. He followed Pat, anxious not to lose sight of her. He watched from the doorway as she rushed down the street.

* * * *

Thinking furiously, Pat considered her options. If they could really do those voiceprint things, she was in big trouble. She'd better talk to Sandy, now. Too bad she'd left her cell phone home to charge this morning. Scanning the area for a telephone, she saw one at the next corner. Fumbling in her wallet for the right change, she fitted the coins in the slot and then punched the number. Her body, rod tense, she waited. The phone rang, once, twice, three times. Damn, maybe Sandy had gone home.

"Hello." The deep voice reassured her.

"Sandy, this is Pat." She leaned against the side of the post slightly more relaxed. "Did you know they record 9-1-1 calls?"

"I sort of remember something about it. So what?"

"Paul Counts says the police can take a voiceprint, and will know I called them when Stan convulsed. He also knows about my buying drugs from Harley and that Stan left the club with me. You've got to do something."

"Did you mention me?"

"Of course not. What do you think I am, stupid? I told him he was wrong and left." She drummed her fingernails on the small shelf below the telephone.

"Good, let me think about this and see if there isn't some way to sidetrack him."

"You'd better. I don't intend to go to jail for this. If I get hauled in, you're with me—don't forget that."

"Have I ever let you down?"

"Once or twice, but you won't this time. Little Patty knows too much, and you value your skin and your job. Just get this guy off my back."

"All right, give me a little time and I'll take care of it. Where are you now?"

"I'm at a payphone on Main and Third. I have to get my car out of the County Garage and then I'll be heading home."

"Okay, I'll talk to you there later. Just take it easy and drive carefully." The voice, warm and soft now, reassured Pat. "There's nothing to worry about, darling. I still love you."

"And I love you, bye." She hung up the phone, feeling a little better, and walked briskly to the parking garage.

* * * *

Patty had just become a definite liability. With her out of the way, Paul Counts would be left with a jealous lover who decided to do away with her main squeeze, and he'd find no link to anyone else. Thank God for self-preservation and secrecy. Neither drugs nor Patty could be traced to anyone except to Harley Donovan, and the file tampering could only be linked to Stan. Yes, being careful clearly paid off. The big problem now remained what to do about Patty. It would have to be clean, quick, and accidental, although an apparent suicide had distinct advantages. Time to move or lose one opportunity.

* * * *

On roads stick with rain, Pat drove towards home. As she came around the curve to merge in from the left hand lane, a large car with tinted windows pulled alongside. Going the same speed, the driver, a blob dressed in a black-hooded sweat jacket, wouldn't let her in. She hit the brake, but her car started to skid. Out of control, the car headed for a cement divider. Pat fought the wheel and struggled to turn into the skid.

Time ceased as the car drifted toward the cement pier, and she prayed. The pictures of one horrific recent crash flashed through her thoughts.

Afraid to take her hands off the wheel, she mentally crossed herself. "Father, forgive me for I have sinned."

Then, all at once, the car responded to the wheel. Pat just hit the gas, released it, and managed to steer the car past the pier. At last able to slow down, she changed lanes and pulled off the side of the road.

She slumped forward over the wheel, her foot pumping up and down in nervous reaction. *My God, that was close. What ever had possessed that fool?* Okay, she shouldn't have been trying to merge so fast, but that entry way was poorly designed, and, if you weren't up to speed, it was hard to merge with oncoming traffic. All the locals knew that. The driver must have been either a screwy kid or an out-of-towner.

She sat on the berm for ten minutes. Finally her leg stopped jumping, and her hands grew more or less steady again. She restarted the car and pulled back on to the road. Keeping just under the speed limit the rest of the way home, she also waited longer than normal at the stop signs. No more chances for her.

As she stepped into the house the phone rang. Dropping her purse, she automatically grabbed it.

"Hello, Patty?"

"Yes? Oh it's you, Sandy." She leaned against the wall, relaxing.

"It's been awhile since we've had an evening together, and I need to make a few things up to you. I know you've felt I've been distant, but with Stan and work, we had to stay apart for a bit. I miss you, Sweetums."

"You mean it?"

"Of course I do, I always have. Maybe dinner and a little hot tub to relax us—a nice fire and a little love. I could do with some."

"So could I. Some idiot almost creamed me on the way home."

"You're kidding? You okay?"

"Yeah, I'm fine, just a little shaky. I'll expect you about seven. How about a nice white wine?"

"You're on, I'll see you then. Love you, Sweetums."

It was all so simple, just make sure Pat drank a lot, and then once they were in the hot tub, make sure she stayed underwater long enough to stop breathing. It should be easy. The suicide note to the police had already been mailed, and they would receive it by tomorrow afternoon.

Chapter Thirteen

After the disconnect, Pat replaced the telephone handset. She and Sandy hadn't seen each other outside of work since before Stan died. She worried if Sandy's affections had cooled. Oh, Sandy always had the best excuses, but loneliness dogged Pat, and she wanted things settled. Stan had eased her depression and provided companionship. At first she had balked at using a drug overdose on him, but Sandy insisted she choose between them. Stan knew too much and could put them all in jail. Sandy said he would, if Pat dumped him.

Thinking about that wouldn't change anything, better to concentrate on dinner and later. She would make Sandy's favorite lasagna, and afterwards—Sandy knew all the ways to satisfy her. Warm and tingly, Pat congratulated herself they suited each other so well.

After putting the lasagna in the oven, she showered and changed into a brightly printed silk caftan. In the kitchen tossing the salad, she looked up when a familiar tap sounded at the door. Unlatching it, she embraced her lover and relished a deep kiss.

Heart racing, Pat finally came up for air. "Umm, that's nice; I've missed you." She twined her arms around the smooth neck and pressed her body against Sandy's firm one.

"And I've missed you," Sandy hugged her close with one arm. The other held a paper sack. "Let me put these down, shut the door, and do it properly."

Setting the sack on the counter, Sandy pushed the door shut with a foot and pulled her close. The hungry and demanding tongue roused Pat at once.

"Whoa." She pushed the enveloping arms down. "Do you want dinner or no?"

"I had dessert in mind." Sandy grinned. "But all things in their proper order. I'll take off my jacket, and we'll eat first." Sandy let her go, and hung the jacket over a kitchen chair. Pat set the salad on the table as

Sandy grabbed her around the waist from behind.

One hand massaged Pat's left breast. "What do you feel?" The lithe body moved against hers.

"You are in the mood tonight, aren't you." Pat laughed, pushing back against Sandy, rotating her hips up and then down.

"I told you, it's been too long. Just think what we have to enjoy later."

"I am, but keep that up, and there'll be no dinner."

"Okay, okay, I'll be a good kiddie." Sandy let her go and sat at the table. "Feed me, mommy."

Pat laughed and went to the oven to remove the lasagna. She placed it on the trivet and returned to the counter to leave the potholders and retrieve a serving spoon.

"All set." She sighed in satisfaction as she took her place opposite Sandy.

Eating with relish, her lover savored every bite. "More wine, Sweetums?"

Pat nodded and held out her glass. Sandy knew wines and always chose the best. This mellow Cabernet slid down her throat and left a warm, relaxed feeling.

"Superb as always, Patty," Sandy raised the wine glass. "A happy life." Looking sated, Sandy leaned back in the chair. "Now what about that hot tub?"

"So soon after eating? I thought we might have coffee first."

"I was thinking more like a little dessert. Come now." Sandy lifted her hand, kissed it, and pulled her to her feet.

"I'll put the dishes to soak first."

"No, I'll do them for you later. Right now, I have other things in mind. Come." Sandy drew her close and walked her toward the entrance to the basement. When they reached the stairs, Sandy swept her up and carried her down the steps, stumbling on the last one.

"Damn, maybe I drank too much."

"Hardly, I had two to your one. I've put on a few pounds."

"Yes, but that only makes more of you to love." Setting her down, Sandy raised the caftan over Pat's head, drawing her close. Skimming fingers lightly over Pat's ribs and across her back, Sandy unfastened Pat's bra and then slipped it from her shoulders. Kissing her ears and then her neck, Sandy nibbled at her heavy breasts. Caressing hands slide down Pat's generous hips and pushed her panties downward, teasing her flesh.

"Now into the tub with you, while I get the wine." Sandy lifted her over the edge, and Pat sank with a happy sigh into the warm bubbling water. "I'll be right back; just relax."

The water lapped Pat. Leaning against the tub, eyes closed, she let the soothing warmth envelope her. She savored the coziness, and anticipated sharing it with Sandy. She had almost fallen asleep when footsteps on the stairs made her shake her head.

"Wine, my sweet," Sandy murmured, handing her the glass.

Pat sipped, letting the wine permeate her body like the warm water flowing over it. "I'm so drowsy, Sandy. All that wine I guess. I feel so relaxed" She smiled up at the loving face hovering over her. "We haven't done this for too long."

"I know, Patty, that's why I came. Now just lay against my arm and rest."

She lay with her head against the bare arm and almost floated.

"That's it, easy," the soothing voice crooned.

* * * *

Waiting a minute as Pat nodded, quiescent, Sandy then shoved the top of her head under the water almost to the bottom and held her there. Pat struggled for a minute or two, splashing water and spilling it on to the floor until the warmth, wine, and the drug took effect. After holding her down for several minutes more, Sandy then released her.

Picking up a towel, Sandy dried dripping hands. Pat kept the mop in the hall closet, so Sandy went upstairs and retrieved it. After mopping the floor, Sandy added a little more water to the tub to ensure it remained reasonably full and then replaced the mop in the upstairs closet.

Using Pat's rubber gloves, Sandy ran the dishwater and scrubbed the dishes, placing the clean dishes in the cupboard. Wiping the table, cupboards, and doorknobs to remove all traces of anyone other than Pat came next. Sandy left a half empty bottle of wine and Pat's glass beside the hot tub. *Yes, that should do.*

After a quick check to ensure everything touched had been wiped clean and that nothing looked out of place, Sandy dressed and buttoned the white shirt with deliberate care. Leaving by the back door as usual and walking through the alley to the car parked in the next street, Sandy noticed the rain had stopped, but the streets remained wet and glistened where the scattered street lights reflected from the pavement. No one lurked about as Sandy got in the car and drove off. Yes, it had all gone according plan and nothing tied them together, nothing.

* * * *

Brooke's doorbell chimed right on eight-thirty, signaling Sam's arrival.

"Hello," she said, opening the door and leading him into the living room.

"I wouldn't want to keep a lady waiting, especially one as lovely as you and wearing my favorite color."

His appreciative smile pleased Brooke and gave her a pleasant rush of warmth. uncertain what to wear, she finally settled on a royal blue knit with a fitted bodice and a flared skirt. Its flattering shape and comfortable fit in her favorite color made it a natural choice, but not so dressy as to indicate avid interest.

"Have a seat. I won't be a minute. I'll collect my purse and coat."

"There's no hurry. We've plenty of time."

Brooke returned in a few moments to find Sam standing before a painting she had bought at a local arts show. The abstract watercolor always reminded her of a whirlpool somewhere in mid-ocean.

"Nice painting. Do you know the artist?" He took her coat and held it for her while she slipped it on.

"No. I have a card somewhere if you're interested."

"He's a friend. We occasionally play golf. It's nice to see someone else appreciates quality work." He accompanied her toward the door where she set the lock and then the walked to his Accord.

"I like to encourage local talent and find the prices much less at the art shows than in the galleries."

"And the money goes to the artist." Sam held the car door for her. "Eventually the good ones grow beyond the art shows and only appear in the galleries. Jim is having a show later this month only a building or two away from where we're going this evening."

Sam's car offered comfort and suited a mid-level banker. Its dark blue exterior, color-coordinated with gray-blue plush upholstery, soothed the eyes, while a quiet engine did the same for the ears. Brooke found him a set of fascinating contradictions; a banker who liked jazz, an accountant studying Russian literature, and a football fan knowledgeable about art.

The short drive down High Street to the Short North, mainly through the University area, passed quickly. Near the University, groups of students milled about, clustering around the pizza joints, the bars, and the fast food restaurants. As Sam drove, they passed boarded-up shop fronts, and the farther they went, the worse the neighborhood became, but gradually as they neared the Short North, the character changed. They drove past galleries and boutiques that drew the yuppies and the intellectuals. Several bars featured musical combos catering to modified country and western, Irish music, and jazz. Unlike the usual neighborhood bars secretively turning inward, hiding from the eyes of passersby, and protecting their customers' anonymity by dimly lit interiors, these bars featured large, well-lit windows, a remnant of their former role as shops.

Sam had trouble finding a parking place, and they drove down several side streets. Finally he parked a few blocks away and they strolled back to the club. He paid the cover charge as they entered, and the owner escorted them to a table and a pair of chairs, one row back from the small area reserved for the musicians.

"Did you tip him well?" Brooke looked up and whispered to Sam as he held a chair for her.

He smiled down on her. "No need to, I'm one of his regulars. I always sit here."

She wondered whom Sam had brought before. She doubted he came alone.

They ordered drinks, and she glanced around the large, open room. A long wooden bar ran the length of one wall with a mirror behind and paralleling it. The mirror reflected the bottles of liquor and the serving glasses. *Anheuser Busch* in large gold Gothic script stretched across the center. Round tables and bentwood chairs reminding Brooke of a turn-of-the-century soda fountain filled the remainder of the high-ceilinged room.

Sipping her white wine, she wondered how to encourage Sam to talk about Pat and settled on the direct approach. "Did you ex-wife like jazz?"

"Pat?" He shook his head. "No, not really. I'm not sure she liked music much besides disco or a bit of swing. She prefers dancing."

"And you don't?"

"I wouldn't say that. It depends on the partner, but let's be honest, for most men, dancing is a means to an end." He smiled and held her gaze until the intimacy of it forced her to break away. She looked toward the band for a moment, uncertain how to respond.

Raising her eyes again, she stared back at him, arching one eyebrow. "In other words, if you ask me dancing, then I know what your intentions are?"

"Well, I suppose you could say that, but I didn't now, did I?" Sam teased her, arching his left eyebrow to mirror her. "I'd have to know more about you first. You've been asking me all the questions, so how about answering a few yourself?"

"Like what?" She smiled at him over the rim of her wine glass.

"Well, I know you're a writer, so tell me about your ideal man."

Brooke laughed and gazed toward the mirrored wall. "I'm not sure I have one. I guess I like someone a little different, independent, self-confident. Someone who could take care of himself."

"How do I fit?" His dark eyes challenged her.

"Let's see…" She gave him an appraising look. "So far I'd say you had distinct possibilities. You're single, studying Russian Literature, like jazz, are physically fit…" She paused, frowning. "Although, I don't know about banking. You're right about its stodgy image."

He grinned, an impish gleam in his eyes. "Before the evening is over we'll set that image to rest, I promise." Sam took her hand and gave it a light squeeze. He didn't release it.

The jazz performance surprised Brooke with the players' verve and skill. She hadn't realized the local jazz scene produced such quality. The best jazz players carried improvisation to new heights with their ability to take a theme into unfamiliar areas, creating excitement for both the players and the audience. She remembered one of her Early Music friends saying jazz players excelled at Early Music. Most of the written music surviving from that period contained only the main melody line and little else. By contrast, classically trained musicians expected to have fully developed arrangements, although some musicians were equally adept at both classical music and jazz.

Drawn into the music, she savored her wine and realized with a start she was well into a second glass. After that she ordered tea. Alertness and alcohol didn't mix well, and if she expected to learn anything more about Sam or Pat, she needed all the acuity she could muster. This wasn't the time for mellow.

When the combo stopped for a break, she tried again. "Sam, you're something of an enigma to me. I know the facts and your public persona as a bank manager, but I'm not sure I know the real Sam. For an effective profile, I need to understand you better. Would you mind answering some personal questions?"

"And here I thought we were finished with that."

"Not quite, besides, don't you want me to know the real you." She quirked an eyebrow at him.

"My life's an open book to you. Ask away." He grinned at her.

Hesitating for a moment, Brooke decided to take the plunge. "Why did you and your wife split?" She observed his face looking for any false notes and studied his sad eyes as his mouth twisted into a grimace.

"I told you that—she was having an affair with her boss, and it wasn't the first time." His face remained neutral as if closing inward, away from her, and his voice carried a hard edge.

Guilt struck Brooke. She hated pushing for such personal details, but she and Paul needed to know everything she could learn about Pat Jensen. She owed it to Stan. That required facts, as many as she could muster.

"But how did you know that? Did you follow her?"

"Hardly, that's not my style." He picked up his beer and drained the glass. "Sure, I could've hired a detective, but for what? She told me what she was doing and with whom. She said 'If I'm good enough to sleep with a Vice President, I'm good enough to marry him, and I will.' She made no bones about what had happened and asked for a dissolution. What good would it have done to make her behavior a matter of public record? It probably would've destroyed another marriage—one of the men was married—and it certainly wouldn't enhance my image or my standing at the bank, would it?"

"No, but are you really finished with her? Is it over?"

He set his empty glass down and turned to look at Brooke, searching her face and perhaps wondering why she asked. "Yeah, it rankles a bit. No one likes to be played for a fool, but if you mean do I think every woman is like Pat, the answer is no. I know most aren't. It all goes back to the value system. One of the things I liked about your ideal man was that you didn't mention money, job status, or title in the things you wanted. That gives me a lot of hope."

He gazed at her with an intensity that surprised her, and he took her hand, stroking it with his thumb. Brooke couldn't find any words to respond to his unasked questions about her own feelings, and she lowered her gaze, afraid to prolong the contact, but she returned a gentle squeeze, hoping it conveyed her sympathy.

The combo returned and the music eliminated the need for conversation. Brooke kept time with her foot and finally forgot Sam continued to hold her hand as she marveled at the intricacies of the solos. The combo finished its second set ending with a rousing rendition of "Satin Doll."

Glancing at her watch, Brooke noted with surprise it read almost eleven and gently withdrew her hand to pick up her purse. "It's time we left. I've enjoyed this Sam, but I have some interviews tomorrow and need to be downtown early."

He smiled wryly. "So you want to turn into Cinderella?"

"Not want to, have to. I've enjoyed the music, but it's late and I won't think well tomorrow if I'm tired."

Sam sighed, rising. "Well, if you insist."

He helped her on with her coat and his hands rested lightly for a moment on her shoulders until Brooke moved. He paid the bar tab, and they strolled slowly back to the car.

"Would you join me again—for more music?" They had reached his car and stood facing each another.

"I would." Brooke grinned at him, but then sobered when she remembered her promise to Paul. "But not for the next few weeks. I'm behind on some articles I promised the editor a week ago, and if I don't get them in, he won't use my stuff. Besides, I don't want the editor to reject my profile on you because we've gone out a few times. Once I've got my work schedule back on track, I'd like to see you. Right now it's no distractions." All valid excuses and, hopefully by then, this business with the bank and Stan would be finished.

"And I'm a distraction?" He smiled down at her.

"Most definitely, and a very tempting distraction at that." She returned his smile.

"Well, that makes me feel better. I'll give you two weeks and then I'll call, okay?" He held the car door as she slid onto the seat.

"Yes, I'd like that."

After Sam dropped her off, Brooke remembered to call Paul. She punched the number and waited for him to answer.

"Paul? Brooke here; I just got back."

"Kind of late isn't it?" He sounded a touch sarcastic.

"A little, but Sam said Pat had been involved with a married man. I didn't mention Vavor, but I'm pretty sure that's whom Sam meant. Pat said something to the effect, that if she was good enough to sleep with, she was good enough to marry."

"Okay, I have to think about the Vavor aspect and see if it makes any difference. I talked to Pat earlier today and suggested to her the police could do a voiceprint on the 9-1-1 tape."

"Can they?" A spasm of hope flared for Brooke.

"I don't know, but it upset her. The next time we talk, I might get something out of her." He paused a moment. "Did you...uh...enjoy yourself?"

"Yes, I had a pleasant evening and loved the music."

"That isn't exactly what I mean." He sounded annoyed.

"I'm tired, Paul; nothing happened. I'll talk to you later. Right now I need some sleep. Good-bye." Brooke hung up the receiver before he could protest.

She didn't like the tone of his voice. Okay, she liked him, and he seemed to like her, but that didn't give him any territorial rights.

Brooke brooded as she undressed. She hadn't learned much more about Pat. She'd found Sam attractive, more attractive than she'd expected, and if it weren't for Stan's unsolved murder, she could be interested in knowing him better. And then, too, there was Paul. For the present she had to be put Sam aside. She would talk further with Paul about Sam, but she hoped he realized her primary interest just now was not Sam, but Pat Jensen.

* * * *

Late the next afternoon, Brooke's phone rang jarring her out of her work.

"Hello, Miss Beldon? This is Detective Meyers, Homicide."

Meyers? What did he want? Had he learned something about Stan's death? Unreasoning hope overwhelmed her. She'd heard nothing more from him since he had told her the police had classified the death as an accident.

"Yes, have you discovered anything more about my brother's death?"

"I have some news for you. We received a note in today's mail from a woman named Pat Jensen admitting she was with your brother when he died. The note says his death was accidental, but it has been on her conscience. Someone told her we might do a voiceprint on the 9-1-1 call, and the note says she couldn't face the public exposure as a drug user possibly implicated in a death. She committed suicide last night—drowned herself in her hot tub after imbibing a lot of wine and taking some pills."

Shock held Brooke silent for a minute.

"Miss Beldon?"

Scrambling for something to say, she struggled to stay coherent. "Oh, I'm so sorry to hear that." How would Sam take the news? And Paul? He'd met with her. With Pat dead, who remained?

"Would you have charged her?"

"It's doubtful. These things happen all the time. If she'd been a dealer, maybe, but as a user also high, probably not. I'm not sure whether we would get anything useful out of a voiceprint anyway. You wouldn't happen to know who might have told her that?"

"Well, uh…no. I never met Ms. Jensen." Should she tell him about Paul? No, that would only make Meyers more suspicious of him. "Thank you for calling."

"You're welcome. This will close our investigation into your brother's death. We appreciate your cooperation and your patience. I'm glad there are no loose ends. Good-bye, Miss Beldon."

"Good-bye."

No loose ends? Brooke doubted that. They hadn't solved John Pierce's murder. As she hung up the phone she wondered exactly what Paul had said to Pat. Perhaps she should call him because the police certainly would. She keyed his number, waiting impatiently for him to answer.

"Paul? Brooke here; the police just called to say Pat Jensen killed herself and wrote a note saying she was with Stan when he died."

"What?" He paused for a moment, as if the unexpected news surprised him. "When I spoke to her yesterday she acted nervous, but I'd never have thought she was the suicidal type."

"Detective Meyers says she left a note saying she couldn't face public exposure as a drug user and the responsibility for Stan's death."

"Somehow that doesn't ring true." The doubt in his voice came through. "She didn't appear all that concerned about Stan yesterday."

"Detective Meyers said the note mentioned someone had said the police could make a voiceprint. Didn't you tell her that?"

"Yes, and it made her leave in a hurry. I followed and saw her telephone someone. If she were in this alone, why call anyone? What about John Pierce? The police are looking for a jealous lover, but I still feel all three deaths are related. Somewhere I missed the key to this. I'm going to have go over it again."

She hoped he didn't feel responsible for the deaths. "Why not do it together? You can bounce your ideas off me, and, maybe between us, we can work it out."

"Okay, my place or yours?"

"Mine. Come over and I'll fix us some popcorn—we missed that last time."

"Yeah, the night John Pierce died. Be there in a half hour."

* * * *

Brooke had fresh popcorn and cold beer waiting when Paul arrived. They sat side-by-side on the leather couch sharing the large bowl of buttered popcorn on the coffee table.

"Okay, let's review it again." Paul took a large handful of popcorn. "We have three victims: Stan, a programmer; John Pierce, an accountant; and Pat Jensen, a personnel representative. All of them worked at First Bank and all of them frequented the Lido." He paused to eat a handful of the richly flavored popcorn.

"Do you think the link with the Lido is accidental or really important?" Brooke, who already had eaten several handfuls, helped herself to another.

Paul frowned. "I don't know yet. Stan worked for Morgan Jones. John worked for Walter Vavor. Pat Jensen worked for both Vavor and Morgan. It's also rumored, and, Morgan admits it, Pat had been in love with him. We know Vavor is linked to the Lido, but Morgan isn't. Stan did something strange with some subroutines and some auxiliary files. So far, I've found they created an account in the name of Sandy Jovanoski. The bank sent weekly checks to that name care of General Delivery. Depending on how long this has been going on it may have resulted in several million dollars."

"What?" Brooke stared at him, wide-eyed. "I thought you were talking about siphoning off odd cents."

Paul nodded. "Yes, it was, but do it often enough and on enough accounts, and it soon amounts to dollars and to large dollars. Treating it as a rounding error, made it almost impossible to detect. That and the account number." Thirsty, he reached for his glass of beer.

"So somebody made lots of money?"

He nodded again. "So it seems. Now, who has or needs lots of money?" He paused for a swallow of beer. "We suspect Vavor is buying drugs for his daughter, that he lives well, but is also paid well, but these days drugs aren't that expensive in small doses. He could use the money, and, as a financial officer would understand what was involved, but has a reputation of impeccable integrity. Morgan said he would make a ruler look crooked. So he is possible, but questionable."

"Don't forget that Sam Stephanowsky said that Pat had affairs with two vice presidents. The second may have been Vavor."

"Okay, that's possible, but what about Stephanowsky?"

Frowning, Brooke jumped to Sam's defense. "We don't have any links to him with anyone else except Pat and, perhaps indirectly through her, to Vavor and Morgan."

"True, but we can't exclude him. Maybe he hated her or she threatened to tell the police about Stan's death."

Brooke shook her head. "The police never spoke of anyone, but a woman. Besides, he's not the type. The divorce happened several years ago. No one else has ever mentioned him." She paused a moment trying to think of an alternative. "What about Morgan? I know he had no tie to the Lido, but he had ties to Pat Jensen, although supposedly not recent, and he is in charge of Stan's division." Brooke picked up her beer and sipped it.

"Agreed, and he also has the knowledge, both as a senior officer and as a technology guru. I've kept him informed about all the suspects and what I've learned except for Sandy Jovanoski. He lives well, but also has a good salary. I don't know about a tie to John Pierce. If we could find one, or there were some way to tie him to the Sandy Jovanoski account, it might be possible. Jones and Jovanoski begin with J. So far he seems even less likely than Vavor."

Brooke scrounged a small handful pf popcorn from the bottom of the almost empty bowl. "What else do we have?"

"Nothing, I can't see any way or motive to tie in Donna Sanders or Kent Carpenter. I wonder about Sanders and Sandy, but it doesn't fit in any other way. Kent was supposed to be Pierce's lover, so maybe he knew about the scam. For a while, I even wondered about Jensen, formerly Stephanowsky, and Jovanoski, but Pat and Pierce are dead and we still don't know who killed him. He drowned in his hot tub like Pat."

Paul set his glass down and stared at Brooke. "Do you think maybe Pat didn't commit suicide, but was killed to shut her up and that the same person killed Pierce?"

"I thought you were aiming at that earlier." Brooke wiped her hands on a napkin.

"Yeah, but we should question everyone and everything. We could argue Pat killed Pierce, too, but the note didn't say that, and I doubt she did."

He picked up his glass and drank more beer. Staring at the picture over the fireplace, he chewed his lower lip. "Who's getting the money? That's the real question, and the answer to that will probably also answer who killed Pat and Pierce."

Brooke frowned. "So far we can tie Vavor to the Lido and to two of the three dead people. We've nothing about Morgan and the Lido, but he knew Stan and Pat. Carpenter is linked to Pierce and the Lido; and Sanders only to the Lido. Numerically that puts Vavor one up on Morgan and way ahead of Sanders, although Carpenter sounds like a possible. We don't know anything about Jovanoski and how he or she relates to the others."

"Yeah." Paul twisted his empty beer glass in his hand.

"You don't sound convinced."

"I'm not. Maybe I shouldn't, but I trust Vavor. If what Suzy and Topaz told you is true, he did a stupid thing over his daughter, but maybe that's it. He didn't impress me as the type to murder someone in cold blood; in anger maybe." He set his glass on the table.

"Well, how about Carpenter and Morgan?"

"I've heard Carpenter is furious with me and, if he wrote the notes and called me, it's true, but I can't see he would have killed Pierce, unless it was a lover's quarrel and he's trying to cover up. There's no reason to suspect Morgan, except for Pat, and, as far as we know, they aren't still involved. Obviously, I trusted him enough to tell him my suspicions, and he seems to have been honest with me. He didn't try to hide his past involvement with Pat, and he urged me to find out what Stan was doing,"

Brooke sighed and rubbed her arms. "Are Vavor and Morgan honest men?"

"That's a hell of a question to ask." He stared at her wondering how to respond. "How should I know?"

She turned to face him. "But isn't that what it all comes down to? We're faced with someone of questionable ethics who doesn't value human life, a manipulator who uses people and disposes of them when they get in the way,"

"Yeah," Paul nodded, "I guess that about sums it up; a cold-blooded, ruthless son-of-a-bitch."

"Well, we have to settle on Vavor, Carpenter, or Morgan, find Jovanoski, or add somebody else to our list. More beer?"

"Not at the moment, I've had enough of this. Let's let it rest for a bit." He laid his left arm on the back of the soda behind Brooke. "Have I told you how attractive you are?" He grinned at her.

"Not lately that I remember. You've been a bit preoccupied." She smiled back.

"Well that has to stop." He moved his arm onto her shoulders, pulled her closer, and kissed her mouth slowly, tenderly. She waited, wondering what he would do next. His tongue traced the outline of her lips and then he hugged her against his chest and kissed her thoroughly. Engrossed in his kiss and the warmth created by his encircling arms, she stopped wondering at that point and let her physical and emotional responses blot out her too logical thoughts.

* * * *

The next day, Paul keyed in the phone number from Meyers' card. He hated calling the Homicide Squad. If you weren't reporting a crime in progress, it always resulted in being routed upward through the chain of command until, if he was lucky, he finally reached someone who would take a message, or he had to use the blasted voicemail. Finally, a familiar voice answered.

"Detective Meyers?"

"Yes?"

He'd hit the jackpot first try. This must be his lucky day. "This is Paul Counts, the man those notes were about. We met in John Pierce's apartment the night he died. I found the body."

"I remember you, Mr. Counts. What can I do for you?"

"I'd like to talk to you briefly and share some information with you. Would it be convenient for me to stop by your office?"

"How about two o'clock?"

"That's fine, I'll see you then."

* * * *

That afternoon when Paul reached the Homicide Squad quarters, it still had that same cluttered, overworked, understaffed look. He walked toward Meyers' desk with quick steps. Meyers rose as he approached.

"I've arranged to use one of the interrogation rooms. If you'll follow me, Mr. Counts." Meyers, carrying a pad of paper, walked toward the wall of doors.

"This will give us more privacy," he said, opening one of the doors. The long, narrow room had barely space for the gray rectangular table and the four straight-backed chairs, two on each side. Meyers sat in one and faced Paul across the table.

"Now what is it you want, Mr. Counts?"

Taking a deep breath, Paul crossed his fingers. "Did you have Pat Jensen's suicide note tested for fingerprints?"

Meyers shook his head. "No, we didn't see any reason to. What are you suggesting?"

"I think she may have been murdered."

As if looking for a motive, he studied Paul's face. "Why?"

"Because she knew who killed John Pierce."

"Pierce, how does he fit into all this?" Frowning, Meyers gave him a hard look. .

"It's kind of a long story that actually starts with Stan Beldon."

Meyers let his pencil drop and stared at Paul. "Beldon? That was months ago, and Jensen admitted she was with him when he died."

Paul nodded. "I know all that, but I talked to her just before she died, and, after we talked, she phoned someone. I think she called the person who killed her. She acted scared, and probably convinced the killer she would talk if pushed too hard. The killer couldn't afford that."

Sighing, Meyers picked up his pencil, doubt clear on his face. "So far, there's no reason to suspect anyone killed her. Are you sure you aren't looking for a scapegoat, so you won't feel you caused her to commit suicide?" He tapped his pencil on the pad.

Paul shook his head, frowning. "I don't think she killed herself, and if you don't find her fingerprints on the note, then why aren't they there, if she prepared it."

"It was either photocopied or done on a laser printer, probably the latter."

Paul leaned forward, resting his arms on the table. "But she would have handled it and her fingerprints would be on it. Right?"

Meyers nodded. "Yes, but several people here have handled it."

"Okay, but there should still be a set of her prints on it somewhere. Don't you think it's at least worth looking at?"

"I guess we can do that." Meyers made a note on his pad. "Is there anything else you want to tell me?"

Paul shook his head, "Not yet. I might know who the killer is, but I don't have any evidence."

Meyers put his pencil down and stared at Paul. His face had a red tinge. "Evidence is for the police to find. Withholding information can get you prosecuted. Don't you think it would be better if you let us do the job?"

"Probably. Look, if what I have in mind doesn't pan out, I'll tell you what I know and leave it up to you. The problem right now is that it involves some confidential information I really can't tell you about. You let me know about those fingerprints, and then maybe I'll be in a position to tell you more."

Meyers sighed. "I'm beginning to wonder if you weren't the reason both Pierce and Jensen are dead. You talked to both of them shortly before they died. Maybe I should place you in protective custody for the safety of the community. We don't need any more dead bodies."

"I don't think there will be." Paul rose, walked to the door, and then stopped. He turned toward Meyers. "Please, just check those fingerprints."

Detective Meyers watched as Paul Counts left the Interrogation Room and then he strolled slowly back to his desk. His partner, Blaine Watkins, an unlit cigarette dangling from the corner of his mouth, looked up as Meyers sat down.

"What's up?"

"It's this Jensen case."

"The suicide?"

"Yeah, but this Counts guy seems to think there's something strange about it. He thinks she was murdered and that it all ties in with the Beldon and Pierce cases."

"Well..." Blaine twisted the cigarette in his mouth. "She said she was with Beldon, but what's this bit about Pierce? We still have that on the books as unsolved."

"Yeah." Meyers sighed. "And this Counts was found with the body."

"Does he know something he isn't telling us?"

Meyers nodded. "That's what I think. I'll have that suicide note checked for fingerprints, and if Jensen's don't show, I'm going to give this amateur detective hell. Put the screws on him to find out exactly what he knows, and why he's withholding it. I'm guessing it's tied up with the bank."

Blaine looked thoughtful. "Do we have any contacts there?"

"No, but we keep getting these notes about Counts, and it's just possible that eventually the writer will tell us what we want to know." Meyers rubbed his eyes. "What puzzles me is whether Counts is guilty and trying to divert us, or whether he's trying to play detective."

Blaine snorted. "Just what we need, more bumbling amateurs. TV makes 'em all sure it's easy and they all know more than we do."

Meyers nodded as he pulled out his chair and sat at his desk. "Yeah, well I'd better find the note and have it checked. After that we should have a little talk with Counts and really grill him."

"Sounds like fun. Let me know when. I want to sit in on that." Blaine stuffed his cigarette in pocket and smiled.

* * * *

After work, Paul went to Chiquita's, hoping to catch Kent alone. When he arrived, he saw him sitting at the bar with a beer, looking even more rumpled than last time, and still wearing the same Reds' baseball cap.

Paul ordered a Beck and strolled over to Kent. He slid onto the adjacent stool. "I hear you and John Pierce were buddies." Paul sipped his beer and waited for Kent's answer..

"You might say that." Kent gave him a sullen glance and faced forward.

"I imagine you were upset when he was killed."

"Wouldn't you be?" His tone didn't invite comment.

"If it was a close relationship, yeah, I guess I would." Paul watched as Kent took a long swallow of beer. "Was it?"

"None of your business, bud." Kent refused to look at him.

"Perhaps, but then again, maybe it is my business. You see, I found Pierce's body, and someone's trying to convince the police I killed him. Maybe it's you."

Kent swiveled on the stool to face him. "You asked him a lot of questions and leaned on people, including me."

"That's true, but Pierce called me that evening to say he had something to tell me. I didn't know where he lived until that call." Sipping his beer, Paul watched Kent's reaction.

"He had something on you, so you killed him." Kent glared at him, his eyes narrowed and dangerous.

Paul shook his head. " No, I didn't kill him, but someone else did, perhaps Sandy Jovanoski."

"You bastard. I'll see you hang." Kent grabbed Paul's shirt with both grasping hands and pushed his red face close to Paul's. The smell of the sour beer on Kent's breath almost choked Paul. "You killed him so you could keep the money."

"What money is that?"

"You know what money, the money your friend Stan Beldon salted away in the Jovanoski account."

"So who takes the money out?"

"You." Kent shook him with so much force he almost tore Paul's shirt.

He reached up to loosen Kent's grip. "I'd hate to have send you the bill for a new shirt. Have you looked at my bank statement lately? I'm not wealthy, no sudden inheritance, no lottery win. I haven't any major assets, and I have no access to the Jovanoski account."

"But you know about it." Kent balled his empty hands into fists

"Yes, but I found that out the same way you did, by going though Stan's program files, not because I was in on some scam. Your friend Pierce was in it up to his neck, and I'll bet that whoever has access to the Jovanoski account is the one who killed Pierce. Pierce was going to tell me; that's why he called me. His buddies must have found out and decided to silence him. Besides, I'd already talked with at least two of the senior bank people about it, and they had begun a review of Pierce's accounts before he was killed."

Kent slumped like a flat tire.

"I want Pierce's killer as badly as you do, because I believe the same person killed Stan Beldon." Paul omitted any mention of Pat, her suicide, or the note.

"Stan ODed," Kent mumbled.

"That's what the police think, but he wasn't a drug user. As you said, he was into a scam, and at least two other people were also involved: John Pierce and Sandy Jovanoski."

Kent sat in silence, as if considering what Paul had said, weighing the words and trying to decide what to believe.

Paul leaned closer to him. "I can use all the help you can give me. I haven't had any luck in finding out what happens to the money once it's sent to General Delivery. If we could only find out Sandy Jovanoski's real identity, we could solve both Stan's murder and Pierce's. You want the killer caught, don't you?"

"So what are you proposing?" Kent looked up at Paul with a beginning of hope.

"That instead of sending notes to the police, you help me find out who Sandy Jovanoski is."

"I'll think about it." Kent paused. "I'm still not convinced about you."

"So what? If you can link with me Jovanoski, go ahead. Meanwhile, two heads might just be able to solve this puzzle."

"Could this Jovanoski be a woman?" Kent played with his beer glass.

"What makes you ask that?"

"Nothing really, it's just that the name, Sandy, could be either a man or woman."

Always coming back to a woman it seemed. First there had been Pat Jensen. Her suicide note claimed she was the woman who had called 9-1-1. Had Sandy Jovanoski killed her or was she Sandy? That still left him with the problem of finding the real person. The bank employed no one by that name. The closest he had was Sanders, Donna Sanders, but that was still a far cry from Jovanoski.

Chapter Fourteen

Compelled by his conversation with Kent to consider women who might be Sandy, his thoughts naturally turned to Donna Sanders. She had the brains and the daring to plan such a scam, although he wasn't sure how she would have convinced Stan to cooperate. He knew of no link between her and Pat. Sexual seduction didn't appear to be her strong suit, but stranger things had happened. It was time to talk with Ms. Sanders again.

He wondered how she would respond this time, particularly when he asked about the credit reports. The phone stopped ringing. "Hello, Ms. Sanders?

"Yes?" She snapped out the word with brisk economy.

"Paul Counts, I spoke to you a week or so ago about Stan Beldon and Harley Donovan."

"I remember very well, Mr. Counts, and I thought I made it clear I had no intention of being subjected to blackmail." Frost iced the phone line.

"Yes, you made that clear, but we still have one or two things we to discuss, like those lists for Harley."

Silence. "Umm...yes, perhaps we should."

"Waldo's, five-fifteen?"

"Yes, I'll meet you there."

A sharp click sounded as she replaced the receiver. At least Harley gave him a lever to use with the cool Ms. Sanders, but was she Sandy Jovanoski?

It took Paul a moment to adjust when he entered the dark and empty Waldo's. After picking up a Beck at the bar, he selected a place as distant from it as possible. At precisely 5:15, Donna Sanders entered and peered into the gloom. Sighting Paul, she strode toward, him and sat on the facing ottoman.

167

"A neat Scotch?"

"Yes, thanks." She settled herself, straightening her skirt and smoothing it over her knees as Paul walked toward the bar.

He returned with her drink and placed it in front of her.

"Well, Sandy, I'm sorry to have to bug you again, but there are a few points we didn't discuss at out last meeting."

"Such as?" She raised an eyebrow at him and waited without apparent anxiety for him to continue.

When she didn't react to the name hope rose. "Such as those lists you give Harley. He gives you the names, you check them for him, and provide him with credit reports."

Raising her Scotch to drink, she studied him over the glass, and then sighed. "So, I gave Harley a few reports on people."

"It's against bank policy to provide such information unless the requester comes from an organization with a legitimate reason to want the data and has the customer's permission. Policy restricts the use of the big three credit bureaus to bank business."

"That's what the company manual says. However, Mr. Donovan is a bank customer." She set her glass down and looked at him, waiting.

Paul savored the mellow liquid of his beer and took his time before responding. Donna sat in watchful silence. "Yeah, but he's also a drug dealer. If I remember correctly, the manual says improper use of those files and of customer data will result in summary dismissal."

"So what do you intend to do, Mr. Counts?" Her hand steady, she picked up her glass and sipped the Scotch.

"That depends on you, Sandy." He accented the last word.

A half-smile crossed her lips. "How did you know my name was Sandy?"

"Well it's a likely nickname for Sanders."

"Not necessarily, unless you go to an elite prep school or a place like Harvard where only last names are used."

Certain he had her, Paul leaned forward to deliver the coup de grâce. "And Jovanoski?"

"Jovanoski?" She set her glass down and stared at him. "Who's that?"

"I'm looking for a Sandy Jovanoski connected with Stan Beldon, and since you're Sandy, have already been involved in some questionable activities, and..." Paul let his words trail off, knowing she would get the drift.

A broad, amused smile crossed her face. "You just naturally assumed I'm this Sandy Jovanoski." She peered at him over the glow of the small candle and then shook her head. "I'm sorry to disappoint you, but I'm not Jovanoski, and I don't know anyone by that name. As far as I know, no one at the bank knows I was called Sandy in college. I have never used that name since, and no one here knows it."

She sampled her Scotch. "Well, Mr. Counts, what do you plan to do about the reports?"

Stumped, Paul sighed. "I don't know. Frankly, I'm not concerned with them, but eventually someone else will find out and tell your boss. When they do, you'll be out of job."

She put down her glass and leaned toward him. "What if I tell Harley I won't do any more?"

"And if he threatens to call the bank?"

"It would be his word against mine, and he has as much, if not more, to lose than I do." She shook her head. "No, Harley won't do anything. Most likely, he'll just look for someone else to get him the reports."

Paul sipped his Beck, finding it hard to let go. He hadn't found any other Sandy. "And you're sure you don't know this Jovanoski?"

Donna smiled. "Quite sure, Mr. Counts. Would you like me to do a credit check on this Jovanoski for you?"

"Umm..." Paul paused, wondering what might turn up there. "I suppose it wouldn't hurt. Yes." He nodded, glad he might get at least one piece of information since everything else led nowhere. "Do that and send me the results."

She studied his face in the light of the candle flame. "And you won't say anything to anyone at the bank about the reports?"

"Not unless I find out you've lied to me and are tied up with Stan's death."

"Good. I believe I can rely on you, Mr. Counts, and you can rely on me." She stood and picked up her briefcase. "Thanks for the Scotch. I'll send you that report Monday. Good evening, Mr. Counts."

Paul drank his beer as he watched her stride toward the door and leave. A very cool customer—no hysterics, no tears, just a calm acceptance. She had only shown surprise when he had asked about Jovanoski. His gut said she was okay, but he still didn't know who Sandy Jovanoski was, and so far only Donna Sanders admitted being called

Sandy.

He wished he could cross some of his suspects off his list. They just kept coming back, unless like Pierce or Pat they died. He couldn't believe Kent had murdered Pierce. The death had affected him too much and he had accused Paul of being Jovanoski. On top of that, who had killed Pat? It couldn't be suicide; that was too pat and too convenient. She'd called someone after leaving the bar, but who? Sandy Jovanoski? Always back to the same puzzle, who the hell was Sandy Jovanoski?

He hadn't yet eliminated Walter Vavor. He could be Sandy Jovanoski. He had the opportunity and Pat had worked for him. Paul worried that he had missed something. Vavor had never told him why he went to the Lido.

With both Pierce and Pat now dead, Vavor might reveal his involvement with Harley. Paul pondered how to catch him off guard and decided approaching him at home might be best. If he didn't attend church, Sunday morning would be a good time to reach him. It would upset Morgan, but he didn't have many options left.

* * * *

Paul had finished his Sunday paper and realized he couldn't put off calling Vavor much longer. Might as well get it over with. The number rang several times and Paul almost gave up, thinking Vavor probably attended church when the ringing stopped.

"Mr. Vavor?" He'd lucked out.

"Yes?"

"Paul Counts, we talked several weeks ago."

"Yes, I remember." His tone implied it wasn't a pleasant memory.

"It's important I talk to you."

"Mr. Counts I recall our last encounter only too well. I have no desire to pursue further discussions. Didn't Morgan speak with you?"

"Yes sir, he did. I appreciate your feelings, but after I talked to you last, John Pierce and now Pat Jensen have been killed."

"What?" Paul could almost hear the wheels churning. "The newspaper said Pat committed suicide." His surprise sounded genuine.

"The police thought so at first, but now they're beginning to see a connection between the two deaths. I suspect the police will want to talk to you." Paul paused for emphasis. "Especially, if I tell them about Harley Donovan. I'm in a difficult spot with the police. They consider me a suspect, and I can't withhold information, if they ask me. I'd rather talk to you first."

A long-suffering sigh came over the wire. "Meet me at Antrim, same place, in say thirty minutes."

"Thank you, Mr. Vavor. I'll be there."

It took Paul only twenty-five minutes to reach the park entrance. Vavor stood by the walkway watching for him. Paul followed as Vavor led the way to the lake area beyond the freeway.

Striding at a moderate pace, Vavor looked toward Paul. "Explain what you meant about John Pierce and Pat Jensen."

"John drowned in his apartment hot tub, and someone tried to frame me, because the police arrived to find me with a dead body."

Surprised, Vavor stared at him. "Did you kill him?"

"No, he called me, apparently to tell me about something happening at the bank. Did you find anything in reviewing his accounts?"

Vavor stared long and hard at Paul, as if assessing his motivation. "It's not finished yet, but so far nothing has shown up."

"Then the police found Pat Jensen dead, also in a hot tub. At first they thought it suicide, but I'm sure it was murder."

Vavor frowned. "Why?"

"Pat Jensen was with Stan Beldon when he died and called 9-1-1. It's even possible she gave him the drug overdose. I can prove Stan was siphoning off bank funds in a scheme that also included Pierce, Pat, and perhaps a fourth person."

Vavor appeared dazed. "Who?"

"That's exactly what I want to know, and I need your cooperation. One scenario says you might be the fourth person. After all, you and Pat were lovers."

"What?" Vavor's eyebrows shot up and he blinked. "Who told you that?"

"Sam Stephanowsky, Pat's ex-husband." Wary, Paul waited to see Vavor's response, hoping for some telling reaction beyond shock and surprise.

Vavor snorted. "I wouldn't take that seriously. He probably didn't like the long hours Pat put in and just jumped to conclusions."

"No, Pat told him. She taunted him with the fact he wasn't ambitious enough for her tastes, and if she could sleep with a Vice President, she could marry one."

Stopping, Vavor faced him "Now just a minute, Pat may have said that about Morgan, but not about me. I've got a wife, and I've no intention of divorcing her, never have had."

"I believe you, sir, but Pat may have felt otherwise, and then with the scam, you were forced to kill her."

Vavor stopped in mid stride and faced Paul. "Listen, Counts, and listen well, I'm not a murderer of Pat or anyone else, and I'm certainly not involved with any bank scam."

"You haven't told me the truth about Harley Donovan so why should I believe you about murder. Maybe I should just tell the police."

Sweating, Vavor ran a hand through his hair. He gazed at Paul and then toward the lake perhaps weighing his choices.

"The last time I asked you about Harley Donovan, you refused to discuss him. You can either tell me or the police, it's your choice." Paul shrugged, absolving himself of responsibility and started ahead.

Vavor reached out to stop him. "No, Mr. Counts, stay." He said nothing for a moment, but looked troubled. "God, how complicated things get! You leave me little choice, but please, I ask you to treat what I tell you in strictest confidence." His look pleaded with Paul.

Reassured, Paul relaxed. "As long as it has nothing to do with the murders or with the bank, I'll agree to that."

"It doesn't. Sometime ago I learned my daughter smoked crack. She used money from her allowance, and even stole from her mother. I was afraid of what might come next. We tried to get her into a treatment program, but she refused. I even considered committing her to a mental health clinic, but she ran away. Her mother and I finally persuaded her to come back, but only on her own terms. One of those was a continued supply of crack."

Vavor looked straight at Paul. "I know this sounds crazy, but you have to understand, she's our only child. My wife couldn't have any more, and we love her. I probably should have committed her to the clinic, but I couldn't deal with my wife's unhappiness and my daughter's hatred, so I agreed."

Hands balled into fists, Vavor implored Paul for understanding. "The crack from Harley was for her. I'm at my wits' end. It never seems to stop. I'm worried eventually she'll OD. I don't know what to do."

"I'm sorry for all of you, but it won't any better, and dealing with slime like Harley will probably end with the police arresting you both. Besides, the OD danger is real—look what happened to Stan. It takes more and more to get a high, and eventually the body can't tolerate it. You'd be smarter to face up to it and put her in a clinic before she's dead. I won't say anything about this to anyone, but please let me know if you turn anything up in Pierce's accounts. You are having them reviewed?"

"What? Oh, yes, the review is underway."

Paul stepped forward and then stopped. "Oh, Sandy…" He paused, alert for Vavor's reaction.

Vavor's face registered only surprise. "What did you say? Sandy? Who's that?"

Paul released his pent up breath. "Someone told me Pat worked for someone called Sandy. She worked for you, didn't she?"

"She worked for me for several years and was an excellent assistant. I was sorry to lose her to Morgan, but she never called me anything but Mr. Vavor. When I was a kid, I used to be called Dutch, but by college, it was Walter or Walt. I've never been called Sandy." Vavor appeared mystified.

Paul nodded. "Sorry, my mistake. Good luck, Mr. Vavor. You really need it."

He left Vavor standing by the lake, a lost look on his face. Paul hurried back to the parking lot and his car. As he drove away, he considered Vavor's explanation. He pitied the family, but they had made the mess. They had raised a spoiled brat who probably needed a little discipline and some tough love, but she just got in deeper and deeper, pulling her parents down with her. He hoped they could turn it around, but didn't see much reason to expect any change.

For now, he would leave a question mark next to Vavor, but he didn't act like a cold-blooded murderer, and unless something else turned up, his name could probably be crossed off. The results of whatever the review of John Pierce's accounts turned up should reveal something. The police hadn't responded yet about Pat Jensen's fingerprints on the note. Maybe the credit report from Donna Sanders on Sandy Jovanoski would identify the link needed.

* * * *

Paul had asked Brooke to attend a viewing for Pat at the funeral home to pay their last respects. Black looked good on Brooke. Her simple black dress hugged her curves and then flared into a flirty, swinging skirt. On the drive to the funeral home, he told her about his meetings with Donna Sanders and Walter Vavor.

Brooke eyes reflected sadness and sympathy. "I guess you were right about it being tied in with his daughter, but it's almost tragic, isn't it. Do you think he'll take your advice?"

Frowning, Paul sighed. "I don't know. I hope he does, but I doubt there's much hope. Brenda will have to want to change, and I'm not sure she does."

Paul pulled into the funeral home parking lot located near a small shopping center. They parked and walked to the pillared front entrance. The attendant at the front door directed them to the second room on the right. As they entered the large room, they saw a guest book on a stand by the door, which they both signed. Paul noted Morgan Jones, Walter Vavor, and San Stephanowsky had all signed the book as well as several others from the bank.

A small group of mourners clustered around the coffin at the far end of the rooms. Probably family, Paul thought. As they approached, he noted that one of the women resembled Pat—most likely a sister.

In death, Pat's face appeared relaxed and less lined. The undertaker had done his work well, and she looked more attractive dead, than she had the last time Paul had seen her. Somehow they had erased the brittleness and petulance. Sympathy for her and regret over a too-short life assailed him. A touch of guilt also niggled at Paul. She would have had almost half a lifetime ahead of her. Now she lay in a coffin, just cold meat to be placed in the ground.

"Hello, I'm Pat's sister, Marisue," the woman who resembled Pat greeted them. "Are you friends of Pat's?" Her tight black dress showed her excess weight in several ridges. Her hair flamed, a bright, artificial red.

Paul shook her hand. "I'm Paul Counts. I work at First Bank, the same place Pat worked. This is Brooke Beldon."

Marisue shook hands with both of them. "It's nice to meet you, Mr. Counts, Miss Beldon, and thank you for coming." She dabbed at her eyes with a lacy handkerchief. "We've had several people from the bank stop by."

Paul nodded. "Yes, I noticed in the guest book."

"Mr. Vavor was so nice. He told me how good an assistant Pat had been. Mr. Jones remarked on how much I looked like Pat. Sally Cameron said she and Pat used to eat lunch together." She turned toward the open casket with sprays of flowers behind it and around both ends. "Have you seen Pat?" Paul and Brooke both nodded.

"Yes," Paul answered her. "It's hard to believe she's dead. The paper said something about being despondent."

Marisue trembled. "Oh, that's not true, simply not true. As a good Catholic, Pat would never commit suicide. Besides, she planned to marry soon. She told me they were taking a cruise on the QEII for a honeymoon. I found the tickets in yesterday's mail." Marisue blotted her eyes with the lacy handkerchief.

Paul glanced quickly at Brooke. "I didn't know that. Who was the luck..." He stopped, suddenly aware that 'lucky man' wouldn't do, "Uh...whom did she plan to marry?"

"A man who worked at the bank. It was always 'Sandy this, and Sandy that.'" She sighed. "Now, we're burying her."

"Did you say Sandy? I don't remember a Sandy at the bank. I thought she was upset over Stan Beldon."

Marisue shook her head sadly. "Oh no, she mentioned Stan once, but the man she planned to marry was called Sandy, her pet name for him. I'm not sure what his full name was, but he was an officer at the bank."

"What did you say?" Paul leaned forward.

"I said he was an officer at the bank; Pat used to work for him." Marisue blinked at his interruption.

He waved a hand as if to brush the cobwebs away. "No, before that, about Sandy."

"Oh that, that's what Pat called him, Sandy. I guess it was sort of a pet name."

Frowning, he puzzled again over the identity of Sandy. "You must be right. I don't remember anyone called Sandy at the bank, at least not any men." The name on the account was Sandy Jovanoski. Was it possible? But which bank officer—Vavor or Morgan—Sam again? Or someone else who claimed to be, but Pat would know.

Married, Vavor couldn't marry Pat unless he divorced his wife and that took time. Vavor denied that he was called Sandy.

Morgan was single, but he said he broke up with Pat. No one ever called Morgan anything except Morgan or Mr. Jones. Jones, Jovanoski?

Sam Stephanowsky? No, it would be Sammy, not Sandy, and she'd already been married to him. Marisue knew him. Well, that let Sam off the hook. Too bad. Paul wouldn't have minded pinning something on him. Brooke liked him and considered him much too attractive for Paul's taste.

He wanted to get away and think. Mumbling condolences to Marisue, he ushered Brooke toward the door. Just as they were leaving, a sad-faced man in a dark suit with long sideburns and slightly thinning hair entered.

"Brooke, how good to see you. It was nice of you to come."

"Hello, Sam." Brooke gave him a warm smile, too warm Paul thought. "May I introduce Paul Counts? Paul, this is Sam Stephanowsky, Pat's ex-husband."

"Pleased to meet you, Mr. Stephanowsky," he said as he shook hands. At least Stephanowsky had a firm grip.

"Likewise," Sam responded. "What brings you two here?" He focused on Brooke, ignoring Paul.

"Paul works at the bank, and the police called me because of the suicide note Pat left. Is there anything I can do?" Brooke studied his face, seeking, Paul guessed, to learn how much Pat's death had affected him.

Sighing, Sam shook his head. "Your being here is enough. I came, to help out Marisue. There's not much family, and I felt I owed it to Pat to come. Maybe we could do dinner sometime." In Paul's view, he looked near to tears.

Brooke nodded. "Call me when you have a chance. We have to go. It was nice seeing you, Sam." She rose on her toes, gave his cheek a quick peck, and squeezed his hand. "Take care."

Paul hurried her out the door, anxious to put some distance between the sympathetic Brooke and the grieving Sam.

Chapter Fifteen

Paul's office phone rang, breaking his concentration. He swore as he answered it.

"Mr. Counts? Donna Sanders." Her crisp voice made the wire crackle.

"Yes, Ms. Sanders?"

"I have that report on Sandy Jovanoski; it doesn't say much. It identifies him as male, thirty-eight, current address is General Delivery, Central Post Office, with a previous address of a Parma, Ohio, post office box."

"Anything else?"

"No, but I also checked his account with the bank. A check is sent every week to General Delivery."

"Yeah, I knew that; that's part of why I wanted to know about him. You know how the Feds are these days about money laundering, and I wanted to be sure the bank hadn't gotten involved in such a scheme."

"Oh, I hadn't thought of that." Donna paused a moment. "Is that why you were so concerned about Harley Donovan?"

"No, not really, Harley's small potatoes and only a minor means to solving who killed Stan. I appreciate your checking for me, and I'm relying on your promise to stop doing those background checks for Harley."

"I gave you my word on that, and I've already told Harley no more business." Her tone had dropped several degrees "Is there anything else?"

"No, nothing, but send me a printout of the credit check, I may need to check with the postal authorities on that name."

He doubted the postal authorities would tell him anything, but perhaps when he figured out things Meyers would listen. In the meantime, maybe Nancy, in the library, could locate biographies on

Vavor and Morgan.

The afternoon mail arrived with copies of two newsletter articles from Nancy. Vavor had been born in Pennsylvania and had come to the bank from Cincinnati. Morgan had been born in the Cleveland area and joined the bank after graduating from Ohio State. Paul puzzled over which could be Marisue's Sandy, and, thus, also Sandy Jovanoski. The only geographic clue he had to Jovanoski was Parma. He couldn't remember exactly where that was. Ohio had so many towns and villages named for famous European cities—Lima, Athens, Canton, now Parma. He thought of it as somewhere north.

He pulled out an Ohio road map to look it up when the phone rang again.

"Hello, Mr. Counts? Milton Meyers here."

"Yes?" Paul fiddled with the map and finally got it unfolded.

"We checked the Jensen letter for fingerprints and found none of Ms Jensen's."

"Does that mean you'll reopen the investigation?" Paul located the coordinates for Parma and looked for it on the map. Noting its location, he suppressed a small whistle.

"That sort of depends on what else you might have to tell us."

He refolded the map and set it aside. "I was just checking something now. How about four o'clock in your office?"

"All right, but I expect you to level with me. No more hide-and-go-seek or that fencing you talk about."

"Right, I don't want any more murders. I'll see you then. Bye."

That took care of the preliminaries. Paul sent an e-mail message to Carol Coates asking her to delete Stan's special routine. Since he planned to talk to Meyers in a few hours, the thief was hardly like to detect it and flee. He still had to earn his salary and get a little work done before meeting Meyers.

Noting the time on the bottom of his screen, Paul realized he'd reached the end of his hunt for Pierce's and Pat's killer. He signed out and walked toward the elevators. Once he talked with Meyers, he couldn't turn back. Either the police would make an arrest, or he'd be stuck with some assertions he'd have difficulty backing up.

The biography Nancy had retrieved for him from the bank newsletter stated Morgan had been born in Cleveland, but didn't mention his changing names. Still, Morgan had told him that, so there was no reason to doubt it.

Arriving at police headquarters on time, Paul took the elevator to Meyers' floor. This time Meyers had his partner with him and, after introductions, they accompanied Paul to a claustrophobic box of an interrogation room.

Once seated, Meyers, with Blaine next to him, stared at Paul from the other side of the table. "Well Mr. Counts, what do you have to tell me?"

"It's a long story and involves three murders—Stan Beldon, John Pierce, and Pat Jensen." Paul noticed Blaine's eyes flicker at Stan's name. "And the theft from the bank of millions of dollars. Stan, at the instigation of Pat Jensen, devised a routine to take the rounding errors and store them in a special account. Later, the bank sent money periodically in the form of a check to Sandy Jovanoski, care of General Delivery at the main post office."

Meyers nodded as he recognized the name. "What are these rounding errors?"

"When calculating interest due depositors, it often comes out as a decimal number with more than two decimals. Amounts at the third place after the decimal over five are rounded up, those less are rounded down. We're talking about one cent added to some accounts, but not others. Stan truncated all calculations at the second decimal and stored the results in another account that gradually grew, first to cents and then to dollars."

"So how about these millions you mentioned?"

"Do the truncation many times on a lot of accounts and it eventually adds up."

"All right then." Meyers nodded, accepting the explanation. "Who is this Sandy Jovanoski?"

"I've been trying to work that out. I think I have." Paul laid the copy of the newsletter page and the credit report on the table. Meyers picked them up, scanned them quickly, and handed them to his partner.

Blaine stared at the pieces of paper and then looked at Meyers. "Milt, this guy Jones, he was on the list of people who bought wine the night Jensen drowned."

"Wine?" Paul looked from one to the other.

Meyers sighed, giving Blaine an annoyed look. "We found a bottle of wine with Ms. Jensen the night she died. A special bottle of wine. We traced the tag to a local store. They sold only a few bottles of it that evening, and Jones paid for his with a charge card."

Paul frowned. It sounded stupid, but then Morgan probably figured no one would ever check. He'd expect Pat's death to be accepted as suicide. "Pat's sister Marisue said Pat planned to marry someone from the bank named Sandy and she found tickets for a cruise on the QEII You might want to talk to her and see who paid for those tickets. Morgan and Pat once had a romance."

Meyers made a note on the pad of paper in front of him. "We'll do that, Mr. Counts. Do you have anything else?"

Paul shook his head. "No, that's it really."

Meyers nodded, finished making his notes, and looked up at Paul. "Thank you, Mr. Counts, for the information. If we need anything further from you, we'll call."

Paul shook hands with both men and left. As he closed the door behind him he heard Blaine's excited whisper. "Looks like we've found our killer."

Back at in his office, Paul sat staring at the Delacroix lithograph. Three figures—two fencers with swords in hand and the Devil—held his attention. As he remembered, Faust won because the Devil stabbed Valentin, not because it was a fair duel. Which role had Morgan played—the Devil or Faust? Paul sighed. Faust seemed most likely since the scam focused on amassing power and money. Ambition had been the Devil. Stan, John, and Pat had been the not-so-innocent victims.

He debated about calling Brooke and decided to wait until the police acted. An outside chance existed he might have figured wrong and Morgan was innocent, but he doubted that. How had he described the killer to Brooke? 'A cold-blooded, ruthless son-of-a-bitch.' Was Morgan that? Manipulative and arrogant, he matched most of the senior executives. However, murder took ruthlessness to another level. Had he murdered?

The next afternoon as Paul walked past Marilyn Johnson's desk, she beckoned to him aquiver with excitement. "Say, did you hear the news?"

"News? No, what's up?" Her agitation caught him off guard.

Leaning forward, Marilyn lowered her voice. "They arrested Morgan Jones for Pat Jensen's murder. They say she didn't commit suicide. He murdered her."

"Morgan?" Paul's surprise wasn't entirely faked. He hadn't expected the police to move so fast. "How about that?"

She gave him a solemn nod. "Yeah, Sally Morris, his assistant heard it all. They arrested him right here in the bank."

"Did they say anything about Stan?"

Marilyn shook her head, clearly puzzled. "Not that I know of. Say, do you think he was in on that, too? I thought Pat's note said she was with Stan when he died."

"It did, but that was supposed to be a suicide note, and if..." Paul let his words trail off, reluctant to spell it all out.

Looking thoughtful for a moment, Marilyn then opened her eyes wide. "Oh, yeah, I see what you mean. If she didn't commit suicide, she didn't leave the note."

Paul walked on as Marilyn pondered the implications of Pat's murder. From his office, he tried to call Brooke, but only got her answering machine. Disappointed he hung up without leaving a message.

As he got ready to leave work, the phone rang again. The computer operator on the line said something had gone wrong with the backup routines and they needed help. Paul sighed. Well, he could always call Brooke later and maybe take her out for a drink or a pizza. Hopefully, the computer problem could be fixed quickly.

* * * *

Late in the afternoon, Brooke dialed Sam Stephanowsky's number. "Hello, Sam? Brooke Beldon."

"Good to hear from you, Brooke." His voice still had that rich, warm timbre that sent a delicious thrill through her from head to toe.

The memory of his eyes as she had seen them at the funeral home, sort of dark and lonely and almost lost, still haunted her. "Are you all right? You looked so down at the viewing for Pat, I thought maybe you needed cheering up. I have a copy of your profile. Would you like to see it?"

"Yes, I would. How about dinner? I should warn you, however, I'm not the best company these days. Pat's death came as a shock."

"I can understand that. We don't have to do dinner. I can send the piece to your office."

"No, no, I'd really like to see you. It's just that I'm not likely to be bright and sparkling. Actually, I'd...like someone to talk to, about Pat that is."

Brooke wondered whether she might learn anything more about Pat now that she was dead. Anyway, she liked Sam, and if he needed to talk, so why not? "Think of me as your Aunt Oprah. Writers have to be good listeners."

"You are, I remember that. I feel like a heel taking advantage of you, but since we talked about Pat and what happened, I feel you know a lot about both of us, and I've got to talk to someone."

"What time shall I expect you?"

"Seven, if that's okay?"

"I'll see you then." Brooke replaced the phone and went back to her writing. She had an article due in a few days and wanted to get it into shape. She spent the hour or so remaining on it until it was time to dress for dinner with Sam.

His grief-filled voice made clear he wouldn't notice what she wore. Bright colors would be out of place, but she didn't want a color that would be too poignant a reminder so black was out. She chose a simple dark blue dress.

Sam arrived at seven, and they drove to Salvatore's. This particular restaurant sat on a site not far from the river. The interior, done in shades of cream and gray, used dark green vinyl for booths and on chair seats with occasional accents of red to provide a reminder of Italy without the more typical red check tablecloths—Salvatore's preferred plain white cloths. The booths lined two adjacent walls, while tables and chairs filled the center of the room. The dinning area had two sections with a wall between them.

Sam asked for a booth at the far end, suitable for quiet conversation, and they waited a few moments until the hostess had cleared and set it. Once seated, he immediately ordered a Jack Daniel's while Brooke asked for hot tea. When the waiter returned with the drinks to take their orders, Sam finished the whiskey in two swallows and held his glass up for another.

Brooke sighed. As she poured a cup of steaming mint tea, she studied Sam, telling herself the food would absorb the alcohol. At the worst, the Lido had given her plenty of practice in dealing with inebriated men, and she had promised him a sympathetic ear.

She ordered the Chicken Dijon and Sam ordered Pasta Marinara and a bottle of white wine as a suitable accompaniment for both entrees. She breathed easier when he didn't order another Jack Daniel's. The waiter returned quickly with the wine, and, after trying a sip, Sam nodded. The waiter poured a glass for each of them.

Brooke sipped the crisp Chardonnay. "Nice wine."

"Not bad," Sam agreed.

Salvatore's made a delicious salad, and she particularly enjoyed the fresh mushrooms and spinach leaves. The vinaigrette dressing provided just the right touch of sharpness. Sam drank his wine and hardly touched his salad.

"It's a good salad," Brooke said as she watched him pour more wine.

"I'm not much for salads these days." He gulped down half his glass of wine.

The waiter arrived with their entrees and they ate; rather Brooke ate as Sam moved the pasta around on his plate. Finished, she wiped the corner of her mouth with her napkin and leaned back against the back of the booth. "Superb."

Sam nodded and gulped the rest of his wine. He frowned as he poured the last from the bottle and then signaled the waiter for another.

Frowning, Brooke gazed at him. "Drinking doesn't help, not really."

He glanced at her and grimaced. "I know, but it blunts the edge. Makes pain a little more bearable. I loved Pat. Even though we split, I still loved her." He knocked back the wine in his glass.

The waiter brought a fresh bottle and filled Sam's glass. Brooke covered hers. One of them needed to stay sober, and, the way Sam was drinking, he'd be in no condition to drive.

"She wasn't a bad wife, you know, not until she started working for that son-of-a-bitch Jones. He took advantage of her and then dumped her. Oh sure he got her an exempt position all right, but he got her out of the Executive Suite. Pat loved him and it really hurt her. I tried to help, but she wouldn't let me. Said I had no drive, no ambition." He stared down at the glass in his hand.

At a loss for how to comfort him, Brooke didn't know what to say. "A lot of women would say you'd done quite well for yourself." He didn't seem to hear.

"Pat wanted money, lots of money. Said she was going to get it, too, and she was going to get that bastard Jones. Said I was just in the way. But Donna knew how to do both. Donna loved her and was going to take care of her."

Brooke had trouble believing her ears. Did he mean Donna Sanders? "Donna?"

"Yeah, Donna. How about that? I lost my wife, not to another man, but to another woman. Not every man can say that, can he? Here's to women!" He raised his glass in a toast.

Confusion held Brooke silent for a moment as she struggled to sort out the implications. "Sam, what are you talking about? I thought you said you divorced Pat because of Morgan Jones."

He shook his head slowly. "No...o, no...o, that business with Morgan Jones was over." He waved his glass about. His words sounded slurred and made her wonder how much he'd had to drink before he picked her up.

"He dumped her. Made her bitter as hell about it even though he wangled her an exempt position. 'I'll get that SOB," she told me. 'He'll be shor-ry, you wait and see-ee.' But she didn't. She killed herself inst'd." Big tears rolled down his face.

That's all she needed, a crying drunk. Shades of the Lido! Brooke took a deep breath. "It wasn't your fault, Sam. Don't cry. You can't help her now."

He shook his head, forgetting to stop. "No...o, no...o, I can't help her or hurt her... anymore, not anymore."

She struggled to sort through the jumbled thoughts Sam had poured out. "Why did you divorce Pat?"

He shook his head again, like a nodding bobble doll. "I didn't divorce her, she... she divorced me."

During the interview, Brooke remembered Sam saying he'd divorced Pat. Had he lied? But why? Pride?

"Because of...Donna. Said she...she loved her. I couldn't deal with that. Some man, eh? He can't hol' his own wife. She'd rather sleep with another woman than with me." He squinted and stared down at his glass.

"Another man I could unders'an', 'specially if he made more money, or had the looks, or...even...if he's a better lover. But another woman? I jus' don't unders'an'. Where'd I go wrong?" He looked at Brooke, begging her to tell him.

Stretching out her hand, she placed it lightly over his. "Sam, it's not you. It was Pat. Some people are different. It has nothing to do with you as a person or as a lover. Don't let it get you."

"But..." He gave a little shake to his head. "But I loved her. I really did. Why couldn't she be happy with me?"

Brooke struggled to find the right words. "People...have

different...needs. Just because you love someone, doesn't mean they have to love you. My brother Stan loved Pat too."

Sam stared at her, and his face crumpled, as he appeared to remember how her brother had died and Pat's note. "Yeah, I...I sort of forgot about him. I'm sorry, Brooke, about your brother I mean." He patted her hand clumsily.

She squeezed his back and gave him a sad smile. "It's all right. At least I know he wasn't into drugs. His death was an accident. The police said so. Don't blame Pat. It's all right, really it is."

"Why Pat? Why? I can't make myself unders'an'. And Donna, why Donna? I told you about Donna, didn' I? Sure I did. I thought everybody knew that. No....no, tha's right, it's a secret."

He looked around the room and placed a finger to his lips. "Don't tell anybody. How would it look? Good ol' Sam, his wife left him for another woman. Ever'one wanna know wha's wrong with Sam. Can't hold a woman. Poor Sam." He emptied his glass and picked up the wine bottle.

As he tried to get more out of it, Brooke reached over and removed it. "Sam, don't you think you've had enough to drink?"

"Never enuf to drink, not these days." He waved his glass around. "To beautifu' womin."

Sighing, Brooke realized she'd have to get the car keys away from him or get someone to pick them up. She signaled the waiter. "Keep him here," she whispered, "while I phone a friend."

Brooke hurried to the Ladies Room and pulled out her cell phone. Keying in Paul's number, she hoped he was home or to call a taxi. She wasn't about to wrestle Sam for his keys. The phone rang. No answer.

Then on the third ring, she heard Paul's voice, and she breathed a sigh of relief that it wasn't his answering machine.

"Hello, Paul? It's Brooke. Can you come to Salvatore's to pick up Sam Stephanowsky and me? He's had a little too much to drink."

"Salvatore's? Sure I can be there in ten minutes. What are you doing with Sam?"

Sighing, Brooke didn't want to deal with Paul's unmerited jealousy just now. She only wanted to get Sam home. "I'll tell you all about it when you get here. I'd better get back before something happens. Hurry, Paul."

"All right, bye."

With out waiting for the disconnect, she hurried back to the booth to find Sam, his head down on the table.

Sitting, musing, Brooke waited for Paul. She pitied Sam, but she still had a hard time believing what he'd said about Pat and Donna. He hadn't mentioned Donna's last name, but it had to be Donna Sanders. She motioned to the waiter for the bill and paid it, leaving a generous tip.

Sam began to snore. Brooke kept glancing from him to the entrance, annoyed with him and starting to feel equally annoyed with Paul as well. Where was be? She glanced at her watch to discover the ten minutes had only just expired. As she looked toward the entrance yet again, she saw him enter. He came over to the table and stood staring down at Sam.

"A fine mess this is. I thought you gave up drunks when you quit the Lido."

Brooke pushed away from the table and stood. "So did I." She moved to take Sam's arm. "Come on, Paul. Help me get him out of here and home."

Between them, with Sam's arms draped over their shoulders, they managed to walk him out the door and manhandle him into the back seat of Paul's car at the restaurant entrance.

"If you can get his keys, I'll drive his car and you can follow. I'll lead you to his place."

"You've been there," Paul snapped as he fished in Sam's pants pockets for the car keys.

"I always make it a habit to see the places where the people I profile live. Don't worry; I haven't been inside. Sam's never asked me over." A burr of annoyance at Paul's unjustified jealousy rankled, and she almost wished Sam had invited her.

"Thanks," she said when he handed her the keys. "He lives in Karric Place. I won't be a moment." She walked over to Sam's car, unlocked it, and drove up to the restaurant entrance to meet Paul. "Ready?" she called through the open car window.

"Anytime you are," he answered.

As Brooke led the way, she kept thinking about what Sam had said. Did it mean Donna was also part of the scam and, if so, how? Paul said she hadn't been involved. When they last talked, he had been considering Vavor and Morgan. She glanced in the rearview mirror from time to time to make sure Paul remained behind her.

She hadn't resolved anything by the time they reached Karric Place.

Someone had called it an instant executive slum—apartments rapidly built and rented for a high price because of the location, not because of the quality of the construction. For Sam, they provided a good address and quick access to the branch where he worked.

Brooke passed the clubhouse and pool by the entrance to the single story complex and continued on toward the left to where Sam's apartment was located. She parked in front, and Paul pulled up along side.

"We'd best leave him on the living room couch, and then I'll take you home." Paul opened the rear door and began to maneuver Sam out of the car.

Brooke went up to the apartment and tried Sam's keys until she found one that worked and opened the door. After switching on a light, she went to help Paul. He had almost made it to the step with Sam. She grabbed a limp right arm and helped get him inside. They managed to stretch Sam's heavy, inert body on the sofa.

She let Paul wrestle Sam's legs onto the couch. "Boy, I'm glad I don't have to do that every night. Why is a drunk so much heavier unconscious than when he's awake?"

"I suppose that's because he can't help you," Paul said as he released Sam's feet. "Anyway, he'll probably be all right."

"I hope so. He was feeling pretty down." Brooke set the keys on the side table next to the couch and gazed down at the sleeping man, pity foremost. She wondered why she'd thought him attractive. Right now he looked a mess with his clothing in disarray and his hair sticking up. His breath smelled sour and stale as he breathed with his mouth open.

"Come on, Brooke. Let him sleep it off. I want to talk to you anyway."

Brooke gave Sam a last glance and followed Paul out the door, remembering to lock it. She shut it behind her.

Chapter Sixteen

"We need to talk," Paul said as he backed up his car. "How about stopping at Wilhem's for a drink?"

"Fine with me," Brooke answered.

He drove out of Karric Place and down the road to Wilhem's at the end of the strip shopping center adjacent to the apartment complex. The crowd had thinned and they had no trouble finding a quiet table in the almost deserted lounge area.

"What'll you have?" Paul asked as they sat at one of the empty round tables.

"Hot tea, I've had enough wine tonight." Brooke settled herself in a dark wood captain's chair.

Paul went to the bar and ordered the drinks, returning with his Beck's.

"The server will bring your tea." He sat down, tasted his beer, and then studied Brooke. "I tried to call you earlier, several times, but you were out." A faint accusatory note sounded in his voice.

"With Sam; he asked me to dinner. He needed to talk."

"I also called earlier this afternoon."

Brooke looked surprised. "I didn't see a message on the machine."

A server came and set Brooke's tea on the table. "Anything else for you folks?" Paul shook his head.

He waited until she left before responding to Brooke. "I didn't leave one. I called to tell you the police arrested Morgan for Pat's murder."

"What?" She stared at him, eyes wide. "When did all this happen?"

"This afternoon."

"Oh," Brooke poured herself a cup tea, a thoughtful look on her face. "Then maybe what Sam said doesn't really matter."

"Oh? What did he say?" Sarcasm crept into his voice.

"He said that Donna…" Brooke paused and sipped her hot tea then set the cup down. "He didn't say Donna who, and Pat were lovers. Furthermore, Pat planned to get even with Morgan for dumping her." She stopped and then stared at Paul. "If Morgan murdered her, she didn't get even, did she?" Brooke rubbed her arms and shivered.

"Wait a minute." He stared at her uncertain he had heard her right. "Donna and Pat?"

Frowning, Brooke nodded. "Yeah, that's exactly what Sam said. A little hard to believe, isn't it? But he thinks so. He got drunk because he still loved Pat and couldn't face losing her to a woman."

"Brooke, are you sure he knew what he was saying? None of this makes any sense. Maybe Sam was just looking for sympathy."

She shrugged. "How should I know, but doesn't drinking release inhibitions? Don't some people say things when they're drunk they wouldn't say when they're sober?"

Suddenly, Paul had a vision of the Delacroix lithograph in his office with the Devil in bold relief. All the facts had pointed to Morgan. The name Jovanoski, Parma, Ohio, and the charge slips for the wine and the cruise tickets. Stunned, Paul stared at his beer, but if Morgan planned to kill Pat why would he charge cruise tickets?

"Damn!"

"What's the matter?" Brooke blinked, startled by his outburst.

He ran a hand through his hair. "I' think I've been outsmarted."

"Outsmarted? How and by whom?"

He picked up the cocktail napkin and began folding it into triangles. "Maybe Morgan isn't guilty; maybe he's been framed."

"Framed? Why?" Brooke frowned. "You don't mean by Pat and Donna? But Pat's dead."

"Yes, Pat's dead and someone killed her, but maybe it wasn't Morgan." He focused on Brooke. "Maybe it was planned to look that way."

"But that would mean Donna killed Pat. Sam said they were lovers, so why would Donna kill her?"

"I'm not sure." Paul sat thinking and drank his beer. "Remember what I told you about Pat's phone call? What if she called Donna? What if she somehow threatened her? Mightn't that be a reason for Donna to kill her?"

Leaning back in her chair, Brooke looked reluctant to accept his reasoning. "I don't know. It's all so new, I'm not sure it all fits." She tried to suppress a yawn. "Let's sleep on it and talk about it tomorrow." She finished the last of her tea and picked up her purse.

Paul left a tip on the table for the waitress. "We need to tell the police."

"What about proof? All we have is Sam's story. With everything pointing to Morgan, will they believe you?"

He took Brooke's arm as they walked out. "Whether they do or not,

I've got to tell them."

He didn't look forward to talking to Meyers tomorrow—make that today. He owed it to Morgan to do it as soon as possible. Morgan might still have killed Pat, but those cruise tickets made that look doubtful.

Neither said anything as Paul drove. He parked in Brooke's drive and walked her to the door.

"Thanks for coming tonight." She unlocked the door and started to enter. "I'm worn out. Call me after you talk to the police."

"I will." He paused for a moment, his mind whirling. "It's been a long day."

"Tell me." She yawned and slipped inside before he could say anything more. "Goodnight."

* * * *

The next morning as soon as Paul arrived at work, he dialed Donna's number, wondering exactly what he should say. He just wanted to hear her voice to see how she sounded. Maybe he could prod her about the Jovanoski account.

"Customer Services, Francine Williams speaking."

Paul had expected Donna to answer just as she had before. Maybe she was on another line or on a break. "I'd like to speak to Donna Sanders please."

"I'm sorry, Ms. Sanders doesn't work here anymore."

"What?" He almost dropped the phone. "Where did she go?"

"We're not allowed to give out that information."

Paul sighed. That was standard bank policy for anyone asking about former employees. "Francine, this is Paul Counts. I work in the bank, too, in Systems. What gives?"

"Oh, well, she resigned and left. Only gave a week's notice, the bare minimum. I'm acting section head until they get a replacement." Francine didn't sound too happy.

"Where did she go?"

"I've no idea. She didn't say. Just said she had a family emergency, and she had to leave. She said she might be back, but didn't know when, so she resigned instead of asking for a leave of absence. She said the paperwork would take too long and she'd take her chances about getting back on. She didn't leave us a forwarding address. Maybe Human Resources has one."

"Uh, thanks, Francine. If you hear from her, let me know ASAP.

Paul Counts in Information Systems."

"Okay, if I hear anything. Bye."

Stunned, he hung up the phone and sat with his chin resting on his hand. Donna had run. Innocent people didn't run, especially when someone else had been arrested. Why had Donna done it and why now? Had she discovered the removal of Stan's routine, or did she think the police would let Morgan go? Maybe with Pat gone, she had no safe way of processing the money. Whatever the reason, he'd better tell Meyers.

Paul phoned Homicide, but couldn't reach Meyers so he left an urgent message asking him to call. The clock read one o'clock before Meyers contacted him.

"All right, Mr. Counts, what's it about this time," the long-suffering Meyers asked.

"Morgan Jones didn't kill Pat Jensen."

"Oh? What makes you say that?" Meyers' doubt came through loud and clear.

"It's too neat, and what about those cruise tickets?"

"We checked into those. He charged them like you suggested on his credit card."

Paul bet Meyers was smiling. Let him; that would soon change. "Yeah, but if he planned to kill her, he wouldn't leave a trail like that, would he?"

"Who knows? People do strange things. The travel agency that supplied the tickets told us his secretary called to cancel the day Pat Jensen died. They told her they had already mailed the tickets and he'd have to return them to get a refund."

Paul hadn't thought of that. "Umm, maybe, but wouldn't Morgan have tried to get those tickets from Marisue if he knew about them? How did the travel agency know the person was Morgan's secretary?"

"That's what she told them."

"Have you talked to his secretary to confirm she called?"

Meyers sighed. "No, we didn't' see any reason to do so. Anything else, Mr. Counts?"

"Uh, well, yes. We learned last night Pat Jensen and another woman at the bank, Donna Sanders, were lovers. At least, Sam Stephanowsky, Pat's ex-husband thinks they were. He also claimed they planned to frame Morgan for the bank scam."

"And murder?" Meyers snorted. "Look, Mr. Counts, if Mr. Jones knew she planned to frame him, it adds to his motive for offing her."

"Yes, but Donna Sanders has resigned her job and left the bank."

'That doesn't necessarily mean she murdered Jensen. Why don't you let us take care of the detecting, Mr. Counts? We'll talk to Jones's secretary and this Stephanowsky, but I doubt anything they say will affect the case against him. We know he used his credit card to buy the wine Jensen drank before she was killed."

The credit card, it always came back to that. What if someone else had used Morgan's card? "Umm yes, but maybe you should check the signatures; make sure he really signed the slips."

Meyers emitted a long-suffering sigh that as much as said 'save me from amateurs.' "Mr. Counts, we know how to do our jobs. We don't need you to tell us what to do. Thank you for calling, goodbye."

Puzzled and frustrated, Paul replaced the phone and stared at the Delacroix. He slammed his hand against the desktop. Donna Sanders had used and manipulated him, and he didn't like it. Somewhere, she must have made a mistake. He had to find a way to break the frame about Morgan. Anger and depression warred. He hated being played for a fool.

Later that afternoon, determined to clear up the mess even if Meyers did nothing, Paul decided to talk with Morgan. He phoned the county jail where the police held Morgan and inquired about visitors and the visiting hours. The receptionist told him rules permitted prisoners fifteen minute visits between one and four in the afternoon or six to nine in the evening on Mondays through Fridays. As an alleged homicide perpetrator in police parlance, Morgan had been placed in the downtown jail. The judge had set his bail at two million dollars, and Morgan had not posted a bond yet.

About three o'clock, Paul entered the tall skyscraper that housed the county jail. The receptionist directed him to the fourth floor. There, he encountered a sheriff's deputy who told him to sign the visitors' book and asked to see his driver's license. Satisfied, the deputy instructed him to take a seat and wait until someone called his name.

Paul glanced around the small waiting room and sat on an empty chair on the far side. The furnishings consisted of several Danish modern couches in blue and dark green and straight-back chairs with a scattering of low tables cluttered with old magazines. One middle-aged woman sniffled, tears running slowly down her face to drop on the worn purse she clutched to her breast. The denim-jacketed young man opposite her sat with his arms crossed tight and stared at the ceiling.

Uncertainty still tugged at Paul. So far Morgan hadn't convinced the police of his innocence. Guilt ate at Paul; he'd put Morgan here. He tried to tell himself the charge slips provided the evidence and not his suggested suspicions. Telling Meyers Morgan came from Parma hadn't added much, but that failed to ease his conscience.

An attendant called out a list of names including Paul's. He rose and followed the guard along with several other people. Carrying a metal clipboard, the guard conducted them into another room partitioned into a series of small booths. Consulting the clipboard, he directed each of the visitors to one of the partitioned booths, assigning Paul to the last booth on the end.

Paul sat on one of the two chairs provided and waited, wondering what would happen next. A heavy glass partition with a metal grill in it faced him. He saw a door in the back of the cubicle on the other side.

A few moments later, that door opened and a guard admitted Morgan. The prison garb he wore, denims and a blue work shirt, looked casually chic. "Come to gloat, eh, Paul? You helped the police in this, didn't you?"

Paul sighed as Morgan sat down. "Yes, and I'm not proud of it. Morgan, did you kill Pat Jensen?"

Morgan stared at him as if wondering why he bothered to ask. "No, and I didn't take any money from the bank either. We don't have much to say, do we?"

"The police have credit card slips with your signature for a bottle of wine found with Pat and for cruise tickets."

"Credit card slips?" Morgan frowned. "I didn't buy any wine recently."

"Besides that, Marisue, Pat's sister, swears you planned to marry Pat. She insists Pat told the travel agency the cruise tickets were for your honeymoon, but the police say you changed your mind and tried to cancel them."

"Cruise tickets? Why would I buy them? As for marrying Pat, I told you before, I finished with her when I arranged her transfer to Human Resources. We had our fun. Why in the hell would I saddle myself with that hag? I can do a lot better."

That made sense, but could Morgan prove it? If he didn't buy those things, someone using his card did. "Did Pat ever have access to your credit cards?"

"Sure, when she was my secretary. She used to pick things up for me now and then. She also signed all my correspondence." Morgan frowned at him. "You think Pat signed those slips?"

Paul shook his head. "No, or at least not the wine slip. Could she still have access to your cards?"

"I doubt it. As my secretary she did, but that was two years ago."

"And now?"

"No, not now."

Paul slumped in his chair. If Pat had a card and used it, the cruise tickets made sense. Donna could easily have gotten access to the card numbers, but not the card. Besides, if they had used the card earlier, surely Morgan would have noticed.

Desperate for an explanation, Paul scrambled for any possibility. "Would you know if someone else used your credit card?"

Remaining silent for a moment, Morgan then grimaced. "Well, probably not. I don't keep the slips. I just pay the bill each month and, unless, it's outrageous, I don't look at the individual charges. Too much bother."

"But you keep the itemized statements?" Paul strained to find an out.

"No, I toss those. Too much paper. If I kept them, I'd have to file them." He shrugged.

Unhappy about Morgan's casual attitude, Paul wondered if he should get him to request copies of the card statements and look for odd charges. He could probably leave that to the police. Everywhere he turned he ran into dead ends and blind alleys. He had to find something to keep Morgan from being tried for murder.

"Morgan, did you ever hear anything linking Pat with Donna Sanders?"

"Like what?" Morgan stared at him, obviously puzzled.

"Like them being lovers?

"Pat, a lesbian?" He laughed. "You're putting me on, right?"

Paul shook his head. "I don't know. That's what Sam Stephanowsky says."

Frowning, Morgan stared at the ceiling. "Umm, the way Pat came on to me, I doubt it. I can't really help you with that."

Disappointed, Paul pushed back his chair and got to his feet. "Well, you'd better think of something. So far the police are certain you killed Pat. If I find anything helpful, I'll let you or your lawyer know. Bye, Morgan."

Outside the tall building, Paul gulped the fresh air, glad to be in the warm sunshine again. The whole visit depressed him. His part in Morgan's arrest still rankled. He wanted to help him, but he didn't know what to do.

Back at the data center, Paul had not finished with the Jovanoski account. He checked both the audit logs and the scanned check records. Courtesy of Walter Vavor, Paul traced the checks sent to Jovanoski. Some had been deposited to Pat Jensen's account, some to the account of Pat Stephanowsky, a few to John Pierce, and some to another Jovanoski account in another bank according to the endorsements on the back of the checks. Regularly Pat withdrew the cash from all except the Pierce account. What happened after that, he didn't know. So far as he could tell, Donna Sanders' account showed no unusual activity or deposits and none corresponding in time or amount to the Jovanoski, Jensen, or Stephanowsky transfers.

Paul stared at the figure of the Devil in the Delacroix. He had to find some way to tie Pat to Donna. Somewhere, Donna had to have made a mistake. He had to find it, or Morgan was going to have to rely on his lawyer to create a reasonable doubt in the minds of a jury. Paul didn't have much confidence in that. Donna had covered all the bases, sewing Morgan into a nice neat package for the police and destroying all the scraps that might point elsewhere.

Suddenly, Paul sat upright. Maybe, just maybe he could find something. The bank used a networked system of PCs. From time to time, secretaries, clerks or accountants managed to lose files, crash a disk or do other damage to their machines. Systems had established a policy of taking periodic snapshots of activity on the network and of providing a backup service to users, especially for print queues. Pat's suicide note had to have been done sometime after he and Pat had met and before she was killed that evening. That meant a three-hour stretch in the early evening to check. Normally Systems stored the backup files for thirty days. Paul looked at the calendar. He still had time.

Calling the data library, he arranged for access to the logs. Next he called Meyers, relieved to reach him on the first attempt.

"Look, I know you're convinced Morgan killed Pat Jensen, but remember the suicide note? The one without fingerprints?"

"Yes, Mr. Counts." Paul heard the cautious note in Meyers 'yes.'

"I'd like a copy of the note. I think I can find out on which bank printer it was produced. Depending on where, it might provide added evidence either for or against Morgan."

"You sure about this?"

"Pretty sure, and, anyway, what have you got to lose? All I plan do is search our backup files and find out at where it was printed. If Morgan did it, it would have to be on a machine to which he had ready access."

Paul ran a hand through his hair. "I don't think Pat's murder was planned very far in advance. If Morgan planned it, he would've taken care of those cruise tickets earlier. I suspect my talk with Pat precipitated her murder. I told you she called someone immediately after we talked, and later that same evening, someone killed her. If the murder wasn't planned ahead, the odds are the killer used equipment he or she had ready access to. Besides, how can you tell the output of one laser printer from another? In most instances you can't, so the killer didn't feel the need to use equipment anywhere else."

"That makes a sort of sense." Meyers paused a moment.

Paul held his breath, fingers crossed. Meyers must want to catch the real villain and so would agree to his request.

"All right, Mr. Counts, I'll let you have a copy of the note, but I expect you to inform me as soon as possible of what you learn. You can pick it up at the front desk."

"Thanks, Meyers. I'll be back with you just as soon as I process the backup files." Paul hung up the receiver, jubilant that maybe, just maybe he had a means to tie Donna to Pat's note. He signed out and left for Police Headquarters to retrieve the copy of Pat's note before Meyers had a chance to change his mind.

Back at the data center with the note, Paul scanned it to create a file for matching and began hunting for the system copy. First he had to create a data set with the proper time stamps. It took some doing, but eventually he found the right files. Using the scanned copy of Pat's suicide note, he created a routine to search the file for a match. He set the routine in motion and waited for the results.

Drinking a cup of coffee, he sat at his desk staring yet again at the Delacroix. This time he saw Morgan and Pat alternating in the role of Faust and Valentin. Donna was the Devil, manipulating both. On balance, he assigned Morgan to Valentin. Despite his drive to succeed, Morgan hadn't had a role in the scam or the murders. Pat made a better Faust. She wanted money and revenge. She hadn't counted on having to pay the Devil her due.

His terminal beeped, telling him the routine had found something. He called up the results and nodded. The note had been printed on the Customer Services printer in Donna Sanders's section. Paul printed out the data showing the time, printer location, and the content of the note itself. Meyers should find these interesting. Paul only hoped they would convince him to consider Donna instead of Morgan as the murderer.

When Paul entered the Homicide Section, he saw Meyers seated at his desk reading a report. "I've got it."

"Got what, Mr. Counts?" Meyers looked up as he approached waving the printout.

"What I said when I asked for the note. The laser printer used to print Pat Jensen's suicide note was in Donna Sanders' area."

"So you think this means that Sanders wrote the note and mailed it, too?"

"Well, what other interpretation is there? Morgan would have used his own, another on the executive floor, or Information Systems, but why would he use one in Customer Services? No, Donna wrote the note and mailed it. This ties Pat's murder to Donna Sanders. Morgan didn't write the note, sign the credit card slips, or murder anyone."

Meyers looked at him and then at the printout with Paul's notes on the printer location. He drummed his fingers on the table as he sat thinking and then stopped and stared up at Paul. "Well I guess we'll have to show this to the prosecutor. It may change things a bit."

"Did you know Pat used to sign Morgan's name and once had access to his credit cards?"

Meyers sighed. "Yes, we talked to Mr. Jones, too. We also checked the signatures. It's possible someone else signed those slips."

"What about Donna Sanders?"

"We've put out an alert on her. She flew from Columbus to New York, but we're not certain yet where she went from there. She may still be in New York. We'll do our best to find her."

"I hope so. I hate to think about a cold-blooded murderer like her wondering about."

* * * *

Brooke surveyed Paul's apartment with interest. He had invited her over for his report on all that had happened. His decor, strictly functional with all the furnishings in neutral shades, had two things redeeming it. She approved the overflowing bookshelves with the well-worn volumes. The second hung over the stereo, a Howard Pyle reproduction of a duel. A monk sat watching a duel between a young colonial and an unsavory pirate. She had long admired Pyle's paintings and drawings.

Most of all though, she liked his cat Shadow. The loud welcoming purr and the warm body rubbing against her legs signified approval. She bent down and scratched the cat behind the ears. The purring increased.

"You've made a friend," Paul observed.

"Yes, and you have a beautiful cat. I don't think I've ever seen one quite like it. I'm not sure I would have understood about a gray stripped cat."

"I know what you mean. Thanks for coming. I knew you'd want to know what happened. Why don't we sit down while I tell you?"

"I'm glad you solved the murders." Brooke sighed and followed Paul into his living room.

They sat on the nubby beige lounge there. Shadow jumped up beside Brooke and nudged her hand.

"Not as glad as I am, I wasn't sure Meyers would accept the printout as enough to prove the frame-up, and I was at least partly responsible for Morgan's arrest." Paul smiled at her ruefully.

"But he did, didn't he?" Brooke stroked Shadow, and the cat's purring rose a notch.

"Yeah, it made sense even to him. We figure Donna had Pat arrange for the cruise tickets on Morgan's card, to make it look like he planned to flee with the money and not return from the cruise."

"And the wine?"

"Donna's little insurance to frame Morgan for Pat's murder if the police didn't accept the suicide note. She really went for 'the belts and suspenders' theory."

Brooke shook her head. "Why did she do it?"

Paul sat a moment as if trying to put his thoughts in the proper order. "Greedy in part, and I guess also fear her pals wouldn't keep quiet. If she was the only one left, she kept all the money, and no one could point the finger at her. She made her big mistake in killing John and trying to frame me. It gave me a reason to dig deeper and to talk with Pat. When I told Pat about the 9-1-1 tape, she got scared the police might consider Stan's death a murder and tie her to it."

"I see how she might think that, but considering her relationship with Donna, why would Donna kill her?"

"According to Sam, Pat loved Donna, but it looks like Donna only used Pat like she used Stan and John. I doubt Donna ever loved anybody."

Donna's cold-blooded nature made Brooke shiver. She never understood such people. "Okay, that explains Donna, but I still don't understand Stan."

"We may never know for sure unless the police catch Donna and she confesses, but I'd say it was really Pat. Stan fell in love with her and agreed to the fiddle, if she would marry him. Knowing Stan, once he had things working, he probably wanted her to set the date. She loved Donna and wanted revenge on Morgan, so Donna must have suggested they eliminate Stan. If it had been Morgan, Pat wouldn't have cared, but Donna probably forced her to do it."

"You think so? I can't imagine anyone doing that to another person."

"Neither can I, but sociopaths don't care who they hurt. Donna has behaved like one. Pat bought the crack from Harley, and they had a party at Stan's place. When Stan went into convulsions, Pat panicked and called 9-1-1. By then it was too late, and now Donna had Pat's involvement in Stan's death as an added lever. It made Pat's situation worse, but she trusted Donna, and her goal all along had been to punish Morgan."

Brooke frowned, uncertain about Paul's reasoning. "But that didn't happen until after Pat's death."

"True, but she thought the plan would accomplish that. However, once Donna killed John Pierce that left Pat as the last of the original scammers. When she panicked about the voiceprint on the 9-1-1 call, Donna couldn't risk her talking to either me or the police."

Brooke stroked Shadow and mulled over Paul's analysis. "At least that provides a reason for Stan, but I'd have been happier if he'd been the innocent victim. I can't believe he'd steal." She appealed to Paul to justify her brother's actions.

"I don't think he saw it that way. It was the rounding errors, you see. As far as he was concerned, it wasn't anyone's money really, and he wasn't stealing. He just took a little selvage from the edge. He saw it as a simple accounting transfer that would never be missed, and it wouldn't have, if Donna hadn't pushed Pat into supplying him with the crack. In trying to cover her tracks and frame Morgan, Donna hung herself. Anyway as for Stan, he did it for love."

Brooke frowned. "I suppose I should be glad he found someone to love. I only wish she'd loved him too."

"Stan had plenty of company. Everybody seems to have done the wrong things in the name of love: Walter Vavor loved his daughter and bought her drugs. Stan loved Pat so he fiddled the files. Pat loved Donna so she encouraged Stan and helped kill him." He gave her a rueful smile.

"As for me, Donna used me to get Morgan. I fell for her ruse and told Meyers. She made a patsy out of me." Paul's look of chagrin told Brooke how much he hated failing to see Donna's real motives.

"Paul, the police would never have suspected her if you hadn't pushed them. They took the easy way out on all the deaths. Don't blame yourself. If not for you, a jury would have convicted Morgan."

"Maybe, but it still rankles."

"Will they ever catch her?"

"Sometime, someplace. Nobody can hide forever, not even someone as clever as Donna. Besides the money will run out sometime and there's no statute of limitations on murder. I'm kind of sorry for Meyers. He's solved his crime, but hasn't caught the criminal."

"You mean you solved the crime."

"Well, sort of, but I sure fouled it up at first. I don't know if Morgan will forget that." Paul grimaced.

"He'd better. I appreciate all you've done. At least I know now what happened to my brother and how."

"You even got to be a hustler," he teased, a smirk on his face.

"Don't remind me. Say what will it take to make you forget that?" She turned to face him.

"At least I met you, so maybe it was all really worth it." Paul gave her a long, lingering look that sent a tingle racing along her spine. "Maybe a date or two might do it. How about joining me for dinner Saturday night?"

"Okay." She paused a moment and savored the anticipation of a date with Paul free of Stan's death and bank scams. "So long as we don't go to the Lido."

He raised his eyebrows in mock horror. " No way, lady. I thought of

Aldofo's or maybe The Cove."

Pleased at his choices, Brooke smiled. "That's better, I enjoy good food and good wine."

"What about good company?"

She gave him a crooked grin. "That too. Did you have some in mind?"

"You sure know how to hurt a guy. I meant me, of course."

"I know you did, I just didn't want you have a swelled head, solving this case and all. I look forward to a great dinner." She kissed him on the cheek. "And you're the best thing to have come out of all this."

"So are you, lady." He pulled her toward him and kissed her.

His mouth covered hers, and he probed her lips with a questing tongue. Instinctively she responded and leaned into his embrace, savoring his warmth and strength. The fire of his kiss gave her hope that unlike Stan she'd found love after all.

About the Author

Nell DuVall aka Mel Jacob lives in southern Ohio with two cats, plenty of wild birds, rabbits, and squirrels. A world traveler, she has written a variety of books including time travel romance, romantic suspense, speculative fiction, nonfiction, and children's books. She reviews for two websites covering speculative fiction, including fantasy, urban fantasy, and science fiction. She is also active in the Internet Writing Workshop and on Facebook.com.

Mel Jacob (Melduvall@aol.com)--Mystery, romance, and beyond
www.Nellduvall.com

Stories in Anthologies

The Corpulent Chiropteran in Curious Hearts
Saving Christmas in Warm Christmas Wishes

Selvage